Beau Monde

Random House
New York

Beau Monde

Dotson Rader

*Grateful acknowledgment is made to the following for
permission to reprint previously published material:*
Random House, Inc. and Faber and Faber Limited: Five
lines from "Lullaby" by W.H. Auden. Reprinted from
W.H. Auden: Collected Poems by W.H. Auden, edited by
Edward Mendelson. Copyright 1940 and renewed 1968
by W.H. Auden. Reprinted by permission of Random
House, Inc. and Faber and Faber Limited.

Library of Congress Cataloging in Publication Data
Rader, Dotson.
Beau monde.
I. Title.
PS3568.A27B4   813'.54   80-5293
ISBN 0-394-42593-6

Manufactured in the United States of America
24689753
First Edition

FOR
Tennessee Williams

There are few things that cause
greater wretchedness than to love with all your heart
someone whom you know to be unworthy of love.

—W. SOMERSET MAUGHAM

Beau Monde

One

I NEVER told Pearl that I loved her. Even at the end when she needed to hear it, I could not tell her.

She was famous for being loved and, paradoxically, she was hated because of it. Because of it, and because she was the most beautiful woman of our time.

I should have told Pearl many things. I should have warned her, and I didn't, not even about Piers. In the end she gave up everything for Piers.

Pearl talked often of him, from the very beginning, and when she spoke of Piers she changed. Her voice . . . years of life out of the South weakening her drawl, the travel that brought her accent down to social snuff, all at Varina Ransome's expense; that fake and monied hardness to her voice, the verbal patina that like a transparent shield distances you from the world.

"Piers could walk on his hands," she would say, "even as a little boy. He'd surprise me, walking upside down with a book balanced on his shoes, and it always made me laugh. I couldn't help it. Piers loved hearing me laugh."

When she talked of Piers her Mississippi drawl appeared out of nowhere, softening her vowels and absorbing her *r*'s. She became younger, less removed, less amused, more interesting, sadder when she spoke of him. Her eyes would widen with wonder and concern.

Marcel Duchamp, when he met Pearl in Paris, said that her eyes looked bleached, so pale was their blue. When she spoke of Piers they became ineffably beautiful and sad, because she remembered what life had done to him.

This is what Pearl's eyes were like.

They were like Jacqueline Kennedy's eyes at Hyannis Port after John F. Kennedy was buried and she kept recounting over and over again the most painful details; sitting on the floor, dressed in chino slacks and a turtleneck sweater, looking at no one, talking compulsively, redundantly in that breathy, aggrieved whisper about the day they shot Jack down, as if in the telling she were indicting Them. *Them* to the American aristocracy being the common people. Untrustworthy, all of them, treacherous when push came to shove. Something they wiped off their shoes when they entered Quo Vadis for lunch.

Well, Pearl was one of Them, and she never forgot it, all her life. And it was Piers who kept her memory clean.

I like to think that what drew me to Pearl and held me there was her courage. But it isn't true.

Two

SHORTLY before Pearl left New York I walked across Central Park from my place to her co-op on Fifth Avenue.

It was a lovely day in New York. The leaves were yellow and red and beginning to fall. Already one could perceive in the air the coming cold, the sense of confinement and islandedness that autumn brings to Manhattan. It is like Paris in that.

Pearl was getting out.

We had white wine in her living room. We drank it out of large crystal glasses I had given her as a housewarming gift when she first moved into the apartment seven years ago. The glasses were shaped like tulips.

"These are the last two," she said, holding them up to the light. "You gave me dozens, remember? Every time I dodged one flying my way I thought of you."

I laughed. "I'll buy you more."

"Not until I find a live-in pitcher to throw them." She meant it humorously, but it was unhappy.

I asked about lunch, to change the subject. I suggested several restaurants where I knew she frequently ate. None pleased her anymore.

"Let's go somewhere I won't be recognized. I haven't been out of this damn apartment in days. I feel like poor Piers when he was sick in New York, remember? Oh, how trapped he felt."

She looked tired and seemed out of breath, as if she had climbed too many stairs too fast. She appeared on the edge of it and worn through, as she had when I first laid eyes on her years before. I was worried about her.

"I don't want to face it anymore, Beau. I'm a curiosity now, like I have two heads and a forked tail. I hate people staring at me in public. I can guess what they're thinking. How quickly things change. You think life will go on as before with its little ups and downs. That you'll grow quietly older, and see your son become a man, and have your moments of happiness and peace, and then, suddenly, in a flash it's gone bad, never to be the same again. Just like that."

"The bad times pass, too, just like the good."

"You think so?" she cocked her head to the side and looked at me with an expression of wistful disbelief.

I looked around the room and noticed that the round occasional tables were empty of objects, the boxes gone. Her apartment was normally cluttered with cigarette boxes, ornamental eggs, and other nonsense rendered in malachite and worked in gold. Their absence spoke to the derogation of her life. Over the years she had shopped for malachite pieces at A La Vieille Russie and Arpels in New York, or in Paris, where she discovered a dealer stuck away on Quai d'Anjou who specialized in the stuff. When I asked Pearl the reason for her love of the green stone, she replied, "It reminds me of Piers."

She meant the color of malachite was the color of his eyes.

I also noticed white tags hanging from the bottoms of chairs and lamps, all the furnishings, even the paintings marked by the appraisers. Her art was Surrealist. Magritte, Matta, Copley, Tchelitchew. The sole exception being Andy Warhol's famous portrait of her. She enjoyed the fantastical.

"You're selling everything?" I asked.

"Spring cleaning," she answered lightly, as if amused by a situation that must have been painful to her. "They're appallingly efficient, the boys of Parke-Bernet. Thank God I won't be here when the junk goes on the block. They've sold the smaller stuff already, the little pretty things. And my books . . ."

"I didn't know."

"Yes. I hated that the most. Some of them I've had for twenty years or more. Quel fucking dommage. The ones I've saved were the paperbacks, the poems Piers had. I even have that goddamn steamer trunk of his . . . It used to embarrass me the way he'd use any excuse to recite Yeats. Oh, and what was the other? Not

Eliot . . . 'As swift as the seasons roll, leave thy low-vaulted past, and let each temple, nobler than the last—' "

" 'The Chambered Nautilus'?"

"Holmes, yes . . . 'Shut thee from heaven with a dome more vast, til thou at length are free, leaving thine outgrown shell by life's unending sea!' Do you know where he taught me that? Let me tell you. It was at an adolescent shelter, a halfway house in Florida. Piers had been caught stealing tires. The halfway house was run by the State of Florida, and it had a recidivism rate of ninety-eight percent, which must have been some kind of record. I visited him there. He was frightened but he didn't want to show it. So young then. So young."

Her eyes teared. She put on her sunglasses.

"Well, I saved the book of Holmes from the goddamned wolves, at least I saved that."

"What about lunch?" I asked gently, touching her cheek.

"Wait." She stood up. "I almost forgot."

Pearl quickly walked across the room with the hurried energy characteristic of her movements, her sheer print dress clinging to her body. She was thin and, as always upon seeing her after some absence, she appeared smaller and more physically vulnerable than I remembered.

She took a small malachite and gold pillbox off the fireplace mantel and handed it to me. "There's no payment in kind with you," she said, smiling, "But at least it's one gift someone gave me that no grand duchess was shot for." She laughed in a low, mocking way.

Pearl had once owned an emerald necklace that had been stolen from the body of the Grand Duchess Xenia minutes before the Bolsheviks lined up her Imperial Highness against a convent wall in the Crimea in 1921 and shot her quite dead.

"I don't want it back," I told her. I had given her the pillbox many years before. It was made by Fabergé and was also Imperial Russian.

"Take it, please. I told Varina and the appraisers that the box belonged to you, that's why it wasn't sold. It's all that's left. Put it in your pocket, but open it first."

I did, and inside was a Lincoln penny made of gold.

"Do you like it?" she asked.

"Very much."

"It's your lucky penny now," she remarked, pleased by my delight.

"Does nothing remain, baby? Not even the jewelry? Even the emeralds are sold?"

"Nothing," she smiled. "I gave the emeralds back. I was never comfortable wearing them. They were too heavy for my neck."

We took a taxi to the West Side, to a new café by the Museum of Natural History. It was a pleasant and uncrowded place.

"What are they saying about me?" Pearl asked, sounding indifferent.

We had finished eating lunch and were having coffee. She had taken off her sunglasses, and I saw for the last time the beauty of her eyes.

"Who? The newspapers?"

"No. The Pack."

"What you would expect. That they knew all along. That you're crazy to have done it. That you won't get away with it. That you must have been on drugs. The usual crap."

She nodded, expecting no less.

"Truman speaks well of you. But then, he always did."

She smiled, pleased.

"I was at Grenouille last week," she remarked.

La Grenouille is a French restaurant on Manhattan's East Side that has good food, but that isn't why people go there. People go there because they think it's a big deal to be seen eating there. It is one of five or six joints in New York where the Pack eats. Pearl was once a probationary member of the Pack.

"I haven't been going out," she continued, "as I told you. And certainly not to Grenouille. But Cecil was in from England, and I thought he might not have heard about the scandal, living in Salisbury. He called and invited me to lunch. I was very touched by that, even if he didn't know about the murder and the rest of it. Just simply the fact that Cecil would call me after so long a time, after what's happened. Except for you and Cecil, I haven't had an invitation from anyone, just reporters and columnists. It's amazing how they get unlisted phone numbers, and how cruel they can become . . ."

How quickly the press turned on her, and with what ferocity. She was once the darling of the gossip columns and the magazines, really too much so. The Perfect Pearl. The Beautiful Girl. The Woman With Everything. Pearl, who had it all until the murder, until the photographers caught her leaving the limousine to enter Doctors Hospital, still wearing the same bloodied dress. They turned on her, and the Pack attacked, and silence and fear engulfed her. She was in seclusion for nearly a year, in a kind of internal exile shut away from public view. Not even the friends who remained saw her. Certainly I hadn't, not since the murder, not until today, when I would be the last to see her before she fled New York for good.

"Oh, and dear Varina. Once a week now I eat very publicly with Varina so she can let the world know she doesn't believe the talk . . ." Her sentence trailed off.

"You were saying about Cecil?"

"Well, Cecil and I went to Grenouille late. I literally stalled in the apartment feeding him Bloody Marys until after two-thirty, thinking we'd miss the worst of it if we arrived after hours. And I wanted to see Grenouille again. One last time. When I was first in New York, trying to make it, you know, one of the guys I met took me there for lunch, and I thought it was the prettiest restaurant I had ever seen. I still do.

"When Cecil and I arrived most of the lunch brigade *had* left. We sat in back against the wall, I in my movie-star sunglasses. We talked about Cecil's house in Salisbury. He's thinking of selling it, can you imagine? Such an exquisite house, it's a damn shame. And you know, I was saddened when Cecil told me because I thought, well, there's another lovely place I'll never see again."

"There'll be others. Even lovelier."

Pearl shook her head no. "You're a dear fool if you believe that. And I know you're nobody's fool. Anyway, there we were at Grenouille when I noticed someone fat and disagreeable coming toward our table. It was Dudley Conrad. I knew by the assertive,

quick way he walked that he was about to make a public statement, a display."

"Did he?" I knew before I asked. The story of Dudley putting
Pearl in her place was all over town.

"Dudley said, 'I think your conduct is unspeakably foul, Pearl,
not that it surprised me. You may have fooled the Ransomes
and Sabina and some of the others, but *I* was never fooled!'

"He sort of sniffed, waiting for me to say something back. I
should have. Instead Cecil stood up, glaring at Dudley. 'Do you
bloody mind fucking off?' Cecil said in that tony, British old man
way of his. Dudley blanched. He finished his piece, his voice even
higher than it usually is. 'I want you to know, Pearl, that you will
never dine at my house again! *Never again!*' Dudley screeched at me
so the whole restaurant could hear. The volume was astonishing."

"It doesn't matter."

"Never again!" Pearl repeated, mimicking Dudley's voice. "But
what's funny is that I've never *been* invited to his goddamn house,
not for dinner, not even drinks. Not once."

"He's an ass."

"As Dudley left, Cecil kissed me dramatically on the cheek. 'The
dogs bark . . .,' he said—"

I completed the saying for her "—but the caravan moves on."

"Yes. And usually downhill."

I wanted to ask her why she cared what these people thought of
her. I understood her affection for Cecil. He had been the first to
discover her. Where else but at lunch at Le Cirque when she had
no money, and men enjoyed picking up her tab. Things like that
happen. Cecil saw her there, and it was he who suggested her to the
editor of *Vogue*, and it was Cecil's photographs of her in that magazine that first brought her celebrity. For what it's worth.

But what about the others? The Pack? Pearl had moved among
them for years, and whether they liked her and accepted her and
included her counted much with her. All these rich who did no
work, who lived on remittances, who despised the people whose
labor made them wealthy. "Cake-eaters," Pearl called them, the
types who never got fired or faced eviction or knew panic in a
public ward. I think she feared them, with good reason, and be-

lieved that she could sniff them out, and charm them, and bend them to her purpose, and it would be all right. Pearl was no different from the rest of us in this: she was dead wrong.

We taxied back to the East Side.

"How is Philip?"

"I don't know," Pearl answered, her voice barely audible. "They won't let me see him, or tell me where he is. I received a letter from the family lawyers informing me that he will be going to school in Switzerland. He'll never know America, not for a long time."

"Does it matter?"

"It matters painfully."

We got out of the taxi.

I could not bring myself to say goodbye, to say the word itself.

"They gave me enough rope, didn't they?"

Pearl spoke more to herself than to me as we stood under the awning, the wind in her hair.

Suddenly she turned away and hurried past the doorman. I watched her go.

I walked back to my waiting taxi. As I opened the door to get in I heard Pearl cry "Beau!"

She ran back to me, awkwardly, like someone who was never comfortable in shoes. She embraced me, gripping me in fear of a terrible fall. She smelled of sandalwood. I felt her tremble.

"It was worth it," she whispered quickly. "Whatever they say, it was worth it all."

I said nothing in reply. I simply held her to me for as long as I could, and then I let her go.

There was no help for it. I knew we were at the end of it, the goddamn lees of it. It was then I should have said that I had always loved her, and that I always would.

Part I

Starry, Starry Night

Three

I FIRST met Pearl twelve years ago through Bonita.

Bonita was a whore.

I knew she was a whore the minute I saw her, and I also knew that I wanted to go to bed with her, and knowing that she was a whore I figured it would not be a difficult thing to arrange.

Bonita was standing in a doorway by Jimmy Ray's Bar on Eighth Avenue and 46th Street. The area was called the Minnesota Strip because most of the whores who worked the avenue were from Minneapolis and Saint Paul. To this day I don't know why Minnesota was the chief recruitment center for New York City chippies, but there you are.

It was early September 1967. A very hot night. An air inversion over Manhattan polluted the city with the smells of dogs and traffic and garbage and, more pleasantly, the fishy, ocean smell of the

Hudson River as the tide moved up toward West Point. Nights like this in New York, when it is steamy and the air unstirring and filled with the stench of life . . . it makes you feel lonesome and horny and incomplete. You sense you will never finally do in life nor meet in life what it is you long for. Or if you do, you will be too dumb to recognize it until after it's gone.

Bonita was not from Minnesota. But I did not know that when I saw her standing on the Minnesota Strip. All I knew was what I saw: a pretty girl with blond hair done up in a wild bouffant. She wore black leather boots with stiletto heels, a black miniskirt, and a tight tank top that amply displayed her breasts, which were large for a girl of such diminutive size. She looked about sixteen years old. Whores who are very young are called "chickens." The men who buy them are called "chicken hawks." It makes sense.

When I noticed Bonita, chewing gum and swinging her handbag in obvious impatience, I said to the taxi driver, "See that blonde across the street in the black leather boots? Pull over."

I opened the door and shouted at the girl, "Get in, baby."

She said she wanted to go home.

"Where do you live?" I asked.

"Avenue B."

Avenue B was a main street on the Lower East Side, only the Lower East Side was now called the East Village by real estate types. It was largely Hispanic, drug-infected, destitute. A human and architectural ruin. Dangerous.

"Why not come to my place?" I asked. "We can have champagne and cucumber sandwiches."

I have discovered over the years that nothing impresses a whore more than an offer of cucumber sandwiches and champagne. Or even Champale, if you can't spring for the bubbly. They want to be treated like ladies, which is all right. The problem is that their conception of what a lady is involves images of violins playing and tea sandwiches and waiters in white gloves at the Palm Court of the Plaza Hotel.

"I got to get my ass home," Bonita replied. "You my last trick of the night. My father's expecting me."

Fair enough.

"What'll it cost?"

"Fifty dollar." She spoke with a Spanish accent.

As we drove downtown to the Lower East Side, Bonita sat next to me and said nothing. She wore a heavy amount of Chanel No. 5, a perfume the women of her trade seem to like almost as much as cucumber sandwiches.

Abruptly, she took my hand and placed it on her bare thigh. I slid my hand under her skirt.

"You got clammy skin, man. Ice-cold. You feel like a dead man."

She wore no underwear, which was nice. I felt her sex. Her skin was hairless, and I thought that odd. She spread her legs and lay back with her head resting on the seat of the taxi, her yellow, bouffant hairdo looking brittle and absurd, like cotton candy spun out of fiberglass. In fact, she looked like one of my sisters, when they were eight or nine years old, dressing up in my mother's wigs and old clothes to play house in the attic. Only Bonita was playing hooker, and she did not look the part.

She never stopped chewing Double Bubble bubble gum. She blew small pink bubbles, and when they broke she would laugh and shove the gum back into her small mouth with her fingers. Her fingernails were long and painted silver, like fountain-pen points made of aluminum.

"My feet hurt," she complained. "It's the goddamn boots. Man, johns dig boots, but they a real pain in the ass to wear."

That was all she said until we arrived at a high-rise public housing project on Avenue B.

Bonita lived on the fourteenth floor. The elevator was broken.

"Screw it," she snarled, kicking the door.

"Why not come to my place?" I suggested again, not wanting to climb fourteen flights of stairs. I'd been wary of stairs ever since an angina attack the summer before in the National Hotel in Manila. I was in there to research a movie I was writing about Bataan. There was a hurricane knocking out electricity and of course the elevators for four days and I had to use the stairs. One broiling day I collapsed as I climbed to my room.

"No way, man. Come, I show you."

We took the stairs to the basement and entered it, passing scores of uncovered canvas trundles filled with rubbish, and rats and old furniture and other stuff. Bonita pointed to a corner behind a furnace. I could see several mattresses placed near concrete block walls sprayed with obscene graffiti.

"I first got fucked here when I was eleven. Paco, he was the man who bust my cherry." Bonita confessed this news matter-of-factly, but with an undeniable sense of pride, patting her hairdo. "Paco was nineteen. Big, man. He dead now."

"I'm sorry. Did you love him?"

"*Sí.*" And then she shrugged, as if to say, Easy come, easy go.

Approaching the mattresses, she knelt down and touched the soiled cover of one, adoringly, as if it were a holy relic.

"Here we do it," she whispered. "Paco, he love pussy. He a real man."

I misunderstood, thinking that she wanted to have sex on the mattress.

"I don't want to do it in the cellar."

Bonita giggled. She was a good girl. "No, we go to roof and walk down to my place." Then suddenly she kissed my cheek. "You crazy man."

We took the service elevator and it was on the roof of this lousy building on Avenue B that I first encountered Pearl.

Scores of people came there to escape the late summer heat. There was safety in numbers. They sat on folding chairs, or paced in twos and threes along the brick walls, or lay on blankets—entire families together, women in nighties, men in shorts, trying to sleep. They brought to mind refugees from some calamity, gathered in makeshift camps trying to resume a semblance of normal life amid its debris. A teen-age Hispanic couple stood pressed against the outside wall of the stairwell, moving their hands slowly over each other's bodies like gentle waves against a beach. Nearby a drunk leaned unsteadily, his eyes blurred, his torn trousers soaked with urine. He was yelling incoherently in Spanish against the white devils. Small children ran about as two old Jews argued in Yiddish in a corner, gesturing heatedly at each other beside a small pine tree dead in its broken pot.

Below, a block away, Tompkins Square Park lay green and deserted but for the addicts and the pushers doing business under the lamps; the gays and joyboys doing business in the darkened stalls of the comfort station; the muggers walking their beats.

I felt uneasy as Bonita and I strolled across the roof, which covered nearly half a block. In my Brooks Brothers suit and tie I could have been taken for an undercover cop or a bill collector. That wouldn't be smart. And I was wearing a Cartier Santos tank watch with a solid gold band that my old man had given me just before he cashed in his chips. He had received it from De Gaulle's French Republic for wartime service to the Free French. When he died, the French demanded the watch back, after posthumously stripping him of his Legion of Honor. I refused. Now, on this roof, I feared someone might steal the watch, to say nothing of cutting off my hand to get it. They do things like that. I was not part of the neighborhood, not one of the boys. I felt afraid and, like most liberals then, my fear of the poor also made me feel guilty.

We heard Spanish music from portable radios, and rock and roll, and conversations in unfamiliar languages not English. And then I saw Pearl running toward us.

Now, you would think—considering the fact that Pearl would influence my life and touch my heart for twelve years to come, considering the fact that I would love her—you would think the heavens would open up and angels descend and I might even hear a trumpet or two, or a few bars of recorded harp music; you'd think I'd be overwhelmed, and have thoughts—*visions*—that would be special and remarkable and in keeping with the significance of the occasion.

It wasn't like that at all.

Pearl was trying to run across the roof toward us, and she was clumsy about it, taking steps too small and throwing her legs out to the sides as if her shoes kept getting stuck to the asphalt. In other words, Pearl ran the way most women do. Most women when they run are like geese on the ground, totally out of their element. There is something touching in that, as there is in all awkwardness.

"Bonita!" Pearl exclaimed, still several yards from us.

"That Pearl," Bonita said, with undisguised annoyance.

Pearl came to a stop in front of us. She stood smiling there, breathlessly, her hands on her hips like a basketball player in time out. Which was appropriate, since she was wearing satin basketball shorts, green with yellow piping, and a white T-shirt several sizes too large for her. Her T-shirt was soaked with sweat. I could see her breasts heave against the cotton as she breathed, her nipples darkly visible under her clinging shirt.

She had high, lovely cheekbones and a straight, strong nose. Her full lips were puffy and moist, sensuous, even wanton in comparison with the gauntness of her cheeks.

Her hair was pulled back and held in place by a ribbon.

I looked at Pearl with her native elegance and simple beauty, and then I glanced at Bonita done up like a carnival float. And I wondered why I was with one and not the other. Fifty dollars, that's why.

"Did you ask your papa?" Pearl drawled. "Will y'all lend us a hand? We'd be mighty grateful." She had a deeply Southern accent, bayou, Louisiana or Mississippi, an accent one rarely encountered in New York except among welfare blacks.

"He say no. He say Piers no fucking good."

"Now, now, honey," Pearl cautioned.

Bonita turned to me. "Piers a scumbag," she announced in a loud voice. "A shithole."

"Why, that isn't true, honey, and you know it. Piers just needs a fair chance, that's all," Pearl said, a kind of sick smile flickering bravely. "We need your help, no denying that. And it's so little we require, just a place to store Piers's trunk for a few weeks. I'll *pay* you." Pearl sounded desperate, but she was relentless. She plowed ahead. "Here," she was holding money and trying to get Bonita to take it. It was like trying to get a Baptist elder to take a drink in church.

Bonita was unmoved. "Papa say no."

"But we need *help*. Take the money, for God's sake."

"You can no buy *me*," Bonita declared, her voice stern and full of moral rebuke, "Not for a million dollar!"

A million dollar? I looked at Bonita. She was hot off the shelf for fifty dollar, less in winter.

"Hell's bells." Pearl's shoulders slumped, for a moment defeated. "If I can't store his trunk with you, then I'll have to get a car and move it over to Maurice's. I really thought y'all would help me, Bonita. I'll never find a car, goddamn it."

"What's the problem?" I asked.

"What say?"

"What do you need?"

"A car. I need to borrow a car."

"I can get a car," I said. I don't know why I offered. I would like to think it was out of a sense of helping someone in a jam, a disinterested act of liberal charity, a gesture of human solidarity, the usual flimflam.

I offered the car because Pearl was exceedingly sexy, and I was fascinated to know what someone that beautiful, someone from the South, was doing on this roof pleading for help from a teen-age hooker.

"This man with me!" Bonita snarled, making a threatening step toward Pearl. She suspected Pearl was trying to snatch the rabbit from out of her snare.

Pearl flinched and stepped backward.

"So you won't even help me," she said, finally admitting defeat. "That really takes the cake."

"I tell my old man," Bonita warned, possessively grabbing my hand, "You stay the hell away."

"See you later!" I grinned, glancing back as Bonita dragged me away.

Pearl said not a word. She stood where she was, looking offended and angry and bereft, like someone watching her only friend sink beneath the waves. But I could tell she was thinking fast.

"Pearl no good whore. She stay with this Piers, who is shit, man. She come from down South a few days ago. Piers sick now, so she come around expecting everybody to help the faggot. I hope Piers die. I hope he die bad!"

"She lives with a queer?" I found that remarkable.

Bonita shrugged. "He no good," she said, dismissing the question.

We were nearly to the other side of the roof when Bonita pointed to the edge. "That where they offed Paco. They cut Paco's throat, like that." She made a slashing gesture against her throat. "They break his arms. They throw his body over wall and he hit sidewalk. He broke like a fucking melon."

"Good God."

Bitterly: "Oh, *he* know. *He* know who done it. *I hope he die.*"

She meant Piers.

Four

THE PUBLIC hallway on Bonita's floor smelled of urine and spilled whiskey.

A man sat in the living room of her apartment watching a huge color television set. There were five brand-new color television sets in the room, and there were also boxes of stereo equipment, radios, small appliances, silver tea sets, musical instruments, and more.

"Papa, I see Pearl up on roof," Bonita snitched as we entered the room. "I tell her no. We don't want Piers's shit here. Piers no good."

Her father nodded, not taking his eyes off the television set. He was dressed only in a pair of boxer shorts. He kept pulling at his crotch as he watched television and drank wine from a bottle. He looked about my age, in his early thirties. He had acne on his chin.

"Better they go," Bonita continued. "That way they no come back."

Her father snorted in agreement, and pulled hard on his crotch, like someone pulling on a bell cord. "*Puta,*" he grunted, "*puta.*" He lasciviously smacked his lips, and then glanced at me, his eyes narrowing. He looked like a Mexican bandit, which couldn't have been far off the mark.

Bonita tugged playfully on my ear. "He very pretty, no?" she said of me, smiling flirtatiously at her father. I wondered if they had sex together. Pimps usually taste their piece of cake.

"Fuck her quick." He was addressing me.

I nodded.

"You give money."

"Later," I said.

"No later."

He shoved his hand down the side of the chair cushion and pulled out a ten-inch switchblade. He flipped it open. Bonita giggled. He ran the blade against the palm of his hand like a barber sharpening a razor on a strap.

"Money now. Fuck later." He was a man of few words.

"Absolutely." I gave him a fifty-dollar bill.

He studied the bill. He held it up to the light. He spit on the front of it, right smack into the face of former President Ulysses S. Grant. He rubbed his spit hard against Grant's beard. Then he grunted in satisfaction, stuffed the money under the chair cushion, and his gaze went back to the television set, where Joan Rivers, a nightclub comic, was doing jokes about her suburban kitchen.

Bonita and I went into the small bedroom, and I was astonished and moved by the sweetness of it.

It was like a little girl's room, like my daughter's might have been if she had survived. My daughter was eight days old when she breathed her last. Eight days, think of it. I guess that was long enough for her to know she wanted out.

There was a vanity table and stool covered in pleated white cotton, the material attached to the wood by staples that had rusted. Dolls were piled everywhere. The bedspread was made of pink Dacron. On it was sewn a large white and pink appliqué poodle with a rhinestone collar.

On the walls was a poster of Elvis Presley, who was also wearing rhinestones, and several unframed oil paintings, the kind you paint by number. The paintings were of puppies, and the Ascension of the Holy Virgin Mother, and the Sacred Heart of Jesus. The Sacred Heart looked like a fat red brandy flask. It was on fire.

On the window ledge was a plastic bust of John F. Kennedy, the kind sold in dime stores everywhere. Someone had painted his face and hair in Day-Glo colors. Around his neck hung a plastic garnet rosary. It seemed both grotesque and reverent.

I had briefly worked for Kennedy, and I am proud of that fact. I wondered what he would think of the plastic bust with its rosary collar, and the room in general, and my being there. He would probably think, It's okay with me.

"You a sexy man," Bonita allowed, kissing my cheek. "What you want to do?"

"Whatever you like."

Bonita looked undecidedly at me. She exhaled tiredly, seeming very young all of a sudden, like a little girl after too much play. I wanted to tell her about my daughter, whose name was Rose, and about finding her dead in her crib two days after she was brought home from the maternity ward at New York Hospital. The grief that followed, the hysteria, and the blame. It was in the shock of her early death, so unexpected and unaccountable and dreadful, that my marriage began to unravel. Suspicion was born between her mother and me, and we never quite trusted one another again because our first baby had died. We never learned the cause. Sudden crib death, common enough. She simply gave off breathing, for no discernible reason, and that was that. But in the lack of knowledge, in the why of it, guilt flourished, and with it rancor.

So I wanted to tell her how much I missed little Rose, and how often I imagined what she would be like now, if only she hadn't decided to check out early. But the moment passed and Bonita fell into her whore's role.

She yanked the pink Dacron spread off her bed and roughly pulled back the top sheet. It was stained, and gray from need of bleach. Then she turned her back to me and started to undress, pulling off her tank top.

"I want to watch," I said. I always want to watch. Usually I would rather watch than do anything. It's safer.

Bonita turned to face me, her expression hard.

"Don't look so solemn," I said. "Smile for me. You're prettier when you smile."

The game had started. She smiled, held her smile for a second or two, and then dropped it. A look of professional boredom, weariness, and remove took its place.

I thought of Pearl. I wondered if she was still on the roof. For a fleeting moment I considered calling off the game and leaving and trying to find her. I didn't leave. I remembered the fifty dollars invested, and I saw Bonita cupping her breasts in her hands and lifting them toward her face. I think she believed that that was arousing, hoisting them like huge water lilies toward her nose. But she did it too abruptly and coldly, like someone examining damaged goods.

She unbuttoned her skirt. I watched it fall to the floor.

"Leave your boots on. It's sexy when you're naked and wearing boots."

I undressed.

She went to turn off the ceiling light. I told her to leave it alone. It was a very bright light, like light in a surgical theatre, and it was good because it gave a severe edge to the room that worked against any intimacy and humanity in the situation, and that was useful because I did not want to feel for the girl. I wanted it to be cut and dried, and to the point. I wanted to play the hawk.

I wanted to feel no affection for Bonita, or even pity, and less respect, because if I felt any of that I chanced feeling guilt about what I was doing and about the transaction between us and about who she was and about the grinding, unremitting sorrow of a future she was helpless to avoid. I had better things to feel guilt about than an Avenue B tart whose father was her pimp. Not that it mattered.

I had a child lost to me, and a father strung up, and much more. And all of it sat on my mind like concrete that never moved.

Only now, in the last few years, had I been buying sex. Only now, since my wife ran off, only now, since I closed tight the rooms she filled, I mean the ones inside me, only now had I been buying girls. I was attracted to them to the degree that they did not resemble my wife. And yet, at times, even with them I would find myself thinking it was my wife I held and loved and was inside. I needed bright lights to keep the thought of her away.

After our marriage collapsed I didn't want to love anyone again.

We had both hurt each other, and the hurt was as deep as our love had been. I didn't want to be in that position again, made vulnerable to pain by love.

Through it all I found it increasingly difficult *not* to feel. That was the key to pulling it off. Not to feel. The trick to keeping your balance.

I could have been a sap and taken to drugs, or to rough sex, or to the rituals of violence, or lost my self and feeling in radical politics and the oppositionist fever. But that wasn't me. I was a pushover for affection, for sentiment, even as I feared the hurt it invited. Ibsen once said that the strongest man in the world was he who stood entirely alone. I thought that about said it all, only I wasn't that strong. But that's a long story, and not a very interesting one, yet it had a heap to do with why I was in a crummy apartment on the fourteenth floor of a public housing project about to have carnal knowledge of a teen-age girl who would not take the gum out of her mouth.

I lay back on the bed. Bonita would not kiss my mouth, even if I paid extra. It's a hell of a task getting a prostitute to kiss you on the mouth. They'll kiss you anywhere else, and do, but when it comes to your lips they think of germs. Or affection, because kissing implies that sex has become love-making—and that you can't pay them to do.

She knelt over me, her buttocks over my face, her sex above my mouth. I could smell her sex and the horsey odor of her leather boots. And I could smell the scent of a day's worth of semen on and in her body. It had the approximate odor of one's hands after handling fresh fish, or the odor of the sea when it shoves its tidal body up into the Hudson River toward West Point. The smell of a working girl at the end of her day.

The Chanel No. 5 didn't help.

Through Bonita's legs I could see her breasts hanging full above my erection, and I could see her pink tongue touch the tip of it, and watch her small hand, its fingers covered with expandable rings that you win in bubble-gum machines in Playland, pull back my foreskin, and her warm, sugary mouth coat its head and then take it all at once.

I thrust slightly. I felt her gag. I felt her thighs involuntarily tighten and her body tremble. She removed her mouth, and the bubble-gum stuck to my rigid penis. She giggled and pulled the gum off and shoved it back in her mouth.

She slipped down on the bed and her sex pressed over my mouth.

She sat up and squatted over me. I put my tongue inside her. That is how we did it to each other, she faking orgasm with no conviction.

Just before I ejaculated she turned around facing me and stuck my penis inside her and rocked on her heels. She lay bent over on her knees with her head resting against my shoulder. I could feel her warm breath against my inner ear.

Her indifference was staggering, and I came.

I felt guilty and lonely and disconnected and missing out, and I felt sorry for her, and that was the worst of it.

When we were finished we lay there for a few minutes while I smoked a cigarette. I touched Bonita's body lazily with my hand. It was hot in the room, yet she shivered.

"Do you shave it?" I asked.

"I don't have to, man. I'm only thirteen."

Five

I WAS amazed. Hell, I didn't even know what sex was when I was thirteen. And here was Bonita, going at it like gangbusters since she was eleven, selling the family jewels like it was the most natural thing in the world.

I didn't know how babies were made until I was fourteen. I was visiting my mother and two sisters in Santa Barbara, where they lived on the side of a small mountain overlooking the offshore oil rigs polluting the Pacific. My mother lived with a man named Bob, who made his money selling machines to pollute the air, to wit: he had an Oldsmobile dealership in Los Angeles. Bob was only home on weekends, which was all right by me because Bob was a real ass.

This is how I discovered the Great Secret: my mother was sitting on the toilet. She called me into the bathroom.

"Do you know where babies come from?" she asked.

I said not a word. What I knew was that they came from inside female stomachs, but for the life of me I could never figure out how they managed to get in or out. There had to be a secret door to which I hadn't a clue.

I was a city boy, and it wasn't until I was seven that I learned to my utter astonishment that Dairylea Milk came from moo cows. At eleven years I still believed that marshmallows grew on bushes in marshes. I was disfigured by shyness, by an inexpressible panic, a terror that got worse after my old man tossed in the towel, and so I wouldn't ask questions. If I didn't know something, like how milk was made, I just let it go by.

"I didn't *think* you knew," my mother said in disgust. "Just like your father not to get around to it. Well, they come from here." She bumped her pelvis up. "Right here. Daddy puts his peter inside Mama's glove and shoots in the sweet stuff, and that's how it happens."

"Oh."

"Now, that's over with," she said.

I liked the fact that Bonita was only thirteen. There was something incestuous about it, looking back, something incontrovertably sinful, and that gave it a real kick. And supposedly that is what the 1960s were about in the good old U.S. of A. Getting your kicks.

But they were about something deeper than that, and worse than that, and unhappier and more cruel.

The Sixties were about Death.

Six

I FOUND Pearl on the roof sitting on an upended orange crate. Her long legs were crossed at the ankles, and she was staring down at the street like someone at a wake that had gone on too long. She was watching two black men fighting each other under a street-lamp twenty stories below while a crowd of fifty people or so enthusiastically egged them on. We heard police sirens in the distance. It would soon be over.

"Hi," I said, smiling at Pearl, giving her a little salute. I remembered John-John Kennedy saluting his father as they carried his flag-draped casket down the Capitol steps. Too much memory, public and private, too much waste and ruination, enough to make you gag.

She looked startled, and then she smiled. I sat down on an orange crate near her.

"I knew you'd be back, I just knew it." She brushed back her hair with her hand. She had removed the ribbon that held it in place. "How was Bonita?"

"She chews a lot of gum."

"That's the least of it, honey," she laughed. "She chews on a lot more than gum."

"She's only thirteen. I didn't know that."

"Does it matter to you?" she asked. I said nothing in reply. "I didn't think you'd mind. It's real common, don't you know, in the South anyway, to start young. Most girls are around the block before their first training bra. I know a few girls who upped and married and had kids before they were thirteen, and ten years later they look like old women bent in the back. I'm twenty-three and I was saved from that, thank the good Lord."

The subject of teen-age sex made me uncomfortable, or at least discussing it with Pearl did. I don't know why, unless it was because I wanted to believe that she was different and better than I and wasn't open to intimacy on first meeting. Certain women, when you first encounter them, seem made to be courted. You don't want it to come easy. You want it to be earned, like something precious you save up for years to possess, and when you finally have it you discover that it is as good as it promised to be. There is very little in life worth the wait. I thought Pearl was worth the wait, right from the start.

"When do you need the car?" I asked.

"Oh, I need a car right now."

I looked at my watch. It was after one.

"I think I can borrow one, but we'll have to hurry."

"Thanks, honey." She stood and stepped toward me and she mussed my hair with her hand. She smelled of sandalwood cologne. "You're right good in a pinch. I need someone good tonight."

Impossible line, but I believed her. Not only that, I was flattered by her trust, and made to feel strong by her very need. It made me feel decent. It's not bad, on a hot night on a New York slum roof, to find an angel inviting your help.

Pearl took my hand and we walked to the stairwell and started down a flight of stairs to the floor where she was staying. It was dark, most of the lights smashed by vandals.

"What the hell are you *doing* here?"

"Piers."

"That the guy Bonita hates so much? Watch your step!" I grabbed her arm as she stumbled. "Why does she hate him?"

"Piers? Because she thinks he killed Paco, her boyfriend. Or if he didn't do it by himself, he knows who did. That's why." She spoke very quietly, like someone who feared being overheard.

Now I stopped. I was suddenly nervous. "*Did* he kill Paco?"

"Let's sit and visit a minute, honey."

We sat on the landing in the dark. She continued to hold my hand. I offered her a cigarette. Then I took one and lit them both.

In the light of the flame I thought I saw tears in her eyes. She looked away.

"What's wrong?" I asked.

"Sometimes it's so damn hard just going down the road. Each step. The morning, and then you got the afternoon to get through. And then the night, the hardest of all. Lord in heaven, some days don't I wish they'd thrown me out with the bathwater."

I took her hand and lifted it to my lips and kissed it, because I did not know what to say.

We finished our cigarettes.

"You married?" she asked.

"Was. And you?"

"Almost, but wasn't."

"What happened?"

"Oh, what you might expect," she said. "He fell for someone else. His name was Tommy Lee Davis, and he run a motor court in Panama City, Florida. I was about sixteen at the time, and he was the first man I ever did meet who had himself his own car and television, and who wasn't mean. I lived with him for a few months and I worked in the café at the motor court, and we got along just fine because Piers was off working a fishing boat in the Gulf, don't you see, and I was awful lonely. Then Tommy Lee turned around and married someone else, the woman who bought the motor court. Money calls the tune. Money always calls the tune."

"And you had none?"

"Not so much as a lucky penny in my shoe."

"Does Piers have money?"

"Piers?" she laughed bitterly. "Piers is flat busted, and Piers is dying. Now, don't that beat all? My Piers dying?"

Seven

I CALLED Hayton Ransome. I had known him for a very long time, since we were boys together. He reluctantly agreed to lend me his car.

We couldn't get a taxi on the Lower East Side, so we took a subway to midtown and walked from there to Beekman Place, where Hayton lived on the first three floors of a Federal town house owned by his mother. He lived alone. Hayton was twenty-five, and he had been overindulged and overmothered, and much too rich too early—he was very American in that.

I rang the bell. A few minutes later, Hayton appeared at the door in a blue velvet smoking jacket and black trousers and petit-point carpet slippers. He bought his slippers at Harrod's in London. They were sewn by young girls in Hong Kong, who slowly went blind in the process. No one dressed that way anymore, just Hayton and a few old British actors in Hollywood who were trying to maintain standards. Nobody cared.

"C-Come in," he said irritably. "It's a horrid hour to be borrowing a car." And then he saw Pearl, still dressed in her basketball shorts and T-shirt, and he exclaimed, "I say!" brightening, sounding like an old actor. "What have we here? Do come in, come in!"

He pulled the door wide open, and made a small bow, and ushered us in. The foyer had floors and walls of imported Italian marble taken from the same stone quarry where Michelangelo used to get his stuff. An early Roman bust of a patrician stood in a niche. The foyer was as antiseptic as a men's room in a deluxe restaurant. You expected a porter to hand you a scented towel and begin brushing your coat.

Pearl seemed in awe.

"We're in a damnable hurry, Hayton," I said, as we followed him up the stairs into the living room on the second floor. It was a long room, the rear wall solid glass affording a pricey view of the East River and the Pepsi-Cola sign and the dreary barred windows of the public madhouses on Welfare Island.

There were Rigaud candles burning everywhere, giving the house the smell of a perfumery on overtime. I glanced at Pearl. She was enchanted.

"You have time for a drink. So stay while I hunt the bloody car keys. Haven't the vaguest where I could have tossed them." He smiled at Pearl. "Do sit *down*," he said, gesturing to the raw silk sofas by the fireplace.

It was a very hot night, but Hayton Ransome's fireplace was blazing away in the coldly air-conditioned house. Richard Milhous Nixon would have felt right at home.

In fact, Nixon once remarked in this very room that he felt right at home, and then laughed sheepishly, fearing that he'd gone too far. This was in 1960 when he was plotting to seize the Republican presidential nomination from Nelson Aldrich Rockefeller, and he was talking to Ambassador Orin Ransome, Hayton's illustrious father. Rockefeller was a social and business friend of the Ransomes, and while the Ambassador was a lifelong Democrat, he was considered neutral in that conflict and acted as mediator between the two ambitious Republicans. Which wasn't surprising. Ambassador Ransome had mediated for Presidents and would-be Presidents since the days of Joseph Stalin, another acquaintance of his. He made a career of being useful to men who wanted to cut each other's throats. He was always neutral. That's where the bucks are. Just ask the Swiss.

"Introduce your stunning friend," Hayton prompted.

"Pearl . . . ?" I was embarrassed. I had never asked her last name.

"Pearl Oxford." She smiled. "And you're . . . ?"

"Hayton Ransome. You're Southern, Pearl. How splendid. Mississippi, I trust? We have a country place there, east of Natchez. You must fly down and visit when the weather cools."

The place was called Timberton. Two thousand acres, a mansion, and two swimming pools.

"The *car*, Hayton." I was getting tired of all the soft soap. I knew he was excited at meeting Pearl because when he got excited his voice went from a cultivated baritone to an unsteady tenor, and he forgot to stutter. He had learned to affect a mild stutter at Eton. In Britain many of the bluer bloods and the old fat-cat families—but *only* the males among them—affect a stutter. Only God knows why.

"Can't tell you how pleased I am to see you. Only got in myself about an hour ago, just before I got your call. Went with Binky to this new club on the Brooklyn waterfront. Tawdry, actually. Topless dancers and longshoremen, that sort of place. Amusing in its way." He couldn't take his eyes off Pearl. "But I wouldn't take someone as lovely as you to such a place. Good God, no. But let me take you somewhere special for lunch this week, La Grenouille perhaps? Or Lutèce?"

"We need your car, remember?" I was annoyed by Hayton's pass at Pearl, who was, after all, with me. "The *keys*?"

"Oh," he said, still looking into her eyes as if I weren't in the room. "First you must see my new Ellsworth Kelly. You'll love it, darling." They stood. "It's actually sort of marvelous. Very cool, greens and blues, very primary shapes, fiercely hard-edge," he cooed, taking Pearl's hand and leading her from the room. "In a word, fabulous. Like you."

That is how Hayton talked when he was trying to impress. He talked like most of his friends in the Pack, men and women, like a piss-elegant patrician high on ludes.

"There's some wine and caviar in the fridge at the bar if you want to drag it out. Pavlavi stuff."

They left the living room.

It was golden caviar, the kind only the Shah of Iran was allowed to eat when he ran the store. The Shah liked sending batches of it to his friends, like Imelda Marcos and Andy Warhol and senators on the Foreign Relations Committee. He sent it regularly to Hayton's father.

I opened the wine and sat on the sofa and watched the fire. After the first glass I looked at my watch. They had been gone for ten minutes. Why did we have to borrow his car, why did she have to meet him? Because you couldn't get a taxi on the Lower East Side at night any more than you could in Harlem or Bed-Sty. And you couldn't rent a car at that hour. So here we were. Or rather I was, with Pearl upstairs examining expensive paintings in his bedroom. I didn't like any of it.

I waited another five minutes, and then started up the stairs. When I reached the top I saw them coming down the hall. Hayton's arm around her, and he was giggling and whispering something in her ear.

"Where the hell's the car keys?"

"My, my, aren't we feisty!" He had adopted Pearl's Southern drawl.

He pulled the car keys from his jacket pocket and dangled them in my face. "D-Drive carefully," he advised, smirking. "Varina would absolutely *hate* having to buy her little b-boy another Jensen this season."

Hayton laughed, and then Pearl laughed, a beat too late.

As we left, Pearl thanked him, and he pecked her on the cheek. "Remember: Mind and Matter." He howled with laughter, and she laughed too.

Eight

I DROVE Pearl downtown in Hayton's car, saying very little. I was angry, and I was confused by my anger. Face it, I was jealous. Simple as that.

"You never had your wine," I said, breaking the silence.

"I had a glass in his bedroom."

"What else did you have in his bedroom?"

"What are you all fired up about? Good Lord, I kissed him once or twice, if it's anything to you, and I don't rightly see what business it is of yours."

"Sorry."

"What was his name again?" she asked.

"Hayton."

"No, his last name."

"Ransome. Hayton goddamn Ransome. You want me to spell it for you?"

"What's got into you? I just thought he was nice, if a little wacky. I like wacky men. You know he has a bar in his bedroom? In the brass bookshelves. Can you imagine? It opens automatically. The books move and there it is, big as life, made of mirrors and with a tiny sink and running water, like in a trailer house. And an ice box."

"Big deal."

"He must be mighty rich."

"His parents are. Filthy rich."

"I never been in swatting distance of the rich before, and it does seem miraculous when you think about it, I mean, that they exist, and that you can meet and touch them. The only rich folks I ever met were preachers, Baptists mostly, who owned their own churches and buses and big cars. But they never lived as good as Hayton. Is he married?"

"Why do you want to know?"

"I'm just curious," she said, defensively.

"No, Hayton is not married. He's what's known as a most eligible bachelor. A major catch. A goddamn gold mine."

"Oh." She thought a moment. "I think he fancies me a tad, not that I care. Still in all, when you think about it, he must get lonely being in that big house all by his lonesome."

She was fishing, and I did not like it. "No, Young Master Ransome has a veritable stable of overnight guests to comfort him. He's known as a ladies' man."

"A rich playboy?" she laughed.

"What were you two laughing about when we left? Did someone die and leave Hayton a bundle?"

"It was a joke," she said. "I didn't think it was funny, but I laughed anyway. The German commandant says to the Jews, 'Let's play Mind and Matter. It's a joke. You'll love it.' So the Germans take the Jews to the edge of a cliff. They machine-gun them. The last Jew left in the line scratches his head and says to the German commandant, 'I don't get the joke. Mind and Matter?' The German commandant laughs, 'Ve don't *mind*. And you don't *matter!*' "

It was the kind of joke you would expect from Hayton. Most of the Pack were anti-Semites, especially the Jews in the Pack. It was the rich Jews who usually told the most bald-faced jokes to gentiles. They laughed hard and long, the Jews did. They wanted to be one of the boys. They wanted you to forget that they were cut.

I never understood that. As I never understood why some of the most liberal rich holidayed in Franco's Spain, or in Haiti, or other oppressed places.

We parked Hayton's Jensen in front of the housing project on Avenue B. For a moment I was afraid that the car might be stolen, and then I thought, Screw him.

When I was around Hayton, and when I was around a lot of other young men who had money they never earned, I thought of F. Scott Fitzgerald and I remembered that he said, ". . . I could never forgive the rich for being rich."

Nine

I T TOOK some time to drag Piers's trunk from the apartment foyer to Hayton's car, but we did it. The damn trunk must have weighed a hundred and fifty pounds. By the time we were outside, and I had stopped pulling in front, and Pearl had stopped pushing in back, it finally occurred to me to ask, "Baby, is it really necessary? My back aches like hell."

We were sitting on top of the hood of the car resting a few minutes before lifting the thing into the Jensen's trunk.

"Beau," she said, all out of breath.

By this point in the proceedings Pearl had named me Beau. When I asked her why she called me Beau when my given name was Michael, she explained that every woman needs a beau in her life, she more than most.

Anyway, I hated my name. Michael. Mike. Mikey. Mickey. Mick.

"Long, tall Mick/sucks his own dick" was a refrain I heard in the school showers.

The man who betrayed my father was also named Michael. Michael Garrett. It was during the troubles of the 1950s when men grown middle-aged in sweet-ass jobs in Washington, D.C., became frightened of losing retirement benefits and government life insurance and federal health care and mortgaged split-levels in the suburbs. Cowardice was patriotic. It still is. So to save his split-level, along with his ass, Michael Garrett spilled the beans about my old man, and that was that.

After my father's funeral Garrett told me he thought it would all blow over.

He said, "I didn't mean any harm. Goddamn it, you have to believe me. I didn't think they'd carry it *that* far. I believed Ike would put his foot down. Goddamn it to hell, your father and I were pals. We were buddies, soulmates. We loved each other! We were as close as you can be. Believe me, I meant no harm."

"I understand," I said, embarrassed by his pleading, by his hurried explanation punctuated by quick glances over his shoulder. Of course, I didn't understand because even then I didn't believe that intentions counted for much. Acts mattered. They announced character and most everything else worth knowing about a man. Intention declared after the fact was only camouflage spun of remorse to conceal accountability. Something like that.

"What can I do?" he continued, gripping my shoulder hard. " 'The Moving Finger writes,' you know, 'and having writ moves on.' " He shrugged sheepishly, as if having made a poor joke.

But I wondered why he didn't come to the funeral to tell me. Instead, he cornered me on the street a block from my house when no one was around.

"Listen," he patted my shoulder roughly like a drunk at a bar, "if you need any help, a few bucks maybe, just call me anytime. I try to do what I can on my salary, but I can stretch things a bit if you need help. I mean, for your father's sake. He probably talked about me a lot, right?"

I didn't know what he meant.

"*Right?*" he repeated.

"No, not much. Just about fishing with you."

"That all?" he asked, obviously relieved. "Well, we had a great time going after the trout, I tell you that. Your father always kept his mouth shut about company business. That's why we were friends. Remember, call me anytime. But not at the office, okay?" Michael Garrett added before he ran down the street.

He worked at the State Department.

"Beau," Pearl said, sweat running down her face like it ran down mine, "if we don't get this damn trunk safe in storage at Maurice's apartment, Piers won't leave on the plane tomorrow morning. And if he misses the plane, he'll die. Sure as shooting."

We hoisted the trunk into the car, and as we did its identification tag tore off. I picked it up. "Denton P. Goodpasture," it read, "1046 Dumaine, New Orleans."

I handed it to Pearl. "You better tie that back on. Who's Denton Goodpasture?"

"That's Piers, silly. Piers is his middle name. He hates Denton."

"And who's this Maurice?" I asked, as we drove uptown to East 78th Street, where Maurice lived.

"He's a friend of Piers's. I haven't met him, but he's been good as rain to Piers. Saved his life, I reckon. He's agreed to store Piers's trunk until other arrangements can be made."

"What's in old Piers's trunk?" I inquired.

"Books, I expect. I never did open it. He fancies books. Poetry mostly."

"You mean it could be a dead body for all you know, or illicit drugs, or gold bullion."

"It wouldn't be gold. Piers hates gold."

I was overly fond of gold. I owned two gold bracelets, anniversary gifts from my wife. *To Sweet Thing from His Buttercup.* Four gold pillboxes, very small, given to me by my lawyer after I wrote and sold the scripts to four B movies. I also owned my father's gold Cartier Santos tank watch, his gold cuff links, his gold stickpin, his gold money clip, and his gold watch fob from which hung a gold-plated .38 magnum bullet that had been removed from his left thigh by a surgeon at the Walter Reed Army Hospital in 1946. That was quite a haul for me after Michael Garrett spilled the beans.

"I bought Piers a gold watch once," Pearl continued.

She seemed happy now, or less anxious. Moving that trunk was very important to her, and she was relieved that things were under way.

"It was in Florida. I was living in a motor court with Tommy Lee—the man I thought wanted to marry me? and one of the patrons claimed he found this old watch in the men's room at a gas station on the Interstate. I rightly knew it was hot, but I made an offer anyway. It cost me all of ten dollars. I gave it to Piers on his birthday. He's a Capricorn, just like me. Then one afternoon we walked along the beach, and wouldn't you know he yanked that old watch right off quick as lightning and tossed it smack dab in the ocean. Just like that. Why, you'd of thought it was an empty pop bottle, worth nothing at all. When I inquired why he done such a mighty foolish thing, he said 'Bourbon Street.' "

"What'd he mean?"

"If you ever been to New Orleans you know that on Bourbon Street's where the hustlers and the whores are. The boys wear lots of them gold chains, even gold earrings. That's how you spot them, by the gold. Piers, because he's truly beautiful, did hate anybody thinking he was selling boodie. I swear, he'd like beat the living daylights out of any soul that tried to get his boodie."

"Really?"

"Why," she continued, "I can't tell you the very many occasions I seen ladies, and even *men*, lusting after Piers. I seen their hungry looks. Perfect strangers with some hellish itch they desire him to scratch. Mind you, Piers smiles some, and he may give them a kiss to put them off, and then wink at me to let me know it's his way of being polite. Or he'll shrug and laugh some. It's like Jesus almost, the way they do follow that boy about."

"Jesus?"

"He has them eyes of Jesus, don't you know," Pearl replied in the most straightforward way.

"Once in New Orleans we was in Jackson Square on the river, just hanging out in the cool, and a couple come up and offered Piers fifty dollars if we was to go to bed with them. *Fifty dollars.* I don't believe we had a plug nickel between the two of us. You know what Piers did? Why, he stood there looking as serious as a deacon, like he was considering it, and he bid them *up*. One hundred, one-fifty, two hundred! Land's sakes, I couldn't believe my ears. And not only that, he took ten dollars down on account! Don't that beat all? We still laugh about it, ten dollars down on account."

Pearl giggled, amused by the memory of Piers outwitting a pair of longing souls in some public park.

Then quietly, as if speaking to herself, but determinedly, indeed fiercely, as if she were confiding in me some vital fact about which she entertained no ambiguity whatsoever, she said, "I love Piers. I won't ever let him be broken, I swear I'd kill for that boy and not look back. I truly would. I'm never going to let Piers be hurt again, not as long as rivers flow to the sea."

Rivers to the sea.

"What does that have to do with his dislike of gold?"

Pearl smiled condescendingly, like a teacher to a pupil asking a dumb question. "Piers hates gold because it's the whores' metal."

Ten

I SHOULD have caught on to who Maurice was before I saw his black face peering at us through a crack in the door of his Upper East Side apartment.

Once we were inside, he recognized me, although neither of us said a word about seeing each other around town, at parties and in the bar he owned.

Maurice. He had a one-name name. He was a cabaret owner and man-about-town, very popular with the Pack. In fact, his place on East 54th Street was named Le Gratin, a French word with a meaning roughly equivalent to "the Pack."—The upper crust, the social cream, the rich and fancy. For years he had run it and gradually built a following. He featured black blues singers and jazz greats, always women; passable food and a handsome if somewhat stuffy décor. It was said he had Mafia connections, and that he was very helpful in a discreet way in obtaining drugs and other illegal pleasures for the Pack. And to it all there was an air of seedy elegance, of a kind of hushed 1930s restraint, a sense of whispered indulgence, of expensive pampering. In short, Le Gratin and Maurice were a refuge for the rich in Manhattan, a combination supper club, cabaret, and procurement station that functioned quietly with understated, almost languid, efficiency.

Maurice was fifty years old, but looked thirty, and as the Sixties stomped in, smelling of mary jane and sounding like rock and roll, he became increasingly valuable to the Pack. A reassurance in the alcoholic night. For the rich were disquieted by what was happening around them. As well they might be, since it was as plain as the nose on your face that most of the known world hated their guts, and most of their children did too. They didn't like it, and they didn't understand it, and it was comforting to go to Le Gratin, where black tie was never out of place, and to find good old colored Maurice standing glued to his spot by the door and welcoming you, with proper deference and dignity, as if money conferred special value on your person, as if nothing ever changed, no civil rights and antiwar movements, no assassinations and terror in the streets, just the fashionable rich, and everyone else who happily paid them their due. The place brought to mind better days, in particular the Great Depression, when the rich danced through the worst of it in white tie and tails. Just like Fred Astaire. When they were with Maurice at Le Gratin, they knew they'd be dancing again.

And Maurice found himself to be chic. In demand. The only chocolate drop on the pavement you could trust to come to your dinner party and act like a white man. He was just right in his overly tailored Savile Row suits and Italian shoes and white-capped teeth and subtly powdered face. He wore Dunhill cologne and gushed, in a nicely modulated, arch, lock-jawed way, words like "Fabulous! Marvelous! Top Drawer! Simply too, too divine!" as if he meant them. As if he had grown up a WASP heiress on the South Shore of Long Island and attended Farmington rather than having scuffed his troubled way out of Harlem and never finished high school.

He had no black friends. He was also homosexual. But that was convenient, too. A dinge queen. At least you didn't have to worry about one black buck going after your white wife or, God help you, your white daughter who smoked grass laced with angel dust and did acid and thought the Black Panthers were the bees' knees.

"It's nearly three o'clock in the morning," Maurice groused, opening the door. "Couldn't you have come sooner?"

"I had trouble getting a car," I explained.

He fluttered his hands in dismissal. "You're Pearl? Ah, and how's dear Piers?"

"The same," she said. "He said to thank you."

"It's really, really nothing, my sweet. And I did so mean to visit him."

"I'm sorry about the hour," Pearl apologized.

"Just leave it by the door," Maurice replied wearily, pointing at the trunk. "I'll have the houseboy put it somewhere in the A.M."

Maurice kept his eyes averted. He wore a velvet jacket, like Hayton's, and white silk pajama bottoms underneath.

"Who's there, Moosey?" A boy's voice from the bedroom.

Maurice glanced painfully at us, flinching slightly. I felt sorry for his embarrassment. So he had a boy for the night. What was it to us?

"Never mind," Maurice called out. "It's a late delivery. I'll be there in a sec."

Maurice rubbed his hands nervously on the jacket above his hips. As he did I noticed how unusually large they were, the fingers long and thick and brown as Cuban cigars, when you could still buy Cuban cigars.

"My cousin's here for a day's visit to New York. He loves Fun City. You know how these youngsters are," Maurice explained.

We dragged Piers's trunk inside.

"I'll send for it in a week or two," Pearl offered. "I'm tickled to make your acquaintance. Lord knows, if you hadn't-a called me about Piers in New Orleans, I declare he might have expired. I'm ever so grateful."

Maurice put his hands over his ears as if the compliment was simply too great to endure. "It was nothing, my dear. Nothing."

"Piers talked powerful much about you, and all you done for him of late. He was a stranger in a strange land."

"Aren't we all?" he said.

"Yes, but you were kind."

"He's a fine young fellow," Maurice remarked. "I wish I could do a thousand million times more!"

"*Moosey?*" A whimper. I looked toward the bedroom, and there in the doorway stood Maurice's "cousin." He was about eighteen years old. The Navy dog tags around his neck glinted in the light. His skin was as white as Maurice's porcelain caps. "I got to get my ass on a bus. Let's get *at* it."

"Delirious with impatience, the young," Maurice said. "Killingly so."

Eleven

I WAS surprised when I entered the apartment on Avenue B with Pearl. There was nothing inside the large living room. Even the kitchen was empty, like a vacant place up for rent. The walls were dirty, and the floor covered with dust, and clinging to it all was the smell of insecticide. The one bedroom was at the far end of the living room, its door shut.

"I hope he slept well enough," Pearl said as she unlocked it, taking a key hidden on the doorframe above.

"Why do you lock it?"

"So no one will break in. Hush now, Beau. He should be asleep."

We went into the bedroom. It was dark.

Pearl turned on a small plastic lamp on the floor by the mattress. There was a pink scarf over the shade to soften the light.

The one window was open, but the bedroom was uncomfortably warm, and it smelled heavily of perspiration and soil and sickness. It was a squalid little room with smudged walls.

Piers lay on his side. He was naked. His knees were pulled up toward his stomach and his hands were shoved down between his thighs. His back was to the door, and what I saw first was his curly brown hair damp with sweat. He was excessively thin, and, like Pearl, had long legs.

Between his jackknifed thighs hung his scrotum, unusually large and darker in color than the rest of his skin, which appeared mildly tanned in the pink light.

It may have been his position, or his labored breathing, or his rib cage visible under depleted skin, but he brought to mind some swift animal wounded and fallen in a field.

"Piers, precious," Pearl whispered, sitting on the mattress, placing his head in her lap, caressing his damp forehead and hair with her hand. "It'll be all right. I'm here now, honey. Everything will be all right."

She looked up at me and smiled sweetly. Glancing down at Piers, and then at me again, her eyes expressed concern and love and more than a little pride. He's it. He's all there is. There's nothing better.

Deeply moved, I felt no jealousy. It is a rare thing in life to find anyone so palpably and openly and, yes, *innocently* loving someone else. For her, Piers was the whole ball of wax.

She gestured me over to her.

"Beau, sit here a minute and hold him. Just caress his face so he knows he's not alone. I'll get the shower going. We have to bathe him now."

We? have to bathe him now?

I took her place on the mattress. I felt Piers's forehead and his face and neck. He was feverish.

At first I felt self-conscious and unmanly.

Piers opened his eyes and gazed at me, and then he closed them again and nodded weakly, and it was all right.

His face was extraordinary, childlike in repose; dark eyebrows which, like Pearl's, grew to the very edges of his forehead and drew your vision to his eyes beneath, where the center of Piers was housed. The longest eyelashes, like featherdusters, and high cheekbones and full lips. His handsomeness was fragile and unspoiled, almost feminine in its delicacy. I remembered Bonita's contempt, her conviction that he was complicitous in the murder of her boyfriend Paco, and it made no sense.

I heard the shower going.

Pearl came into the bedroom.

"Is he awake?"

"I'm not sure."

She stood next to me as I gently rubbed his forehead. She touched my neck in affection, her hand cool from the water.

"He's easy to love, isn't he? Easy as pie," she murmured.

She kissed the crown of my head. "But so are you."

She knelt down.

"Piers, sweetheart, are you awake?"

"Uh-huh."

He didn't open his eyes.

"We have to bathe you now. Do you think you can get up and walk, honey? We'll help you."

"I'm too beat," he said, and we could barely hear him. "Hell, I'm so damn tired."

Pearl moved away from the mattress. She pulled off her T-shirt, then her sneakers, and finally dropped her satin basketball shorts. She had nicely shaped breasts, and those firm nipples I first noticed on the roof. Her body was thin and altogether lovely, unreal in the pink light. I thought of the semi-nude nymph on those old soda bottles, and I felt depersonalized, as if it were all happening in another room through tinted glass, or on a movie screen, or in sleep.

Sometimes, when you see something fortunate and extraordinary, and unlike what you have known, something unexpected and beguiling in its simplicity and perfection, a gift undeserved, you are thrown off balance and left breathless, unable to respond normally, except to stare and try to take it all in and never forget it because you sense that the memory of it will see you through difficult times. As friends should and usually don't, as families should but often don't. So I stared at Pearl as she undressed, concentrating what attention and what capacity for memory I possessed on her body and unself-consciousness, on the soft hair of her sex, on her breasts and rounded forms and on her dear face that expressed both strength and grace at its ease.

"I'll hold him now," she said. "Y'all have to undress. We have to give the boy a shower, and you'll have to hold him. He can't go on no plane smelling like a hound with the mange. They'll know for sure he's sickly."

I obeyed.

"You're a right pretty man," she commented.

"Thank you kindly," I responded, attempting a Southern drawl.

There was innocence to it. As pure as good soap or great music or a nap in the shade. It was all right.

Listen. There are situations where people are completely unashamed and at truce with themselves because in some manner what they value most in life is singularly threatened. They are totally absorbed in the task at hand. Something lethal lumbers about, and they must defeat it. All else is armistice. Sometimes, in situations like that, people do things which, in other times and places, would be highly erotic, but that eroticism, one's awareness of it, is deflected by an innocence born of necessity and renewed in peril. Later, when you think back, you remember how beautiful and sensual and indeed sexual it actually was, or is, in recall. How close it was. But at the moment you experience it you are disconnected from it. And that's to the good.

"Can you lift him?" Pearl asked.

"Me?"

"Just take him in your arms, Beau. He's lost so much weight, he isn't at all heavy now. Look at the child. Look at what they done to him."

I raised Piers up and held him in my arms. He couldn't have weighed more than a hundred pounds. I carried him, one arm holding him under his knees, the other supporting his shoulders. His head fell back, his mouth open.

In the bathroom, Pearl said, "You'll have to stand and hold him from behind under the arms while I wash his front."

It was a small shower, not four feet square. I stood holding Piers under the cool water.

Pearl took a cloth and soaped his chest and stomach. She hesitated a moment at his crotch, and then washed him there. Except for his sex and under his arms and on his lower legs, his body was hairless. And he was smaller than I had thought, about five feet eight inches. Like Pearl, he seemed taller because of his long legs.

"Bend your head down, honey. I have to wash your hair," Pearl said.

"Okay."

It was then I noticed that his skin was yellow. Yellow, the color of dandelions. Curry. Margarine. Jaundice.

"Let's turn him around, Beau."

We did, and I held him again, his head resting on my shoulder.

Piers was a good half-foot shorter than I. He was submissive and unprotesting, his will dormant. He weakly put his arms around my neck. He raised his head and smiled at me. I saw his eyes, unusually large and almond-shaped, the irises deeply green, seductive, rich, the color of wet emeralds.

The whites of his eyes were brownish-yellow.

His mouth was open a little, his face wet with water. There was helplessness there, innocence recently routed. It was then that I understood Pearl's obsession with him, the single-mindedness of her love and its compulsion. Or rather, it was then that my understanding began.

"Thanks," he mumbled, "thanks."

I was disoriented, at a loss, as if I had unwittingly crossed the frontier of a strange new country and would never be the same again.

I carried him wet from the shower to the mattress. There I laid him on towels. Pearl wiped him dry.

He was exhausted by the small effort.

"I want to go home, Pearl," he said hoarsely. "I can't take it no more. I want to die back home."

"Nobody's going to die. I won't hear tell of it. You just get that nonsense out of your head this very minute, y'hear?" Pearl glanced worriedly at me.

Piers began to shiver. It was hot and airless in the bedroom, and the heat was made worse by the humidity from the shower. Yet he lay on the mattress shaking like a wet dog in a cold rain.

"We should get him to a hospital," I said, alarmed.

"No," Piers said. "I ain't going."

"We can't," Pearl agreed. She was very firm about it.

"But why? He needs a doctor."

"The police. Them New York doctors report every damn thing to the police. He'll see a doctor in New Orleans. He has to hold on until then. And he *will*, goddamn it."

I wanted to ask why they were afraid of the police, but I let it go.

"Get the sheet," Pearl instructed, as she lay down beside Piers. He was on his side, and she lay facing him, her arms around him, her legs entwined with his, pressing his body tightly to herself, fiercely, as if to impress by sheer will her health onto him.

She kissed his face, murmuring words I couldn't hear.

I pulled the sheet over them. In the light, for a second, I saw the needle track marks on his arm.

I remembered the strangest thing: the maid throwing white sheets over all the furniture in our house in Virginia, years ago after my father died. The rooms looked like warehouses containing hills of snow, pure and silent.

"Get in beside him, please, Beau, please."

Pearl seemed desperate, yet under control. I sensed her immense tension and brave resolve, and I knew then that she believed he was soon to die.

I lay on the mattress under the sheet and embraced him from behind, trying to warm him and stop his shaking.

I was very hot, and yet I knew such comfort.

Stormy night, when I was a child and scared and ran to my parents' room and lay in the night between them as safe as Joe DiMaggio sliding home.

"I love you, I love you, precious. I'll never let you be hurt again, baby. All will be good again, you'll see. Pearl will pull you through," she whispered in a kind of litany, over and over again as she kissed him.

She was rocking her body as she held him, like a mother with a diseased child. Out of the cradle endlessly rocking. "Go to sleep my baby, my baby." She sang off-key, urgently.

Finally he slept. Finally, the shivering abated, and it was all right.

I was happy, and I thought it the most curious thing in the world, that I was happy. Joyous. I wanted never to leave this filthy mattress and the heat and our bodies knotted there together like youngsters huddled against a ferocious wind. The two of them and me, naked as jaybirds, Pearl singing softly and holding Piers, and me holding him from behind and feeling his heartbeat and his distressed breathing, and listening to her sing. I think she sang for me.

She was stronger than me and Piers put together. Stronger and tougher.

"I have to go to the toilet," she whispered.

She left the room. When she returned, she said to me, "Let me get in between you."

I moved, making room for her. Happy, happy man that I was. I thought of pomegranates and golden bells on a priest's robe making grateful noise. She embraced Piers, and I held her from behind. I felt her breasts, her stomach, her incredibly soft skin, and her silky pubic hair, which was long and straight. She allowed me to. No harm.

For the first time I heard the traffic rumble below on Avenue B. I glanced toward the open window and a lightening sky.

I dozed, I don't know for how long. It was daylight when I awoke, feeling Pearl's small hand reaching between her legs and caressing my erection.

She pushed her bottom against my groin, I slid down a little. She took my penis and placed it against her sex, and I gently pressed against her and in. She was wet, and it felt good, better than I had ever known before.

We lay like that, the three of us. I unmoving inside Pearl, clutching her small body against my own, my right leg fallen across her thigh. She holding Piers.

We slept.

Starry, starry night.

Twelve

I DROVE them to Kennedy Airport in Hayton Ransome's Jensen. She was wearing blue jeans and a cotton blouse, and around her neck was a pink ribbon with a small silver locket hanging from it.

I engaged a porter with a wheelchair for Piers. He was too weak to walk. At the concession stand I bought him a pair of sunglasses to hide his jaundiced eyes.

They had coach seats. I upgraded their tickets to first class so that Piers would be more comfortable on the flight to New Orleans. I loved them both, and I was giddy from it.

We went to the first-class lounge. Piers slept in the wheelchair. He had no appetite. All he could take was a glass of apricot juice, and only a few sips of that. Pearl and I ate roast beef sandwiches, and we drank Bloody Marys.

We talked while we waited, or rather Pearl did, and this is what she said:

"I was in New Orleans. I didn't know where Piers was in New York. He just up and left one day, and I didn't hear from him again. It didn't worry me none because he's done that many times before. He was born wearing traveling shoes, don't you know. He said he knew a guy on the East Side. I fancied the notion that he was set up proper. In the Big Leagues.

"After a month I began to worry. I started having dreams about him. About thin knives up his arms and thighs. I dreamed his eyes had turned to green marble and his skin to stone, but he was still alive inside the stone, and he couldn't stop staring out, he couldn't speak, and he was very cold. I always know with Piers, wherever he is, when the troubles come. I sense it inside, and then I have to fly to him.

"Maurice called three days ago. I didn't know who he was. Just someone who liked Piers. He said Piers was sick unto death. I borrowed the plane fare and came here. When I saw him it about broke my heart. I knew I had to get him home or he'd die. I knew it, and it made me angry.

"You can't hardly imagine the hell we been through. What we faced and survived.

"Piers and I been running like hell since I climbed the fence at the Baptist Girls Refuge in Gulfport, and never did look back. I ran from the goddamn place, and the goddamn preachers, and their Bibles and Jesus. They got themselves one cruel Jesus, those bastards.

"If you did something wrong, if you used lipstick or cussed or fell asleep during prayer meeting or listened to the radio on Sunday, they shut you in a tin shed out back in the sun. Little place it was, like an outhouse. An oven. It had barred windows.

"Elder Bobby Joe Owens was the worst sonofabitch I swear I ever did meet. He was the son of the preacherman who owned the Baptist Girls Refuge. He made me his, had his way with me, and there was no saying no. Until Piers found me.

"Piers is better than Jesus because you can count on Piers in a pinch.

"When I was in the punishment shed Elder Bobby Joe came by at night and stuck his dick through the slats, and if I done him I'd be let out.

"I dreamed of escape. I dreamed of dying. Dying seemed sweet to me, like being kissed until it took your breath away. But if I died, what would of happened to Piers? I was only fifteen.

"I escaped at night. I still don't know how Piers made his way to me. I was in Elder Bobby Joe's house trailer, in back behind the partition lying on the bed when Bobby Joe came in holding a beer. He yanked up my slip. I closed my eyes. I knew the routine. I hated it. He poured beer on me. He liked the smell of beer on me, the feel of it. Then he was on top, and he shoved his legs between mine and spread me wide. He started kissing my neck hard, desiring to leave spots. He loved them spots, his calling cards, he called them. Like you brand a calf. I felt his beard scraping my skin.

"There was a light burning in the front of the trailer, and the light went out. Bobby Joe said, 'What the hell?' and then I heard him gasp, and groan heavy, and a choking noise. And Piers rolled Bobby Joe off me, like a gravestone being rolled away.

"We made it over the fence, and away. Piers and me met up in Panama City where he got work on the fishing boats. He's a goddamn good fisherman, Piers is."

Pearl started to cry. "Goddamn. Goddamn."

I don't think it was the memory of Bobby Joe that made her weep. It was the release from all the tension of her three days in Manhattan, the flight about to leave, and being with Piers again.

We sat on a sofa in the first-class lounge, and I pulled her tightly to me as she cried.

I cannot handle people when they cry. "Don't cry, baby." I patted her head. I felt clumsy and inadequate, yet beguiled by her, and I never wanted her to leave, although she would, although there was no help for it, and I would miss her.

"Cry?" She pulled away. Her voice was hard, its tone bitter, as if hard times had come back like acid on her tongue, and she tasted it. "I'll never cry again."

The plane was called.

We stood. I gave her my phone number in New York and asked her to keep in touch. She had no telephone of her own in New Orleans.

"Don't let me down, baby. I'll worry if you don't call."

She embraced me and kissed my mouth.

"I'll surely call, Beau. You're my lucky penny."

She went over to Piers and woke him up.

"We have to board the plane. Then you can sleep again."

He took off his sunglasses and squinted in the light.

I went to him to say goodbye. He smiled sleepily. "You're one good ol' boy," he said as we shook hands.

Thirteen

TWO WEEKS later Pearl called me from New Orleans. I was delighted to hear her voice. She was at a pay phone in the French Quarter. She said she had a job as a waitress at a bar called Hope's Gone.

"And how's Piers?"

"Better. It's hepatitis. Serum hepatitis. He got it from a needle, wouldn't you know? It's not infectious. He'll have to be in bed for months recovering. It'll do him good. Oh, he asked me to tell you to read Auden's 'Lullaby.' Piers said it was written for you."

"I don't know the poem."

"Neither do I." She laughed. "Can you do me a favor?"

"Anything."

"Ask Maurice to send Piers's trunk C.O.D. on Trailways to their bus depot here. Piers is terribly anxious about it. I've been trying to reach Maurice myself, but he's never home. I leave messages on the answering service. It doesn't do much good. We don't have a phone here, so he can't return the call."

"Trailways. To the depot in New Orleans. C.O.D."

"That's right, Beau."

"Anything else?"

"Beau?"

"Yes."

"I miss you."

Fourteen

I COULDN'T reach Maurice at home, but I did find him at Le Gratin. I told him of Pearl's request regarding Piers's trunk. He seemed relieved to be rid of it and invited me to stop by his apartment about midnight for a drink after the last show at his club.

"What can I get you to drink?" Maurice asked when I arrived.

"Vodka. Straight."

"I'll have the same. Liquor's the only thing I take straight." He laughed. "Let me change first. I just got home five minutes ago. I've come to abhor black tie." Maurice was in the evening clothes he always wore when he worked the club.

He went into his bedroom, and I wandered about the living room. It was spacious and decorated in the white and off-white décor then in vogue, with lots of chrome and glass. Even the piano was white, and on it were scores of white frames containing signed photographs. The inscriptions were cozy and too intimate; reeking of insincerity. They were pictures of celebrities Maurice knew, actresses and songstresses once big in the movies or on Broadway in the 1930s and 1940s, who today were reduced to summer stock and dinner theatres in the sticks, and to publishing badly written memoirs that told more than anyone cared to know. Occasionally you saw these faded stars in New York, where the photographers still snapped their pictures at openings and parties, even if they were not printed in the next morning's papers. Their egos, grown fragile as old newsprint, were treated kindly by maître d's and p.r. flacks. In Manhattan they were the First Ladies of the American Theatre, although no producer would give them a job unless they put up their own money. In Hollywood, where the loot was, they weren't even yesterday's bread.

Alone in Maurice's living room, I felt great longing for Pearl. I remembered every detail of our last visit. And I decided that I liked Maurice, because he had helped Pearl, or rather Piers, which was the same thing. Stranger in a strange land. And this too: Maurice was my only link to Pearl.

Maurice returned from the bedroom wearing a short bathrobe, and nothing else. He was more muscular than I had imagined. I could tell by the way he carried himself that he felt sexy.

He smelled heavily of cologne, and seemed a bit stoned. I suspected that he had taken something strong in the bedroom, and the high was just hitting.

He made our drinks. We sat opposite each other on small love seats, separated by a chrome and glass cocktail table. He offered me a joint, I declined, and he lit up himself, making a hissing sound as he inhaled deeply.

As he released his breath, he smiled. He had nice caps.

Maurice shook his head. "I miss him, you know," he began, holding the smile. "Too, too divine, really. The most beautiful boy. A fabulous piece of cake."

"Piers?"

"Yes, my pet. Piers."

I didn't like "my pet."

"He was extraordinary in his silky way. You've seen him so you know, right? It's a shame the boy took sick. Ah, my pet, what I could have done for him in this town; under my wing he would have met the most glamorous, the most heavenly of the beautiful people. The future is so chillingly vast, and I could have . . . I had the key, my pet, and Piers could have made all of New York *gasp!*" He smiled, throwing his arms wide.

"How did you meet Piers?" I had often thought about it, the combination so unlikely and unsuitable.

"Ah, there's a tale. I met him through Paco Moralez, actually—"

"The one who was murdered?"

"The very."

Bonita's dead lover.

"*Très* sad, my pet. Paco was one of our better hustlers and one of our finer drug dealers, and he was hung like King Kong. He was Puerto Rican, but he was lily white. Exquisite combination, yes?"

"Oh?" I wasn't following his meaning.

"Third World culture. First World color." Maurice leaned over, and in a stage whisper he explained, "*I dig white meat.*" It was a brag and a provocation. He sat back, gauging my reaction.

I didn't blink.

And he smiled. Maurice always smiled. Like a train porter waiting on a tip. I'm certain that years later when he died, tied up like a lamb for the slaughter, I am absolutely certain that as the boy slit his throat from ear to ear, Maurice was smiling.

"And Piers?"

"Oh, Paco brought him along. Or actually, sent him over. Piers was living in the housing project where Paco lived."

"On Avenue B?"

"Yes. Piers was staying with some fellow, don't know who, and the fellow split, as the kids say. And Piers soon ran out of money, as pretty young things do. And Paco, always one to turn a commission, suggested that I buy Piers. Paco should have been an agent."

"I'm not following you," I said.

Maurice was enjoying himself. There was a tease to his talk, a sense of mischief, and it wasn't pleasant.

"Well," I said, 'Paco, darling, if he is as you say, send the boy to me at one in the A.M., and have him do what I like you ofay boys to do."

Maurice took another drag on his joint. I no longer liked him.

"I prefer simple things," Maurice said, expansively, "fabulous, simple things. And Piers was to die over. Fabulous! And at one in the A.M. I opened the door of chez Maurice, and there the divine Piers stood, with his blue jeans fallen to his ankles, and he snarled, just as I like them to do, 'Suck it, nigger!' Heavenly! And I did, right there in the outside hall where anyone getting off the elevator could have seen us." Maurice gestured lazily toward the outside door. "Thrilling, actually. And I handed Piers three crisp new twenty-dollar bills. It was cheap, believe me. It was cheap at any price."

I said nothing. It was not what I wanted to know. I did not like knowing it, but I listened. I wasn't sure I believed any of it. No, I believed every word.

"Piers and I became friendsies in our way," Maurice continued, smiling implacably, "two, three times a week. Always the same format in the hall. When you find the too, too perfect song, you sing it over and over again. It never bores you."

I finished my drink.

"Don't go. Not quite yet." Maurice flapped his long fingers like a bandleader directing his players to sit. "Let me finish. I cared for Piers. I loved him in my way. I never had better sex, not with any-one that *charmant*. And when he became ill and I didn't hear from him, I taxied to his place. I had never been to a ghetto before, well, not in years and years. Impossibly tacky, actually. Too, too dreary by half. Piers was in bed and as yellow as cat pee. He told me to call Pearl, his girlfriend. Do you know they're the exact same age, and born on the same day at the same hour? Fabulous, no? That's why Piers loves her so insanely. It's all in the stars."

I stood to go. I felt disgusted. I had had such a sweet vision of Piers and Pearl, my head full of nonsense, but I needed that in-nocent nonsense, and Maurice had soiled it. I knew he had intended to do just that, and I hated him for it.

"You're really a dirty bastard," I said as I left.

He feigned shock, hands flying to his face. Then he laughed very loudly, the sound full of contempt.

"It's all in the stars, my pet. Ask Piers, the sixty-dollar lay."

"Bastard."

He laughed again.

"You don't mean *bastard*, my pet. You mean *nigger*."

I went home, and got drunk. It didn't help. Something had shifted inside me. Something was defeated.

Innocence is a racket we play against ourselves.

Fifteen

TWO DAYS later I called Hope's Gone, the bar in New Orleans, and asked for Pearl. They said she had been fired. No, they did not know how to reach her.

That afternoon, after I called New Orleans, I went to the Gotham Book Mart and found the book of Auden's poems.

I read "Lullaby," the poem Piers had said was written for me.

> Lay your sleeping head, my love,
> Human on my faithless arm;
> Time and fevers burn away
> Individual beauty from
> Thoughtful children, and the grave . . .

Part II

The Ambassador

Sixteen

A MONTH later I was in London living in a rented house in Belsize Gardens, near Hampstead. I was drinking a great deal.

One night, soon after arriving, I had dinner with friends at a private club called Annabel's. We sat at a table by the dance floor. One of those in our party was named Joan Maizner. A very pretty woman, and I wanted to make a play for her. And then I smelled her cologne. Sandalwood. And I couldn't take the lonesomeness that swept over me. I left early.

I was working for the BBC on a British-American co-production about the Founding Mothers and Fathers of the American Nation, and the colonial Indian Wars.

I stayed in London for six months, and by the time it was over I was convinced that the American colonials were a pretty nasty bunch. Bullies. Religious fanatics. It was news to me. It shouldn't have been.

I used to feel very proud when my old man reminded me that from the time of the Revolution until now members of my family had died in every war that the United States of America had ever fought. On *both* sides of the Revolution. On *both* sides of the War Between the States.

But now I didn't get the point anymore.

I had an affair with an Irishwoman from Belfast named Lily. She was a Protestant, and she hated Catholics the same way the Nazis hated Jews, and the Founding Mothers and Fathers hated redskins. She wanted them all to drop dead.

Lily edited a trade magazine on British antiques and auctions, and as a happy result she knew a lot of aristocrats and others with old stuff they wanted to sell on the sly without the Labour Government's getting its cut. It made her very popular. She edited this magazine, and she was a high-class fence on the side.

Many of the people Lily did business with also knew Ambassador Orin Ransome, his wife Varina, and their son Hayton Childs Ransome, he of the Jensen automobile. I met Lily through friends of the Ransomes.

She was pretty, and divorced, and childless. Her husband was a Presbyterian minister in Belfast. He exhorted Protestant children to emulate their Catholic peers and kill the bloody buggers. After a while the strain of living in a war zone got to be too much. Lily walked.

She was given to tears, and excessively fond of gin, and altogether hopeless in her way. The bus had passed her stop, and she knew it.

Lily's breasts had been inflated by silicone at a Milan clinic. They were like great hams hanging from a smokehouse wall. She regretted the result, and talked constantly of saving up enough pounds sterling to have them surgically reduced, as if smaller breasts would do the trick. It was like Americans saving up for a college education for their kids.

When I decided to go back to the States, Lily became hysterical, sobbing that I was leaving Great Britain because I had never really loved her. Not even a little bit.

"No, baby. My work permit expired. I have no green card anymore. That's why I have to leave."

In truth, I had never loved Lily. Not even a little bit.

Seventeen

THREE DAYS before returning to America, I ran into Sir Cecil Chard at a party in Eaton Square. It was a boring affair, and I was anxious to leave. Cecil was equally bored, and so the two of us took a taxi to his club, White's. We planned to have dinner and play a few sets of backgammon. I detested the game, but Cecil was an ace at it, as he was an ace at photography, and part of the bargain of spending an agreeable evening with him was the promise of backgammon at its end.

Over dinner we talked about New York, which I missed and where Cecil had been working for Vogue until the week before. He told stories about mutual friends and discussed the theatre at length. In addition to being one of the world's leading photographers, and unofficial photographer to Britain's Royal House, he was a leading theatrical designer and had even won an Oscar for costume design. I think he much preferred designing to snapping pictures, a pastime he refused to consider art.

"I met the most delightful creature in New York," he announced, his speech a kind of lilting, slurred music. In any given sentence Cecil's voice was likely to travel up and down a full octave and a

half, and be accompanied by little squeaks and snorts along the
way. It made his speech, as well as his fussy mannerisms, fair game
for every three-martini impressionist on two continents.

"I was lunching with the head of Condé Nast at Le Cirque, and
for one bloody reason or another we had fallen on the subject of
whores. Parlor whores, to be exact, the ladies that cost you forty
pounds a kiss. And I said to him, 'My dear fellow, I don't know
about you but I hardly think it's worth two minutes of ecstasy to
have to spend thirty minutes afterward trying to find your pocketbook under the bed.' He agreed completely. Then he said, 'Do you
think any of the women here in this room are whores?' Le Cirque!
'My good man,' I shouted, 'we are in one of the most reputable, the
finest restaurants in what remains of the civilized world.' '*Exactly*,'
he exclaimed, 'the place must be crawling with tramps.' " Cecil
laughed, or rather he twittered and wheezed.

He was old even then, in his late sixties, and he had lived a life
that encompassed friendships with the most renowed artists of his
day, including an alleged affair with Garbo. He had great staying
power, and had been a famous figure in society and the arts since
the Thirties. This was to his credit, since his origins were in a spartan
Anglican orphanage in the slums of Manchester. He had recently
published the second volume of his memoirs, full of stories of Noël
Coward and Maugham and the Sitwells. He was a charmer, Cecil,
and between magazine assignments and books he paid his rent
by beating the rich at backgammon in country houses around the
world. He endured.

"Did you spy any whores?" I asked, the idea of call girls working
the room at Le Cirque being very funny to me.

"No, dear boy, that's not the bloody point of my story. What I
spied, as it were, was the most beautiful woman I have ever seen,
and I have seen very many. I had put on my glasses—you know I'm
blind without them though I detest the damn things because they
shield the glory of my azure eyes from the world. I do have glorious
eyes, don't you think?" Cecil smiled, batting his eyelashes at me. "I
was looking around the restaurant, trying to ferret out the more
obvious ladies of the evening working the lunch shift, and all I saw

were the usual bores and matronly divorcées and phony titled continentals of the gossip columns. And then, in the front of the room, at a quiet side table, I saw this ineffably beautiful young woman, sitting quite alone, dressed in some cheap copy of last year's Dior, looking somewhat frantic, as if she had booked for lunch and her date, with the credit card, had stood her up."

"What did you do?"

"Simply this. I told our man from Condé Nast, 'Look there! *That's* the most refreshingly beautiful young woman I have seen since Garbo tripped off the boat. And if you don't permit me to photograph her for *pages* in your dreary magazines, you're a cad and a fool.' He laughed."

"And?" I prompted.

"Her date never showed. Or if he did, it was too late. Because I cleverly sent a note to her table via a waiter asking if she would join us for a drink. She accepted and stayed for lunch. The following day I shot her portfolio, engaged an agent, and spent the ensuing delightful week shooting her everywhere, from my studio to Central Park. Her name is Pearl, like a treasure . . ."

"Pearl? Pearl Oxford? My God, I know her!"

Cecil giggled. "You do. You are what we talked about. I assured her that I was bound to run into you sooner or later, because we both seem cursed with the same acquaintances."

I beamed with the news. "I've thought constantly about her, and worried about her, and I hadn't the slightest idea how the hell to find her again."

"She's gone off somewhere—New Orleans I believe, but she said to tell you she'd be back. Remarkable woman, don't you think? So open to experience, although I think she's a trifle too hungry for it. Vastly ambitious. I sat her down and told her about the probable life she would be entering. Already, after I had taken her to a few parties and given several lunches, she was being keenly pursued. Quite a sensation, I must say, for which I take the entire credit. I advised her never to forget who she was, and where she came from. God knows, *I* never have. Get what you can and get out. I told her, if she ever needs them, she won't be able to count on most of the people she will come to know. But by God, what we and they can teach her! She's so hungry to learn."

"I miss her!" I blurted out.

He looked slyly at me. "And you think I don't?"

Cecil held up his index finger. "But there's more. I have a message for you—and why she should be in such earnest as far as you're concerned is quite beyond me—when I think of the monied young males who now preen in her presence. Be that as it may, she said to tell you not to forget that you're her lucky pence."

I laughed. *"Penny."*

"Quite."

Eighteen

JUST BACK from London, I went for cocktails at the Ransomes' Riverhouse duplex on East 52nd Street. The purpose of the party, and the dinner later that evening at the Plaza Hotel, was to raise money for Senator Robert Kennedy's bid for the Democratic presidential nomination.

Kennedy was running because the war in Vietnam and the general disarray of life in America had become intolerable. There were riots not only in the ghettos but on the college campuses. Things were unhinged in America, and there seemed no decent future for her, although Robert Kennedy envisioned one.

People whispered of military coups, of dictatorships of the right or left, of revolution. There was violence everywhere, in the parks and schools and in the streets. Demonstrations and protests and crimes. The country had gone haywire.

There were riots in Harlem the night I went to the Ransomes'. The party was black tie.

Several hundred people were there, writers and publishers and actors and producers. And there were the heavy contributors, the men who expected to do business with the new government. They seemed nervous and too eager, herded together with their wives at the far end of the long drawing room, near where Kennedy stood talking, looking young and tanned and wiry and on to the game.

He was smaller in person than you expected him to be, and there was to him a physical fragility, a winsome delicacy of line and bone that was surprising. I liked him enormously.

There were few members of the Pack present, very few. Most of the social rich hated the Kennedys, seeing them as traitors to their class. It was the same with the Roosevelts, two generations before.

As soon as I entered the apartment, Varina Ransome pulled me aside.

"I simply must talk to you, darling."

I was startled. She came at me from behind. I turned and kissed her cheek.

Varina was wearing a tight pale-blue dress, which meant that her diet was working, and an invaluable emerald necklace with stones the size of prune pits.

She took me to the library, locking the door behind us.

"I need some information. About Hayton. Orin is being his usual oblivious self."

Varina was married to one of the nation's most powerful men. Orin Ransome had been a special ambassador to Moscow under President Franklin Roosevelt, and an adviser to General George Marshall and President Harry Truman on the rebuilding of Western Europe. He had been a delegate at the founding of the United Nations in San Francisco in 1946, and had remained active in international affairs and Democratic Party politics ever since.

Ambassador Ransome was a liberal. He was one because he believed that liberal democracy provided the safest and most lucrative environment for modern capitalism. He was a liberal because he had a former Etonian old boy's respect for notions of fair play.

In the last century, Ransome's grandfather had amassed the family fortune by starving out striking miners and bombing out competitors and buying off or killing union organizers. He had also carried the balls of the United States Senate in his lunch bucket. It wasn't a heavy load.

Orin Ransome's power came from political connections well oiled by money earned in Southern agribusiness and Northern rails and mines, financial interests his political friends of both parties protected and enhanced as a matter of course.

And what of it? Ransome was a national monument. His profile belonged on Mount Rushmore as the best and brightest of the old school. He was proud of what he was.

Varina and I stepped out onto a small balcony overlooking the East River. To the north I could see smoke billowing above Spanish Harlem. The night was shrill with the wail of sirens.

Varina sat down on a chaise longue. She took a drag on a cigarette manufactured by a company owned by her family. Varina Livingston Ransome was originally from Georgia. Kin to the Rhodes family of Atlanta, she had grown up close to Southern wealth and influence. She had gone to school in the East—Briarcliff—and then was taken to England by her mother. It was there she met and married her first husband, Lord Pelham, the press baron. She got little out of the marriage beyond a vast network of British social connections and a love of English country life. She owned a small country house in Sussex, and a flat on Green Street in Mayfair. She did all right.

I smiled at Varina. The energy and liveliness of her imagination made her attractive and useful to men. She had had two husbands, both powerful. She had single-mindedly worked to advance the fortunes of the first until she abandoned him for the second, like a traveler changing trains. But she was possessed by a compulsion to control events that was incontinent. She was American for all that, and needed to be liked.

I sat beside her on the chaise.

"Hayton's had his head turned by a skirt again. Do you know anything about it?" she asked.

"It's news to me. I've been in London for six months or so."

"Of course. I just thought you might have heard something."

"Not a word," I said.

"I haven't met the girl. Knowing Hayton, she's bound to be common. Will he never grow up? I become so bored having to pay them off. Why can't he find someone suitable, with decent manners, someone halfway presentable? Why are men such bloody fools?"

"I'll talk to Hayton. It may be a passing thing. He's easily infatuated," I said.

"Men either have no wits when it comes to women, or they hate them. Perhaps they all hate women, the lot of them. I don't think there's a proper man left. Even the queer ones can't be trusted."

"There are a few men who love women."

"Not in spitting distance, dear. Do you know what that Sabina Phips told me tonight?" Sabina was her best friend.

"Sabina said that her banker ex-husband hit her in the jaw because she wouldn't shut up. Sabina *does* go on a bit. 'I don't want to know what you think,' he shouted at the poor dear. 'If women didn't have cunts no one would talk to them!' See what I mean about men?"

"What a terrible thing for him to say."

Varina glanced at me. She was lovely there in the dim and gentle light, her skin smooth and unwrinkled and untouched by time, or so it seemed.

"I need a man," she remarked quietly. "Orin's no good at it anymore. At least not with me. He's seventy-one, this October. He has a girlfriend—some pathetic tramp in the wastes of New Jersey. Did you know?"

"No, I didn't."

I took Varina's hand and held it. Her skin was cold.

"Not the first of Orin's paramours, of course. Nor the last. But *New Jersey*? I have to laugh when I think of his taking the car out to the Meadowlands. I hope it works out," she sighed. "I really do."

"You what?"

"I hope the tramp is good to my husband. Did you see Roxanne tonight? She has her claws out for him. She'd love to take him from me, you can bet your bottom dollar."

Roxanne was the wife of a United States senator. She was in her fifties, a few years younger than Varina.

"Why is it so much easier for men to grow older?" Varina asked. "I never understood that. Why?"

"How was your winter?" I inquired to change the subject.

"Boring. And yours?"

"The same."

"And London?"

"The same."

"Pity, that. We missed you, darling, did you know? Orin and I. Since your father died we've considered you our son. How much I wish you were. Poor Hayton, he breaks his father's heart. You can't imagine, when he was a baby, the plans and hopes we had for that boy. Politics and business . . ."

"He'll come out of it on top," I said.

Varina snorted, and looked at me askance. "Don't be a toady, Mikey. Not with me. I look at the Kennedys, and I wonder where I went wrong. Perhaps Orin was away too much when Hayton was growing up, or I was. Or we loved him too much, or indulged him too much. What he needs, I think, is a good woman. Someone strong who can rein him in. Maybe then . . ." She drifted off. I don't think she believed it.

She lit another cigarette. "Oh, do you know, I nearly saw you in London? The Princess Dwarf invited me over for dinner last week at Kensington, as if I had nothing better to do but fly across the Atlantic and listen to her bitch. Come to think of it, I *didn't* have anything better to do." She laughed. "How on earth Tony sticks it out with her is quite beyond me. I never understood why he married the Princess Dwarf. I know it wasn't lust. Perhaps being a royal is lure enough. Tony's changed, you know, since he married Her Royal Highness. Grown bitter, like we all do. He was rather sweet before he received the title, when he used to motorbike around the West End taking pictures and chasing Asian girls."

I glanced up the river to Spanish Harlem.

"How long will it go on?" I asked.

"What, darling?"

"The looting."

Varina pulled her hand away.

"Ask Leonard Bernstein. He'll probably have the mob to lunch."
She laughed hollowly.

Another cigarette, chain-smoking as always, and in the sudden flare of the flame she looked her age.

"I tried to have an affair with Tony once. Did you know? When I was still Lady Pelham. This was before the Princess Dwarf ruined him. I saw him in the country, Wiltshire, I think. At Margot's. He was in bathing trunks, and I watched him get out of the pool. I had never really noticed Tony before. He was very thin, boyish, and one leg is withered from polio or something equally dreadful. I found that sexy, the way he carried himself. His courage . . ." She smiled wistfully at me. "Do you think I'm getting too old for it?"

"No, baby. You're as beautiful as ever. I'm mad for your body."

I meant it humorously. She did not smile.

"I feel as old as Orin, and he's as old as the hills. Isn't that depressing?"

"I'll get you a drink, Varina?"

"What happened to all the men? What terrible thing happened to them?"

"Vodka?"

"Make it light, darling. With tonic. I've got this whole bloody night to shuffle through."

She leaned forward and seized my hand, squeezing it tightly, then kissed it. I felt her emeralds cold against my skin.

"Orin would marry Roxanne, you know, if she played her cards right. Such is his vanity."

"He'll never leave you, baby," I said, although I thought he might. Old men are given to that.

"We were very happy once, Orin and I. We were each other's world. Do you think we'll ever be that happy again?"

"Someday."

Varina laughed. "You know someday never comes."

Nineteen

I LEFT the library and walked slowly down the hall.

Robert Kennedy could be heard still speaking to the crowd in the other room. I thought of the first time I met the Kennedy brothers, in Georgetown after the Presidency had been won. It was a time when we believed that something exceptional and vital was alive in the world, and that we were intimate with it. We believed that the world could be changed. Overnight. Just like that.

Robert Kennedy spoke about the Democratic primary coming up in California.

He said we could make a future worthy of ourselves.

He said we could get the country moving again.

He said many other things that night, and none of them came true.

When he finished speaking I headed toward the bar for Varina's drink and ran straight into Hayton. I hadn't seen him since the time Pearl and I borrowed his Jensen to move Piers's trunk. It seemed as if years had passed since then.

"Are you going to the fund-raiser at the Plaza?" he asked.

"No," I said.

"Good. Then c-c-come with us. We're going to the Rainbow Room to hear Peggy Lee and later to a p-party at Countess Vincennes'. I've a table for six, and you'll be surprised by the girl I'm with. Okay?"

"Sure." The only thing that surprised me about Hayton's girls was how they stayed awake in his company.

I had nothing else to do, and I didn't really dislike Hayton. He was twenty-five years old, he was good-looking in a weak way, and I like good-looking people. But he had no character. He had been graduated from Eton and Ol' Miss and Yale Law, and still Hayton Childs Ransome had no values that were any good.

There was something of the pimp in him. He liked doing for his friends too much. Picking up checks and showing off and talking about his rich life and his sex life, trying to impress. But he talked too much about it, and boasted too much, and so you didn't believe him after a while. He did not know who he was or what he wanted to be. I think that deep inside you'd find self-loathing, gnawing away like a rat on electrical wire.

He was waiting around for someone strong to come along and shake him up and tell him who he was and what he was to do about it. He wanted someone to tell him the score and because of all these things and more Hayton was an easy mark for women. They liked his youth and his good looks, and they liked his money.

I ordered a light vodka and tonic for Varina from the barboy. Varina always had pretty barboys, and you always suspected that they went to bed with her or, if not her, with her friends because they were too handsome by half for the work, and they were never very good at it.

"Darling! How *are* you?"

It was Sabina Phips. She had entered the bar with her friend Giorgio Milano in tow. Giorgio was a dress designer, very popular at the time, and his clothes were very expensive; the two usually go together. Sabina was wearing one of his dresses and around her waist she wore an Army cartridge belt with live bullets in it that she'd bought at Bendel's.

Wearing an Army cartridge belt with live bullets in it over a two-thousand-dollar gown was also very popular at the time. As were long hair on middle-class boys and wearing proletarian clothes purchased at Bloomingdale's and having Black Panthers and other revolutionaries to sit-down dinners. And putting your money in the Islands and Switzerland and Monaco. Just in case.

Sabina Phips's red hair was combed back, exposing her small ears, from which dangled ruby earrings. She wore green tinted, harlequin sunglasses. In the ten years I had known her I'd never seen her once without green sunglasses.

She put her hands on my shoulders, and leaned toward me, whispering, "Kissy, kissy," as her cheek bobbed in the general direction of my lips.

Then she turned to Hayton.

"And *you*, Hayton darling, however are you? I hear you have a new interest, a twinkie fresh off the Greyhound and hot to trot."

"S-Sabina, I—"

She ignored him. "I think Bobby Kennedy's simply *divine*," she exclaimed to no one in particular. Her voice was husky, large and gravelly and inappropriate to her delicate face.

Some days Sabina's voice was more gravelly than other days. It was then that Varina would say, "It must be ratings week again, dear." Sabina was known for having carried on an affair for seven years with the chief of programing for one of the television networks. When things were professionally tense in televisionland, he was known to leave the office and be driven to Sabina for a sex break.

"Don't you think he's fabulous, Giorgio?" she inquired. "Much sexier than poor Jack, although Jack was a lady-killer, and Bobby's merely a good Catholic. And *Ethel*? It's just as well she's not here, poor thing. A trifle too mousey and hausfrau for all their money, don't you agree? She hasn't his éclat, his . . . sex appeal. That's what'll give him the election. I invited Bobby down to Giorgio's place in Nassau for a holiday."

"You did?" Giorgio seemed both startled and pleased.

"After the election. For a rest. Giorgio's place is unspeakably *choice*, even if it's impossibly close to the airport. Perhaps a new President can do something about those ghastly planes."

"I'll have to ask Arlene," said Giorgio, invoking his wife.

Arlene was considerably older than he, and much smarter. She had discovered him waiting on tables in Paris and had made him into what he was. And she never let him forget it.

"Arlene'll pee in her pants to have a President-elect on the property," Sabina countered. "Think of the publicity. And don't forget who arranged it."

"Did the senator accept?" I asked.

"Not in so many words. He *winked*. I've gone to bed on less."

I laughed with her, and winked.

Twenty

I RETURNED to the library with Varina's drink.

"Did you find out anything about Hayton's girlfriend?"

"Nothing." I smiled at her interest. "But I'm seeing them later tonight."

"Good. And did you catch sight of Roxanne slinking around my husband?"

"No."

"Don't you think it's terrifically *odd* that Roxanne is here tonight, uninvited? I mean, why would she come unless she was after Orin?"

"Don't be paranoid, Varina."

"Paranoid!" she snapped. "That bitch Roxanne! She's a Jewess, or did you forget?"

"What of it?"

"Can't be trusted."

"Varina, for Christ's sake. Maybe Roxanne supports Senator Kennedy?" I suggested.

"Supports Kennedy!" Varina barked. Then she laughed. Forcefully.

She had a gallows laugh, totally insincere and chilling, complete with its own echo. It was the laugh we will all hear after we run out of gas and discover that the Lord Almighty has barred us as undesirables from the Pearly Gates. "Neighborhood's restricted," the

Lord will say. "Just like Palm Beach." The Lord will point to the BEWARE BAD DOG sign, and the NO TRESPASSING sign. When we plead for admittance He'll let go a gallows' laugh that will echo through the universe. Only He will laugh much louder than Varina Ransome.

"Are you mad?" Varina went on. "Roxanne's husband is one of the senior Republicans in the Senate, the one who wears the cowboy boots to White House dinners, remember? Bobby Kennedy's a Democrat! God, don't be an utter twit. The bitch wants to be the next Mrs. Orin Ransome."

She had a point.

Twenty-One

FROM the Ransomes' I went to my apartment. I ate a sandwich, and decided not to go to the Rainbow Room to hear Peggy Lee.

I started to work on a play I was writing. I had a couple of drinks because it wasn't going well, and I knew it. I also knew that I would never finish writing it, but I could not admit that to myself. The hardest thing for a writer is to admit that something he is writing isn't any good and never will be. It is harder to stop writing something you feel you need to write than it is to stop drinking, or loving someone you shouldn't love. I've had difficulty doing all three.

With each you have to admit your own limits—that you have come to the end of an endurance, or a talent, or imagination or feeling. That you are human in some definite way that resists confession.

Some writers never know it, or if they do they never do anything about it.

Hemingway did something about it. He shot himself. And he was right to do it. That was the only way he could stop writing what wasn't good anymore.

So I worked for a couple of hours on this play I would never finish, and I had a few more drinks, and then I decided I had done enough and wouldn't feel guilty if I quit.

It was too late to go to the Rainbow Room. Instead I would go to the party at Vincennes'.

The countess was always good for a laugh.

Twenty-Two

YEARS AGO, when I first stumbled upon Countess Hortense de Vincennes, the first thing she said to me was "Darling, do you know the difference between a blow job and a ham sandwich?"

"Do I know the difference between a *blow job* and a *ham sandwich*?" I repeated dumbly. We were at a cocktail party for the Salvation Army's Christmas Appeal, and I had never seen the woman before in my life.

"That's what I want to know, darling."

"No, I don't know the difference."

"Splendid!" Hortense declared. "Then I'll expect you for lunch tomorrow!"

Pause.

"Hahahaha." That's how Hortense laughed, like a machine gun, or a string of firecrackers exploding in a trash can, or a pneumatic drill. Hahahaha.

She was an improbable creature, Hortense. Overblown, exaggerated, sentimental, self-dramatic, naïve in the most appalling way, living on the knife-edge of hysteria. She was intimate with panic, and she fought it with pipe dreams and crazed laughter.

Pipe dreams like: 1) Everyone deserves a second chance; 2) You're never too old; 3) People are basically good if you only give them half a chance; 4) Money doesn't matter to a true artist; 5) Sincerity's what counts; and other equally monstrous falsehoods.

Once upon a time Hortense met Count Jean de Vincennes in London. It was during the Battle of Britain, which should give you some clue to her age and capacity for survival. The count had escaped to England, fleeing his fellow Frenchmen, the Vichy, to join General Charles de Gaulle.

Even when he was hiding out in London, the count was a cocky man. He was cocky and rich, and he looked very handsome and cocky and rich in his tailored French Army colonel's uniform as he strolled through the lobby of the Hotel Savoy, where he spent the war, and as he sat in the café of the Ritz, where he spent lunch. In the frenzied social whirl of wartime London the count may even have known my father.

My father served as liaison between the American O.S.S.—Office of Strategic Services—and the Free French plotting away in Whitehall. But the count and my father wouldn't have hit it off. That's because my father, like his son the writer, loathed the French, considering them martinets at best, imperialist poseurs, arrogant losers, and, in a pinch, cowards. That sort of thing. And my father particularly detested General de Gaulle, with whom he was compelled to associate daily and whose ambitions he was paid to advance. He called de Gaulle the five-and-dime Napoleon. The Trifle Tower. King Charles de Balled. And worse.

The O.S.S. was the American cloak-and-dagger brigade. Later it would be named the C.I.A. and be feared and hated by people all over the world.

My father was a spy.

Anyway, Count Jean de Vincennes, De Gaulle's buddy, met Hortense in 1940 at whatever was the British equivalent of the USO. A dance for the troops. Stale cakes and Twining's India Tea.

The count was slumming that night.

Hortense was the daughter of a greengrocer in London's East End, not the toniest part of town. She was pretty and very sexy. People said she looked like an English Betty Grable. The count thought she looked like Betty Grable too.

Hortense married Count Jean de Vincennes two months after she served him a cup of tepid tea at the dance for the troops. She was free to marry him because her first husband, a young Scottish flyer, had the bad sense to die in the air over North Africa.

Hortense had two children by Vincennes, René, a son, and Germaine.

Bluebirds over the white cliffs of Dover, and Count Jean de Vincennes triumphantly returned to his ancestral lands in Provence to take a freedom-loving people's revenge against the vicious traitors. There he directed a campaign against rich collaborators whose property he seized in the name of Eternal France. He divided up the loot with his friends, who had stayed behind on the Home Front doing business as usual. Never mind that they were also collaborators cozy with the Vichy and the Nazis, selling out the Jews and everyone else for a price. They were on De Gaulle's side now, against the Left, in the club.

What the hell, everyone had been a collaborator in one way or another, except the Maquis, who were largely Communists and therefore weren't worth a pin. It was a new ball game. MISERI-CORD, and on you go.

In 1946 the count died of cardiac arrest. Hortense was not mentioned in his will, nor were her children. It seems the count never found the time to change it.

Hortense married at least three more times—she always had a poor head for figures—and when I met her in the early Sixties she was married to a rare book dealer who was overly fond of Dexe-drine Spansules and resultantly was thin as a three-penny nail.

By then, René had settled on a farm in Canada, a contentedly married man who was known for his great physical beauty and his towering hatred of his mother. Germaine had gone to Paris and become a famous actress. And Hortense had emigrated to New York, where she lived with her book dealer husband in a large loft on Hudson Street in Greenwich Village. The loft contained not a single book.

With her title and charm and decaying beauty and the renown and connections of her famous daughter, Hortense tried to establish a salon of the sort the Bloomsbury group might have had if they'd been living in a loft in Manhattan's meat district in the 1960s. That is, every Thursday night at ten on the dot Hortense had open house, at which various arty happenings happened.

It was to this salon that I repaired the night of the Ransomes' party. Incidentally, these open houses that Hortense staged were a small scandal in New York. In the 1960s there were only small scandals in New York; nobody had the energy for big ones.

Given the ferocity of her husband's drug habit, and her own fondness for the weird, which she confused with the creative, Hortense didn't establish the kind of artistic salon at which Irish Catholic Mary McCarthy, say, or Lillian Hellman, or even Gore Vidal would feel at home. But, by God, she *tried*.

It really wasn't for the money, although you had to pay five dollars to get in. It was for Art.

Hortense made money on the side by designing avant-garde wallpapers. Her rich friends, among them Sabina Phips and Varina Ransome, would commission designs and then have them hung on inconspicuous walls in unoccupied rooms. It was charity for art's sake. They felt obligated because she was a countess down at heel, and the only thing thicker than thieves are the untitled rich and the titled temporarily-without-funds.

And one other thing. Countess Hortense de Vincennes was dying of cancer, and there was no way out.

Twenty-Three

HORTENSE'S loft occupied the top floor of an old building that was once the workplace for hundreds of unionized American seamstresses who made children's clothing there. In 1958 the owners of the company moved the business to Liberia, where the same work was done by prepubescent, malnourished black children at one-twentieth the cost. It's called progress.

I took the freight elevator, after paying Hortense's bouncer a five-dollar donation at the door.

The loft was like a lot of other places then, several huge rooms badly lit, sculptures made out of automobile wrecks and rusted iron beams piled about. A long Mission table served as a bar. Above it four of Andy Warhol's execution lithographs. A black-lighted print of a couple fornicating on one wall. Next to it a large and elegant painting by Jasper Johns.

The room was crowded with affluent young people dressed like day laborers and dancing to rock music that was too loud for conversation. But they hadn't come to talk.

The air was fogged with tobacco and marijuana smoke, and there was to it the faint smell of spilled liquor and amyl nitrite and perfumed incense made from sacred Indian Brahmin cow dung that was the rage among writers and artists then influenced by the Inscrutable East. On the far wall was a large, white bed sheet serving as a movie screen. Warhol's *Blue Movie* was being shown. It had recently been banned in New York.

I got a drink and looked around for Hortense and Hayton. I couldn't find either of them in the crowd. So I stood trying to watch the movie for about twenty minutes, while listening at Nat Lesserman, an editor at *Partisan Review*. He had been at the loft for over an hour, and among the movies he had seen there were Jack

Smith's *Flaming Creatures*, Kenneth Anger's *Scorpio Rising*, and Bob Loomis's *The Check's in the Mail*. He was ecstatic about them all.

There were other rooms in the loft. Small bedrooms illuminated by bare red and blue lights hanging from the ceiling wires, with water beds on the floor. Here people gathered for sex and drugs, shuffling about in the groping darkness like heavily sedated inmates of a madhouse.

"Darling one!" cried Hortense de Vincennes, sweeping toward me dressed in a purple caftan. Around her head was wrapped a purple snood to conceal the loss of hair to recent chemotherapy. Even though she looked like Helena Rubinstein on a bad day, I was happy to see her. I knew that under the forced hilarity, under that too broad smile and animated enthusiasm lay the frigid dread of dying, the one never-spoken and never-silenced reality. She played her part well. She accepted the losing hand she had been dealt and went on. I admired that.

Hortense had a gaunt face, with very prominent cheekbones and false eyelashes that were at least an inch long. Like Miss Rubinstein, Hortense was very short of stature.

She was smoking a joint that dangled at the end of a tortoise-shell holder. One endangered species sucking on the remains of another.

"Do get away, Nat!" she commanded, waving him away.

"How are you, Countess?" I inquired.

"Delightfully aroused, now that you're here, darling one. I do wish these editorial types would stay home, but I'm afraid they're the only ones genuinely interested in art, because the poor dears are paid a pittance to be interested. An unfortunate commentary on our times. Parker is here somewhere, with that sweet girlfriend of his. Parker is terribly keen on the new in film. He is arranging a month-long festival of prewar Korean films at the museum. It sounds breathtaking."

Hortense sighed. Dramatically.

"Oh, have I told you, darling one? The Mother Superior called all the sisters and novices together to make an important announcement. 'Sisters,' she said, 'I have discovered a case of syphilis in the convent!' A case of syphilis! Then one of the little novices raised her hand and said, 'Oh, Mother Superior, how wonderful! We're all so tired of the Sauvignon!' "

Pause.

"Hahahaha."

"Very funny, Countess. You should take your act on the road. You'd make millions."

"Precisely. But what about *art*? Oh, dearest one, do forgive the plastic drinking cups. Not a question of expense, you know. Crystal simply isn't *modern*, my dear. Oh, Christ, they're at it again!"

And off Hortense marched to pull several stoned guests from a sculpture made of railroad ties.

I turned to the bar for another drink.

Nearby on a banquette, a naked girl lay on her stomach, her head resting on a boy's lap. Both were either asleep or in a drug stupor. An older man sat perched on the edge of the banquette, disinterestedly looking away while his hand explored the girl's buttocks.

I recognized him, elegantly dressed, his hauteur unaffected by the surroundings, seemingly unaware even of the action of his hand. Dudley Conrad, largest landlord in Manhattan. A lieutenant in the Pack.

Lucky Dudley. Tonight, while he dug his fingers into the girl, the poor of East Harlem were rioting and looting and burning three square blocks of tenements he owned through paper corporations, and for the loss of which he would receive insurance far in excess of his loss. That's called Free Enterprise.

I watched him a moment, and then turned away.

Twenty-Four

LISTEN. I'm not ready to let it go. I have never been *able* to let it go. That's my trouble. I am saddled with moral feelings, sometimes even moral outrage, and there's no appeal.

The first time I remember crying when I wasn't spanked was seeing a newsreel, during the war, of children—Gypsies or Jews or Poles, I don't remember which—being beaten senseless by S.S. thugs in Germany. It could be *me*, I thought. And moral feeling was born or awakened or whatever the process is that makes us want to weep when innocence is scalped and we are helpless as captives before the horror.

My father thought I should have been a preacher. My father was an atheist and a spy to boot. My father was right. I became a writer, which is the same thing, only it usually doesn't pay as well.

In the late Sixties it seemed that each night there was some new place to go late for drugs and rock music and, for some, sex, and each place was grimier and less attractive and more haunted and stoned than the last, until you finally gave off going. It was democratic in its way, like a burn ward after a hotel fire, or venereal disease, or a Billy Graham Crusade. Anyone with a buck got a ticket, no questions asked.

Slumming was in, and people like Dudley Conrad and Hayton Childs Ransome and other swells with loose change and nothing much to do were eager to discover whatever new joint or loft or drug or bar was hot. It had to do with their boredom and self-contempt.

In New York City and other places around the country with similar values, and there were many, you never expressed moral reservations, not if you wanted to be invited back. That made it tough if you cried at newsreels. Such feeling was considered vulgar by the trendier types. By the Pack. The *beau monde*. The big shots. They thought themselves somehow above human sympathy and duty, and in a real way they were.

Something had perished that Americans needed, that the West needed. It was vision, and it had been canceled for low ratings. We existed for a time in the vacuum of its absence, gracelessly. One morning it was gone, like a long-time lover off to buy cigarettes and never to return.

In the Fabulous Sixties, for the first time in my life, people I knew cleared out. They dropped like flies. They stuck needles in their arms to turn out the lights. They fell from windows like Depression stockbrokers, or drove fast cars into trees. They cashed in their chips like it was closing time at a casino. I had thought that peculiar to my old man, but it had become commonplace, like wearing blue jeans.

There was more, and it appeared everywhere, a cheapening of life, a deadening of the senses so that it required greater exertion and risk at more extreme levels simply to *feel*. If you cared to feel at all, and the sharp ones didn't.

I didn't want to feel. Scout's honor. But I couldn't stop it. I wasn't sharp enough. It was like being born with two noses. You smelled twice as keenly as anyone else, but there was no benefit in it. It only stank up your life.

Twenty-Five

I WAS suddenly aware of how hot it was, I put down my drink and walked to the fire escape. The steel door was open. I stepped out on the iron landing and into the breeze off the Hudson. Odor of ocean.

I remembered Bonita, and the smell of her body, and I wondered who was forking over fifty bucks to taste her tonight. I felt ashamed.

A young couple leaned against the railing looking across the low, flat rooftops and the elevated highway to the Jersey shore.

I lit a cigarette and watched the moon shining on the water, its light shattered into small bits on the surface like a plateful of sequins spilled on a polished floor. I thought of Pearl, who was better than all this, better than anyone I knew.

"Beau."

I felt her hands knead my waist. I smelled sandalwood.

"Beau," she whispered.

I felt her breath against my ear.

I inhaled sharply, not wanting to turn around, not wanting to risk that my senses were wrong, that my brain was playing a cheap trick.

I closed my eyes, like a child wanting to be surprised, and turned around.

Pearl pulled me tightly to her.

"I've missed you, Beau. More than you know."

I said nothing. I stared in dumb surprise at her face. I stood winded and astonished and so very pleased.

"Do it to me, Beau. Tonight."

Twenty-Six

So THIS is where you live?" Pearl drawled, surprise in her tone. "I'd of never believed it. I didn't think you so high and mighty."

"Do you like it?"

I was anxious for her to like the apartment and everything else connected with me, and I was afraid that she would like none of it on close inspection.

"It's swell. It beats the Evangeline Residence for Women downtown. Or that dump in New Orleans, far as that goes. And look at all the books. My, I don't believe I ever did see so many books in one place outside the bookmobile, honey. You and old Piers, both of you crazy about books. And you never did tell me."

I moved to the bar. "Bourbon okay? Or wine?"

"Bourbon, thank you kindly. Wait, Beau. Make it a double. No, a *triple*. I've had me one sorry hell of a night."

I made myself a drink, too, and noticed that my hands were shaking.

"Piers would adore your library," she enthused. "Why, Piers is mad for the *smell* of books. Don't that beat all? I seen him sniff at the things." She smiled. "Bottoms up, honey. To love and money!"

"Here's mud in your eye."

I sipped my drink, and she drank heavily from hers. And I could think of nothing to say. My mind had stopped. I stood and stared like a tourist seeing the Hope Diamond in the Smithsonian. Can it be real?

Finally, "How is old Piers?"

"Landa Goshen!" she exclaimed, "will you take a gander at this!

That's about the prettiest damn thing I ever did see. What's it made of?"

Pearl had taken a small pillbox off one of the bookshelves and she was examining it with delight.

"Well, it's gold—"

"No, the green stuff. I swear that's the liveliest green in the world. How it shines."

"It's called malachite. The green stone. It's not all that rare. It comes from Russia. I mean, the pillbox does. Before the Revolution it was popular to have things made of malachite because the czar and his family were partial to it."

Raising the lid, she found a silver locket inside.

"Don't, Pearl," I cautioned as she tried to pry it open.

"But I want to see. Some old lover's picture, I imagine. Some lost young lady's face locked away inside a silver locket inside a mal . . . gold box."

"Wrong. A few strands of hair. No picture."

"Whose hair?" she demanded.

I laughed. I enjoyed that quality of directness, the absence of dissembling, of evasion, the lack of even trying. She was the only animal in our part of the woods who cared nothing for cover. Ask the Pack. It brought her down in the end. She was what she was, and that was that. Take it or leave it. Without pretense and free of artificiality. Yet she was the most complicated woman I'd ever known. Doors opened on to rooms with doors opening on to more rooms. Endlessly. And when you thought you had come to the last door, you discovered she had another beyond.

In every instance when she contradicted herself, and she did often, each side of the dialectic was true. She held them in balance. While she could.

"Whose hair is it?" she repeated.

"A friend's. Someone I loved."

Pearl narrowed her eyes. She knew. "Dead, Beau?"

"As a doorknob."

"Leave the dead their secrets."

She replaced the pillbox with its locket on the shelf.

Inside were a few strands of my daughter's hair. Rose. The undertaker took it upon himself to clip them from her head and, after her burial, he gave them to me in an envelope. It angered me at the time, I thought it ghoulish and cruel. Now I'm glad he did. It is all that remains of her brief sojourn here among the quick, as they say in church, most of it spent sleeping soundlessly in her crib. The locket with its weightless cargo. Memory like wisps of yellow smoke. A birth certificate on which two tiny footprints are smeared in ink. Nothing more. Not much to leave behind, but kinder than some.

"I had a fight tonight with the fellow I was with. I hate fights." Pearl grinned. "The big lug."

"Who was it?"

"What?"

"Who were you with tonight?"

I was aching to know. I was feeling jealous again. And tell me this: why did the sudden pang of jealousy feel so goddamn good? Because I hadn't loved in years?

"Just business. Can I have more, please?" She handed me her glass. She was beginning to slur her words. "Fill it to the brim, honey."

I filled it.

"Business?" I asked, handing her back her glass.

Pearl giggled. "Yes, suh. Monkey business. I walked out on him. Left him dead in his tracks and went off by myself to what's-her-name's, the princess?"

"Countess. Vincennes."

"I been there before, did you know? Oh, yes, honey. I been around, making the scene. I been took up by the *swee*-els. Eighteen carats, flying first class, honey, and getting dizzy from the speed." She burped. " 'Scuse me. Hell, he likes being hurt. Ain't that sick? The more you push him around the better he likes you. But tonight I had enough pushing. My arms got tired."

"Your date tonight?"

"Weren't no other."

"Maybe he's had enough?" I suggested.

"Why?"

"He didn't run after you, right? He let you walk away."

She smiled. "No, he probably ran after. He was just late, that's all. He's probably still at the Countess what's-her-name's moping about like a hound dog gone supperless. But I saw you first, Beau, and I'm so very glad I did. I missed you something awful, sweet darling."

When someone you love says that, and you believe them, your physical heart suddenly constricts. Flip. Flop. Just like that. You get a little dizzy, unsteady on your feet. It's like you're about to have a heart attack, and in a way you are.

"Say it again, Pearl," I whispered. I wanted to prolong it. I was spinning memory, and I knew it. I knew it was rare, rarer than Russian imperial boxes made of gold and malachite, and far more fragile. It was a feeling held clean within a moment of time, and certain to pass. Memory was the fragrance it left behind.

"I've missed you, sweet darling."

"Come here, baby."

We held each other tightly. It was unreal. I closed my eyes, like a true pushover.

"Pearl, say it once more."

"I missed you."

Twenty-Seven

ON THE terrace of my apartment Pearl and I made love, to employ an accurate if dated euphemism.

Making *love* is what we did.

I had never had sex out there before, I had never done it because a high-rise apartment building overlooked my terrace with about a thousand windows. I was not in the habit of making a public display of myself. I was ashamed of my body.

Everyone said that I had an attractive body, but then everyone tells you they like your wife until after the divorce. Then it seems they never could stand the bitch.

I was also told I had decent equipment, something people those days began talking openly about, each other's equipment. It was about then that the term "basket" came into currency. Until then a basket was something you put candy kisses in. Now it meant a bulge.

There was a joke making the rounds at the time, and it went like this: If you were at a party in Manhattan, people asked you what you did for a living. At a party in Los Angeles, they asked you why you were unfortunate enough to be in Southern California. And in San Francisco they asked, "Are you hung?"

The whole country has become San Francisco.

You could see Pearl and me on my terrace if you lived across the way because of the lights from the street and the buildings. Like most parts of Manhattan, my neighborhood had a permanent five o'clock shadow.

"Fuck me here," Pearl requested. "Outside."

"You're drunk."

"No, I'm hot."

"Let's go inside. It's air-conditioned."

"I don't mean hot in that way, honey."

I was shocked. I looked shocked at any rate. I felt like a prude. I was very nervous.

"Why are you looking at me like that, Beau?"

What could I say? That I had never done it outside? That I was concerned about the neighbors? That my lease was coming due and the landlord wouldn't approve?

"Like what?" I smiled. It didn't work.

"You think I'm a whore? Well, I *am* a whore. And so is Piers. Put that in your pipe and smoke it!" She was very exasperated.

"Don't talk that way, Pearl. It hurts me."

"Everybody's a whore. The whole fucking world. Everybody's got their stinking price. *Everybody*."

"Everybody's got their price" was a cliché that used to be very popular. It isn't true.

"Why couldn't you call me again from New Orleans?" I asked. "I was worried about you. Do you understand that? I missed you, Pearl. I didn't know where the hell you were and I had no goddamn way of reaching you. So you let me dangle."

"Call *you*!" Pearl shouted, pouring more bourbon straight from the bottle she'd carried out to the terrace. Very Southern thing to do, and sensible. "I had to take care of Piers by myself and get the shit out of his life. All by myself. Alone. And then, when the goddamn coast was clear, I called and called and called, you bastard. I came back to New York because I thought you . . . Hell, y'all were in London having a grand old time. You could've let me know. I didn't have a dime when I arrived, did you know that, you prick? I . . . uh, you don't care. You're like all the rest."

"Let's go inside."

"No, damn it."

Pearl kicked off her shoes. She unzipped her dress, and it dropped to the straw matting of the terrace. She was wearing one of Giorgio's very expensive dresses, and I wondered how she came to own it.

There was nothing underneath.

She sat on the wicker table, where I have breakfast in the summer, her lovely bottom seated approximately at the spot where I lay the *New York Times*. She crossed her legs at the ankles, staring defiantly at me. She was angry and frustrated.

I stared back.

"Do something!" she yelled. "Goddamn it. Do something!" She seemed about to cry.

I thought of the neighbors and stood my ground.

She grabbed her drink and took a gulp of it, swaying slightly as she did.

"I'm so goddamn unhappy. I like to die."

"Baby, I . . ."

She looked up. She smiled coyly. "I'm on the cover of *Vogue* next month. And I have a six-page spread in *Bazaar*. What ya think of them potatoes, huh? Don't that beat all? I done right well since I been here, not that you were any goddamn help."

"Please . . ."

I had an erection.

"Goddamn Piers. Goddamn you."

She exhaled loudly, like the wind was kicked out of her, and her body appeared to slump in fatigue. She seemed very small and defenseless and lost.

"I'm a whore, a piece up for bids, and I'm in love with Piers but, honey, you got to believe me, whatever I did, er *do*, I will always love you. There's no future with us, and you know it. But I truly, I truly got to be able to count on someone, and it's *you*, poor baby. You my lucky penny, the net under my wire." She laughed sardonically.

I was getting choked up, believe that, and I felt inadequate before her appeal. I never wanted her to leave me again.

Question: Is it possible, in this best of all possible worlds, that two people *who love each other* will not be able to make love work?

"We have to make it work together, and that's God's truth," I said.

"Truth?" she snapped. "Truth won't buy you a corn roll. All the time I was away, I thought of you. I thought, Beau'll take me in. Beau'll see things through. Beau's different. Beau's after nothing. Beau'll make me one right good life. Beau. Beau. Beau. You didn't."

She finished her drink and tossed the glass over the terrace railing into the street below.

She smiled tiredly. "No, you didn't. What the hell." She shrugged. "It don't matter none. Not a damn bit. Come here, my pretty man. Be my lover tonight."

I went to Pearl. My knees were trembling, my stomach tight. I wanted her so badly I feared I'd pass out.

And I was trying to hold back. That is always a mistake. Never hold back.

"Don't look so plum defeated." She touched my face with her soft, warm hands. She wiped my sweat away. She kissed my brow, and then my eyelids. "I never want you to look defeated," she whispered, holding me gently against her breasts. "I need one friend, dearest, who never looks defeated."

I undressed and stood before her, my thighs pressed against the table's edge. I kissed her, deep and long. She bent forward, licking and kissing my chest and nipples, and then suddenly gripped my head by the hair and shoved it down as she fell back on the table, spreading her long legs before my face.

We ended on the chaise. When I entered her, she made small, weak noises, low squeals, noises like a tired and sickly child renders up unto delight.

When we were spent, I carried her inside to my bed as I had once carried Piers to his. We fell asleep holding each other, one of her hands cupping my sex.

Pearl said nothing more that night before she slept but this: "I love you. Don't you ever forget it."

And this also: in her sleep, I heard her moan and then mumble, "Piers, Piers . . ."

Twenty-Eight

LOOK AT Doris over there. No one has ever lived longer after being told they were dying than she! What cheek!"

Sabina Phips was speaking to me in a hushed voice. We were lunching together at Quo Vadis, a feeding station of the Pack. It was expensive, and fashionable, and it drew glitter like Princess Lee Radziwill, and the Countess de Ribes when she was in from Europe, and Halston, and Truman Capote, all of whom were there that day.

The bar was the chic part of the place in which to sit. It was small and intimate and quite lovely in its way, unlike the back dining room, which was more formal and cold. The décor was red, blood-red. Leather banquettes faced each other and they were status seating because everyone entering or leaving the joint would see you.

"David came by last night," Sabina went on.

David was the television network programing chief Sabina had been fooling around with for seven years. In his late forties, he was powerful in a powerful industry. He was shanty Irish Catholic but, through his wife, heiress to an old German-Jewish banking fortune, he had acquired social standing and a considerable degree of taste.

Doris, his wife, was sitting at a banquette on the other side of the bar room, chatting with Henry Wertz, director of one of the city's major museums. Nearly sixty, he was witty and social and patrician in appearance, and one of the most sought-after extra men in town.

"What did he want?"

"Who?"

"David."

She wasn't listening. She was glaring across the room at Doris. "If she is so sick, why isn't she home in bed?" Sabina hissed. "Instead she's dressed to the nines and lunching with Lord Smack Smack."

Henry Wertz, when he lived in London, was involved in a famous divorce trial. He was an art critic then, and during the trial he had to read in the daily press wildly sensational accounts of the testimony of one mistress after another about his curious sexual tastes. The press dubbed him Lord Smack Smack as a result.

Why was I lunching with Sabina? Because Sabina, at Varina Ransome's urging, was trying to pull together another fund-raiser, this time for the Democratic congressional candidates. She wanted me on the committee. I was good at raising money, surprising as that may seem. I agreed to serve. I also made up my mind to go to California and help in Robert Kennedy's primary campaign.

"Maybe she's recovering? They can do marvelous things for cancer victims now at Sloan Kettering. I saw Hortense Vincennes the other night, and she looks much better. So why don't you leave poor Doris alone?" I asked. "My God, Sabina, all you do is bitch. Having lunch with you is like spending two hours with Dudley Conrad." Conrad was a notorious gossip.

"I'm sure I wouldn't know," Sabina sniffed. "I've been waiting for David to marry me for seven *years*. I'm not getting any younger. David was by last night—"

"So you said. Eat your food."

"I'm dieting."

"Then why did you order it?"

"I don't want Doris to think I have to diet."

"That doesn't make sense."

"I'd love to get up and tell her that David came by last night and we screwed."

"You did? What a novelty."

"Don't be difficult, darling. Do you know"—Sabina lowered her voice—"I usually close my eyes when I blow David. But last night I kept my eyes open."

I tried to picture that. Sabina on her knees, dressed no doubt in a bit of lingerie purchased in Paris, wearing her green sunglasses, her red hair falling over her face. Trying not to gag.

"And I learned something. Did you know, before the penis gets hard, the balls get fatter?"

"Really?"

"That's because the balls fill with water first, and then the penis fills with water," she announced.

"Not water, Sabina. Blood. It's *blood* that makes the penis hard."

"Blood?" she repeated, looking bewildered. "Blood? Oh, how unattractive!"

Sabina was thirty-one years old, married twice and divorced twice. She had undergone three abortions. She had miscarried once. And she had less understanding of the male anatomy than a blind nun.

"Look, there's Roxanne," I said. The senator's wife was walking from the dining room toward the door with Rupert von Tallenberg, a young German prince worth about four hundred million.

"She's spotted us," Sabina said. "Pretend you don't see her."

Roxanne and Rupert walked over to our table.

I stood. "Hello, Roxanne. Rupert."

I shook hands with Rupert. His hand was damp.

"And how are you, Sabina, puss puss," Roxanne cooed in a voice that could chill warm wine.

Rupert said nothing. He merely stared blankly in our direction. He had heavily lidded eyes, and at thirty dissipation already marked his pleasant face.

"Divine," Sabina replied.

Sabina was Varina Ransome's best friend. Roxanne was after Varina's husband. Thus the enmity. Sabina was noble here if nowhere else: she was loyal to her friends. I admired that.

"I was at the White House last night . . ." Roxanne let drop.

Sabina smiled patronizingly. "I didn't know the tour ran that late."

"With my husband, puss puss. We had dinner with the President and a few of the Cabinet. They all know you, Sabina."

"I get around."

It was the wrong thing to say.

"As we all know, puss puss. In any case, Lyndon got drunk, and he started saying the most vulgar things about you, Sabina. Of course, I defended you, puss puss, as any friend of yours would."

"I barely know the President." Sabina attempted to sound indifferent.

"That's not what *Lyndon* said." Roxanne smiled.

It was the kind of smile a banker makes when he forces foreclosure on a house worth five times the outstanding mortgage.

"The President said, putting it charmingly, that you had had more men on your dance floor than Roseland."

Rupert laughed. Roxanne smiled at him.

I wondered if they were lovers. Roxanne was fifty-one years old.

"Well, Roxanne," Sabina snapped. "At least my dance floor still gets *wet!*"

That did it. Bye-bye, Roxanne and Rupert.

"The bitch!" Sabina growled. "I wonder if President Johnson really said that?"

I looked at Sabina. She was flattered. I was amazed.

"He obviously has heard I'm supporting Bobby Kennedy," she continued.

I changed the subject. "I didn't know Rupert was in town."

"Rupert?" She blinked. "Then you haven't *heard*, darling?"

"Heard what?"

Sabina shifted in her seat.

"You mustn't tell a soul . . ." she began.

By that point in my life I had learned that whenever anyone swore you to secrecy, what they were about to confide was already known all over town. Confidentiality was a device for appreciating the value of old news.

"Rupert went to bed with Hayton Ransome's new girlfriend in Hayton's apartment. In his own *bed*. She's living there. And, are you ready? Hayton stood and watched them do it. Why, that's unheard of!"

"Sabina, really," I said skeptically.

She sniffed. She hadn't gotten the reaction she wanted. "It's the absolute truth. Hayton didn't watch for very long, but he did peek in on them nevertheless. Even Varina knows. Poor Varina. Hayton is insane for this girl. It's quite unbelievable, I know, but there it is. Varina's convinced Hayton plans to marry the girl, and naturally she's hysterical. And since Hayton is Orin's only child, he gets practically everything when Orin dies. Millions. There ought to be a law. They're in the dining room right now."

"Who?"

"Hayton and his new girlfriend. Poor Varina's almost daughter-in-law," Sabina said with ill-concealed delight.

Why is it that bad news about old friends produces perverse glee?

"What's his girlfriend's name?"

"Name? I can't remember. Something untoward."

"More wine?" I asked. I wasn't much interested in Hayton Childs Ransome and his girls and nocturnal habits.

"Just a touch."

I turned and glanced toward the door to catch the captain's eye to order another bottle of wine. And as I did I saw Hayton standing by the entrance putting a Chanel jacket over the shoulders of a young woman.

Just before they left, the woman turned her head toward me for a second.

"Pearl," I said quietly. I was astounded. "Pearl."

"Yes." Sabina lit up. "That's her name. Pearl. That's Hayton's new flame. Pearl. Good God, that's the kind of name your nigger maid has."

Pearl.

Twenty-Nine

THE MORNING after my lunch with Sabina, Pearl called me. She said she loved me. She also said she was going to marry Hayton Childs Ransome. When I asked her why, she replied, "Honey, I'm doing it for Piers."

I was miserable. I thought, I should have married her myself. Even today, knowing all I do about what would follow in her troubled life, knowing that, or rather despite knowing that, I should have married her in 1968.

But I couldn't marry her then, or I couldn't bring myself to ask, because I was gun-shy. My marriage had been so painful at the end that I didn't have the courage to risk that kind of commitment again. I had thought marriages were for life. I was wrong. I had thought a married couple, with good will and a little effort, grew into love. Wrong again. I even believed in fidelity. And that was strike three.

I learned all this, about how wrong you could be about the State of Holy Matrimony, in the months that followed my daughter Rose's death. We fought all the time then, my wife and I, fights followed by icy silence and pointed avoidance. Even the sex wasn't good anymore. Actually, the sex was the first to go, and what replaced it was heavy drinking for both of us. Sometimes, when we were both plastered, we'd get horny and drunkenly sentimental and fuck. In the morning we wouldn't mention it, and the silence would descend like a painter's throw over our lives.

We blamed each other for the baby's death, and perhaps understandably so. Who's to know? We were suddenly so insecure and begrieved that we were scared to have another child. Although we desperately wanted another Rose. Moreover, we never admitted that to each other, but it was true all the same. To chance it, we'd get drunk and have sex and try to make a baby. When you want a baby too badly, and you have a lot of other problems interfering, when you hunger for a child and secretly think another kid will make everything as good as it was before, when you want a son or daughter *that* hard, it's very difficult to achieve conception, and I don't know why.

Seven years before I met Pearl, my wife left me. She was pregnant by me when she ran off, an irony that didn't escape my notice. It was in the morning while I was at Paramount Pictures on Times Square trying to sell a screen treatment.

My wife walked out because she fell in love with a teacher of comparative literature at Columbia University, after she had long ago fallen out of love with me. She met him one cold night at the Tak-Home Deli on Broadway after leaving a class in cultural anthropology she was auditing at Barnard. The class was taught by Margaret Mead. I never liked Margaret Mead after that.

A few months later, I saw Margaret Mead coming along 54th Street as I was entering the University Club on the corner. I felt crazed.

She strolled toward me, thumping her long walking stick against the pavement, her tongue darting in and out of her mouth like a garter snake's.

At first I thought she was talking to herself, then I realized that it was an old woman's nervous habit, something my grandmother habitually used to do to check if her dentures were secure.

I looked at her stick.

I thought of my absent wife.

I considered anthropology's empirical bias—all values are culturally relative. There are no universal values, such as it's wrong to walk off and leave a husband who loves you without so much as a by-your-leave.

There are universal values. And that's one of them.

"Shove that stick up your ass, homebreaker!"

Miss Mead glanced at me, rather bored by it all. As the world's most famous anthropologist she had spent years studying naked savages in the jungle. She wasn't impressed by me. She licked her lips and walked on.

The man for whom my wife divorced me still teaches at Columbia. His name is Michael Goldstein. I saw him once on Sunrise Semester at six in the morning. It was a Monday, and a woman I had met three hours before at Maxwell's Plum was tugging at me as I sat on the edge of the bed. She wanted to have sex again. We had done it an hour before, but I couldn't raise the interest for another round. So she was trying to give me a hand, as it were.

The television set was soundlessly on, providing a silver-gray light that I thought would be sexy, since I was out of candles. I hoped the woman wouldn't notice the difference.

In the 1960s the middle class, of which I was a charter member, had discovered the relationship between candlelight and sexual acts. We had also discovered singles' bars, wife-swapping, B&D, S&M, water sports, the clitoris, poppers, grass, Quāāludes, vibrators, the

East Village Other's personal columns, threesomes, foursomes, swinging, and the Frederick's of Hollywood catalogue. That was all quite a find.

I felt sorry for this woman, which was why I couldn't get up an encore. She was cashier at a car wash in Jackson Heights, which was bad enough. Worse, she kept telling me in bed that she had never done any of this before. She was forty years old. I believed her.

While this was going on, I glanced at the television set and saw the flickering image of a middle-aged man with a thin waxed mustache and bald head, dressed in a tweed jacket with round, leather patches sewn on the elbows. And on the screen, running like a luminous tattoo across his belly, were the words *Professor Michael Goldstein*. I started to laugh.

I remembered my wife's leaving me, abandoning our two-bedroom apartment in Park West Village with its plasterboard walls that freely admitted the noise of toilets flushing ten floors below or above our own, and abandoning me, who had very little money but would soon make a great deal writing movies; and discarding our black and white Motorola 12-inch TV and our Spanish-style bedroom and living room suites bought at Levitz's and not paid for. Maybe she had a point. And taking my seed fertile in her belly to White Plains and Comp. Lit. as table talk.

I stayed in that depressing apartment for nearly a year after I could afford better, because its two rooms smelled of her and I still loved her. She had sprayed the bedroom curtains with her cologne, and it remained.

I'd come home half expecting that she had come to her senses and would be there. I finally gave up the place when I conceded she never would, and by then loneliness had gone bad and become self-pity.

Three years after our divorce, I got on the downtown subway at 68th Street and Lexington Avenue, the Hunter College stop. It was two-forty in the afternoon, and there she was, my ex, sitting in the graffiti-marred car looking very lovely.

She wore a beige wool suit, gold jewelry, and large bubble sunglasses. Her light brunette hair was now dyed blond. Nothing else had changed.

With her were two little boys who sat on either side, one about three, the other two. They were dressed in identical navy-blue suits with large white buttons down the front, and short pants and blue knee stockings and black Buster Brown shoes. Their hair was dark blond, as my wife's had been as a child, and it was wetted down and parted on the right.

I sat on the bench across from them, and I couldn't stop staring at the children. At the next station, 59th Street, they left the train. But before they did, she said to me, "You look well. Are you making a lot of money writing for the movies?"

"A little."

She laughed. "I should have asked for alimony."

The smallest child hid behind her skirt, peeking out at me.

The older one held on to her hand and, not letting go, stepped forward and tentatively touched my knee.

She pulled him back.

"We're off to Bloomie's. The boys need shoes . . . Oh"—she smiled and patted the older boy's head—"this one's yours. In case you wondered."

In Bloomingdale's card shop you can buy laminated plastic fake-walnut plaques, with the picture of a pretty woman holding a long-stemmed rose and gazing mournfully out an open window.

Under the picture is printed: "It is better to have loved and lost than never to have loved at all."

A pleasing sentiment. But it isn't true.

Thirty

ON THE WAY to La Guardia Airport to catch a flight to California, I picked up the New York *Post*. Its headline: ANDY WARHOL SHOT!

I had known Warhol for almost ten years, and I was shocked by what had been done to him. A woman, apparently a fanatical hater of men who had authored a feminist pamphlet advocating the extermination of all human males, had walked into the Factory, Warhol's studio in Manhattan, and shot him point-blank. The reason she later offered was that he had not produced a film script she had done.

In Los Angeles I stayed at the Beverly Wilshire. For two days I worked on press relations for the Robert Kennedy campaign in a tiny crowded office in the Ambassador Hotel.

On Primary Day, all of us in the Kennedy camp anticipated victory. The feeling of hope and coming power was ardent and unwavering. We were tensely optimistic, and that optimism turned to joy, at times delirious, as the voting returns were tabulated throughout the evening. Most of the Kennedy family was scattered about the hotel, the children running errands, the victory celebration already beginning in hundreds of rooms and spilling over into the halls. Whenever I left the pressroom I'd be hugged and kissed by people I didn't know, strangers momentarily united in the elixir of triumph. For a sweet and brief season we all felt part of the Kennedy family and through it intimate with history. We were enthralled by the promise of a new presidency and the end to a war.

I was late in arriving at the victory celebration in the ballroom. Robert Kennedy had just finished making his statement. I stood in the back of the room and cheered with the others as he waved and grinned at the throng of campaign workers and press. Then he made his way off the platform, and I lost sight of him in the crowd.

I never saw him again. For, minutes later, Robert Francis Kennedy lay dying on the floor of the kitchen of the Ambassador Hotel. He was forty-two years old. He left behind a wife and eleven children. He left behind a nation.

Part III

Timberton

Thirty-One

THE DAY before Pearl's wedding I flew to New Orleans, and then took a connecting flight to Natchez. I rented a car and drove the sixty miles to Timberton. I hadn't been back to the Ransome estate in ten years, and was surprised at how happy I felt that August as I drove through the iron gates and up the quarter-mile of gravel road, under the branches of the ancient oaks, their limbs dripping sleeves of Spanish moss, up to the great house. Memory was everywhere, in the smell of the fields and the mimosa, in the tree house, on the verandas, under the eaves. From the time my father took the fall, when I was fifteen, until I graduated from Princeton eight years later, I spent every summer at Timberton. Except for Christmas when I was obliged to be with my mother and sisters in Santa Barbara, I devoted all my school holidays to the pleasures and generosities of the great house and the two thousand acres of fields and woodlands surrounding it. Ransome lands. And now, in a day, Pearl's too.

I had spent so many splendid years at Timberton because of Ambassador Ransome's close friendship with my father. As friends often do, he felt guilt in the manner and the reason for my father's dying. And he took me in, like a son. I think he knew what I only suspected, that my mother didn't want me with her. And what of it? She had a selfish and legalistic mind. In their divorce settlement she received custody of my two sisters, and my old man got me as a kind of judicial consolation prize. After he kicked the bucket, my mother saw no reason on God's green earth why she should have to spend good money raising me. And I'm glad she felt that way because it opened Timberton's gates to me.

It was one of the finest antebellum houses in Adams County, Mississippi, and that says a lot because the county was endowed with exceptionally graceful buildings.

The history of the place was the history of the family that built it. It lay east of Natchez, between the Mississippi and Pearl rivers, two hours from the sea, and was constructed in 1831 by Hayton Beaumont Ransome, a smuggler and slaver who became a planter and merchant after he crossed the Mississippi from Louisiana, bought and cleared the woodlands, and put up his marvelous house. All of it paid for with money from the slave trade and smuggling in the Gulf islands and Chandeleur Sound.

Ransome was terrified of malaria, and with good cause. It had carried off his parents and his only sister. And so Timberton commanded the highest hill in Adams County. He thought the lowlands were a death house for whites, safe only for the Indians who settled the land fifteen hundred years before the first Ransome took title; safe too for Negro slaves, three hundred of whom worked his fields.

There *is* justice in the order of things. In 1860 the disaster that Ransome feared rose in another form to confront the South like the Mississippi swollen with Northern waters. Before it was over, four of his five sons had died for the Confederacy: one fell at Corinth, another at the Great Redoubt in Vicksburg, the third in the sweet pastures of Shiloh. None of the boys had seen twenty years when his life was forfeited to the armies of Grant and Porter.

The last of the four went slowly, horribly, of starvation and dysentery in the Union prison at Fort Massachusetts on Ship Island, near the lovely bayous and coves his father once worked. It was a hellhole, as were most Yankee prisons, designed to murder slowly but certainly. Stalin's *gulag* had nothing on Fort Massachusetts, a state crime now all but forgotten.

On the same day that Ransome got word that his captured son had died at Fort Massachusetts, he also learned that the Confederacy had surrendered its life at Appomattox. Hayton Beaumont Ransome went into the library at Timberton, put a Colt pistol to his right ear and pulled the trigger. He was fifty-nine.

One son remained. He was thirteen years old when he faced the enemy on the campus of Jefferson Military College. The Southern cadets, in their gray uniforms, ran to meet a Yankee patrol that had wandered onto their campus. They grouped between the Aaron Burr oaks, where the first traitor to the United States was tried, and called out their youthful challenge. The Yankee soldiers, with a whoop and a laugh, abandoned the field to the jubilant boys. It was the Confederacy's last victory in Mississippi.

His name was Childs Ransome. It was he, after his father's suicide in 1865, who faced the devastation of Timberton and its saddest wreckage, his mother. She was given to lurching about the grounds of Timberton, calling out to her lost sons, litanies of waste . . . Hayton, Loxley, Beaumont, Ayres. They never answered.

Although Childs was the youngest, he was endowed with precocious talents: a keen wit, abundant will, morals always subservient to his ambition, and an intense loyalty to his family, his land, and the South. He made money so quickly and consistently that he was known as the "Southern Vanderbilt." And he was handsome to boot, dark blond and hazel-eyed.

Childs established whorehouses and gambling halls for the Kentucky boatmen in the Under-the-Hill quarter of Natchez, a district comparable to the Minnesota Strip without neon. And to get the boatmen both coming and going he built provisioning stores along the Natchez Trace, the route they had to take north back home. His enterprises were in partnership with a carpetbagger named Colonel Michael Wilson of Fort Snelling, Minnesota. Wilson later died of alcohol poisoning in Bogalusa, cursing the Ransomes as he crossed over to Glory. He was but one of many to damn them to no effect.

Ten years after the War Between the States, using money from his bawdy houses and the Natchez Trace, and the old family vocation of smuggling, Childs Ransome saved Timberton for good from Yankee taxes. That same year he married Abigail Thistle de Lyons of New Orleans. They honeymooned in Paris, where she had kin and bought a small house on the Rue Bixio, which the family owns to this day. I have been there often. In fact, that's where I met Philip de Lyons, Abigail's great-nephew. He runs the French franchising operation for McDonald's hamburger parlors!

In 1872 Childs began to hold "Ingathering Nights" at Timberton, putatively religious evenings devoted to discussions of the Tribes of Israel and the Ingathering of the saints in the Last Days. But the tribes that gathered were the Knights of the White Magnolia. It was through the Klan and Jim Crow, through the Night Riders and the burning cross, the truncheon and the lynch ropes that the Ransomes, like other Southern white patrician families, reasserted their dominance over the county and later over the state.

In the decades that followed Childs Ransome fought with James J. Hill and the Morgan interests for control of railroads, and he invested in mines and more land, always more land. And he became rich, and richer, and richer still.

Childs died in 1927, a hated man. He never held political office, but like the Mellons and the Duponts and the rest of the gang, he controlled those who did. On his deathbed, clutching a gold reliquary containing a silvery lock of Jefferson Davis's hair, he kissed his wife Abigail goodbye. Then he gripped the hands of his two sons, Beaumont and Orin, who stood beside his bed.

"Don't ever forget Shiloh and the glory!" he cried out.

"Papa, don't die! Don't leave us!" Beaumont, his youngest son, sobbed, collapsing on the bed.

Orin, twenty-nine years old, stood watching his younger brother weep beside the body of the old man. He refused to cry.

Childs gave up the ghost. And Beaumont, angry at his brother's restraint, yelled, "Did you hate Papa?"

"No, I loved Papa."

"Then why don't you cry?"

"Did Papa ever cry? After Shiloh? After Grandmama died? Not once. Where's the profit?" He turned and left the room.

On the morning of his father's funeral, Orin Ransome met with his father's bankers to decide what to sell.

Thirty-Two

WHERE's everybody?" I asked Aunt Kattie as I stepped onto the front veranda.

Kattie laughed. "They comin'. They comin'. What you in such a all-powerful hurry for, child? They due sometime soon." Kattie was fat and black and old, and she had run the Ransome household for thirty years. She was a substitute mother to Hayton and me when we were growing up. She occupied the same position that her mother, a slave, had held before her. She felt part of the family, and she was.

"But Mrs. Ransome told me they'd all be here hours ago."

"Don't you know nothin', child? The Ambassador he sick. He hurt in his heart." She patted her great bosom. "He got to take his sweet time in comin' and listen to them doctors. He sure do hate sawbones. Now, you rest yourself, hear? Sit over there on the porch and let me bring you somethin' cool to sip, like when you was a boy. 'Member sittin' on the swing divan and playin' Old Maid?"

"I surely do. And I always beat you and Hayton."

She chuckled. "I don't know about Mister Hayton, but you sure never did beat old Aunt Kattie at nothin'. And you never will. You can write a check on that! Now, where's your bags, boy?"

"In the car."

"Just leave 'em be. I get Jeremiah to take 'em up to your room. It like it always be."

"How's Jeremiah?"

"Same. He the laziest nigger God ever made, and that's the truth." She laughed at her statement. She loved putting her husband down. "If I didn't wake him in the morning, Lord knows, he'd sleep a week. And don't you go listenin' to his complaints. Not a word of truth in anything that man ever say. Now, go set yourself down."

I went over to the swing divan and sat down.

"What you want to drink? I guess you don't drink no brown cows no more." Hayton and I used to crave that chocolate milk with Hershey bar shavings floating on top.

"Not until after five! Can you get me a vodka tonic?"

"Yes, child." But she didn't move. She stood with her hands planted on her fleshy hips, a broad grin on her face, staring at me. "I thought I was never to see your sweet face again until we done meet in heaven. And here you is!"

"I missed you too, Kattie," I said, moved by her affection.

"I just no-account, but I loves you."

A few minutes later she returned with my drink. In the glass she had placed a sprig of fresh mint, and the scent of it incited memories of afternoons in the heat of the day, sitting on this veranda under the turning fans, listening to Ambassador Ransome talk on the phone as he sat and rocked and glanced listlessly at the newspapers. Varina would be playing Solitaire, and every few minutes she'd interrupt his conversation with sharply worded advice about the business he was discussing or the person he was talking to, be it the President of the United States or the manager of his farms. And Hayton, very young, five years old that first summer I came to Timberton, would be asleep beside me on one of the swings as I rocked and drank lemonade with sprigs of mint and waited for the sun to lower enough for Varina to say, "All right, children, you can go into the pool, the burn's gone out of the day."

"What's Mister Hayton's woman like?"

"Well, Aunt Kattie, she's very beautiful, and intelligent, and"—this is what she really desired to know—"she comes from white trash and no money. But she's wonderful."

Kattie thought on that a moment. "White trash!" she declared, "No money! Why, the Ransomes they always done marry money. The first Miz Ransome had money. And our Miz Ransome, she come from Georgia money and good stock. Yes, suh. And Grandaddy Ransome, he married big money, too. Don't see no future for a girl with no money marrying a Ransome. No, suh. She ought to stick with her own kind, if you wants to know. Jeremiah tell me she's a movie star. Now, that don't look good in Mississippi for a Ransome to be marrying a movie star."

"Well, she's not a movie star. She's been asked to *be* in a movie, but she isn't in one yet." Which was true.

Kattie shook her head and went "*unhh*-huh!" showing hearty disapproval. She was a Deep Water Baptist, and Hollywood and all its works were of the Devil, and that was that.

"You'll love her, Aunt Kattie," I said, laughing.

"I got to finish the weddin' cake. Lordy, we got ourselves three hundred hungry souls comin' after the weddin' to eat up the Ambassador's food like this was the Salvation Army at Christmas. I been cooking a week. Got three colored girls in to help just with the food. Working night and day for a movie star, don't that beat all?"

And off she waddled toward her kitchen, talking to herself as she went, her Baptist mind convinced Hayton was about to bring a silver-screen tramp into her house.

I rocked and looked out over the front lawn, which spread green and flat for ten acres and then, abruptly, fell away in the steep hill down which Hayton and I once rolled until we were so giddy and dizzy we could no longer stand upright to make another climb. And it was at the base of this hill, in the lilac arbor, that I lost my virginity at eighteen to a girl from Smith. She spent the Easter break with me here, and even now the scent of lilac stops me dead in my tracks, and I find myself thinking of her and how her body trembled on the arbor ground.

I finished my drink. I was about to get another when I heard a rumble and looked up to see a helicopter in the distance, flying toward the house. I stood and watched as it neared and then, with an enormous roar, settled slowly down, wobbling a few feet above the grass and finally landing on the lawn before me.

I could see Pearl in front next to the pilot, waving happily behind the glass bubble.

I ran to them.

Pearl emerged first and embraced me. She was casually yet elegantly dressed in silk, now her favorite material. And her hair was cut shorter and beautifully coiffed. I was both pleased and surprised by the change in her appearance. Already, like some fantastic bird whose coloration changes with age or season, she was acquiring the look and manner of the world she was about to marry. Varina's hand was in all of it.

Varina next climbed out of the helicopter, followed by the Ambassador, who was helped by a male nurse.

I kissed Varina. "It's good to be home!" she shouted into my ear over the roar of the blades.

"Where's Hayton?" I shouted back.

"Comes tomorrow. Got his bachelor party in New York tonight!"

I glanced behind her. The Ambassador was heatedly gesturing at the male nurse to get back into the helicopter. " I don't need you! Git!" he shouted.

The nurse, confused, climbed back aboard. The helicopter took off with incredible speed.

We stood together in a group, windblown, and Varina glared at Ransome. "What's come over you, sending your nurse away? I can't believe it!"

"I don't need a nurse, and I don't want one. He makes me feel like I'm sick."

"But you *are* sick, dearest. And I am very angry with you."

"He made me feel old and helpless. And I'm not."

"What am I going to do with you, Orin?"

He put his arm around me. "Michael's the only nurse I need. He'll take care of the old man, won't you, son?"

"Sure as hell."

"So will I," Pearl said, standing at his side. He put his other arm around her.

"Bless you, Pearl. I tell you, our young Mr. Hayton Ransome is getting the best of the bargain."

Thirty-Three

THAT WOMAN is driving me nuts!" Ransome said, handing me my drink. We were in the library where his grandfather had blown himself to kingdom come more than a century ago. It was ten-thirty. Dinner was over, and Pearl and Varina had gone upstairs to prepare for bed. "Sit down, son," he said, easing himself into a brown leather armchair. I took one opposite him. "If Varina comes in," he whispered, "tell her we're only having Cokes. She'll believe you. Doctors ordered no bourbon, which shows about how much they know."

"Why didn't you let me know you were sick?"

"I didn't want anyone to know. It's a little thing. Another angina attack. Hell, I've had them before . . ."

"So have I," I said.

"Yes. I'd forgotten. But I'm seventy years old, goddamn it, so they shoved me into the hospital for two days of tests. A blasted nuisance. Anyway, I don't want to talk about it." He took a drink. "Tastes good. Now, tell me what you think of Pearl." Ransome leaned forward, and coughed. And then he held up his hand and smiled, as if to say, I'm all right. He coughed some more.

He was a singularly handsome man, dignified and prepossessing, with extremely intelligent eyes. When he spoke his face stirred with animation, and when he listened his eyes would squint at yours as if, from years of diplomatic training and financial schemes, he was hunting out deceit. Or weakness. He was never entirely relaxed, like someone who is forever waiting for an important call. Now, in his age, his body had become thinner, he was slightly stooped, and his memory of recent events was dulled. While his accent was more Eastern than Southern, his manners were indelibly of the Old South, and his confidence, which was bracing, came from a lifetime of great wealth and high achievement. Little impressed him anymore. Certainly not money. Nor did the Pack, whom Varina courted—or rather, was courted by.

But women, beautiful or not, still enthralled him. I never knew a man whose curiosity and delight with women were as boundless as Orin Ransome's. And for a man who had loved so many, it was natural that his vanity was large. It showed in the care he took with his dress, the hundreds of suits tailored in London, rooms full of clothes in all his houses. He had his barber fly to wherever in the world he was to give his ample gray hair the right shape. There was something endearing in his vanity: the utter openness of it.

"Pearl?" he repeated.

"I think she's terrific. She's got good sense. She's beautiful. I wouldn't mind marrying her myself." I laughed, as if I were making a joke.

He stared at me with his intense black eyes. And then he sat back and smiled. "You're in love with her too. Well, you'd have to be a poof not to be. If I wasn't seventy and married to Varina, I'd hanker for her myself." And then he laughed.

"I never saw anyone as beautiful."

"Varina was, when she was young. But in a different way. Hell, I think she still is. I still pine for her when she's away. I know she thinks I've got a regular harem. I don't. Maybe one or two, just for the spice of it. They make me feel young."

I felt somewhat embarrassed by what he was saying. Ransome had never spoken this openly to me before. Perhaps it was his age, or the thought of his dying. He had always been a very private man, but there was nothing left to achieve anymore. Ambition had run its course, and perhaps with it privacy had lost its compulsion. I don't know.

"I'm goddamn glad Hayton's marrying her," he said.

"So am I."

He smiled again. "I doubt that, son. But I'm glad I'm alive to see him married off. He's my own flesh and blood, but I have to say he's got about six less than a dozen upstairs. There's no drive to the man, no desire to do a damn thing but drink and go to parties and sleep around. A playboy, a *Ransome* who's a partyboy! His grandfather would have horsewhipped him, and then shown him the gate. I should have done the same. Truly."

"He's not as bad as all that. He's still young . . ."

Ransome coughed. "He's a liar, boy. He lies about little things. Under that smile and those phony English ways, he's mean-spirited and petty-minded. Do you know, when he'd come home from England during his school vacations, when we were living mostly in Georgetown, he used to *steal* from me?"

"Why would Hayton steal?" I asked skeptically.

"God knows." Ambassador Ransome pulled on his lower lip, and then shook his head. "Sheer contrariness, I suspect. He'd steal money from my dresser, or go through my pockets or his mother's purse. *Why?* I gave the little bastard whatever damn thing he desired. He only had to ask. Perhaps that was the trouble. When poor Bobby Kennedy got himself killed two months back, I said to Varina, I wish Bobby had been *our* son. What did old Joe Kennedy have *I* didn't have? I'm richer than he is. I think my son was better educated than his. God knows, my family's older and we're Southern to our toenails. What the hell didn't we give Hayton that Joe gave Bobby? I'll never know."

"Maybe it was Hayton's being an only child?" I suggested, having no answer. Many times over the years I had heard both Varina and Orin Ransome draw comparisons with the Kennedys. They didn't envy them. They admired them. Yet after all this time they could not figure out how the Kennedys had turned the trick. It rankled.

"Horseshit. Hayton's simply no damn good. I've always sensed his contempt. *That's* why he'd steal, son. Or shoplift. One sneaky act upon another. Not that he needed the money or the junk he'd lift. But to show me his contempt. Well, tomorrow he's getting himself married off, and I trust that darling girl has got the gumption and the balls *he* doesn't have, enough at the least to take charge. Pearl's bright, isn't she? Hell, she's a beauty, and she'll bear bright and strong and healthy children, and I'll have someone to carry on the blood. That's all I want now. The rest is ash and bitterness."

Ambassador Ransome finished his drink, and started to rise to make another.

"I'll get it," I said.

I took his glass and walked to the bar. It was a large ornate glass and steel affair that looked out of place in the walnut-paneled library with its high, intricately sculpted ceiling, its heavy English leather furniture, the portraits of the Ransomes dimly lit and hanging somberly in gilded frames, the thousands of leather-bound books behind glass doors in the hand-carved cases—the fragrance of old leather and paper and cigar and ancient life. And Persian rugs across which Hayton and I erected our toy railroad so long ago.

On the bar, as on every other available surface, stood framed photographs of the family and of their eminent and powerful friends. The rich, like no one else, have an addiction to cluttering space with their own images. Churchill, Roosevelt and Stalin at Yalta, seated together, Roosevelt alone smiling. Behind him, Ambassador Orin Ransome with his right hand resting lightly on the wool cape on the President's shoulder. Orin and Varina with King George VI and Queen Elizabeth; with the Duke and Duchess of Windsor; with Tito; with Gary Cooper; and on and on.

I turned to carry back his drink, and paused a moment by the bar looking across that dark, enormous space at the figure of the Ambassador, sitting slumped in his leather wing chair in a single pool of light from the standing brass lamp, his hands thin and gnarled, rubbing the sides of his brow as if in reflection, or pain. Soon over, that life, over and gone and what an emptiness—what a vast hole his passing would dig. With the exception of Harriman, Bradley, Tito, and Mountbatten, he was about the last remaining of the great men of that generation whose achievements and follies had created our age. They had done their best, such as it was. It wasn't good enough.

"You're only tired, sir. That's why you feel badly about Hayton. I think you're being a little unkind. His marrying Pearl says something about his good sense," I said lightly, trying to lift his dour mood.

"Unkind?" he barked as I gave him his drink. "When you know your life is reaching its end, you see things clearly. I haven't time to lie to myself anymore or lie to you, Michael. It's time to face up to things. And that brings me to your father."

He pulled his body straight in his chair, and then leaned toward me once more. My stomach tightened. *My father.* I don't know why, but except for pleasant asides about my father, Orin Ransome, in all these years, had never spoken in concrete detail of him, and I had never asked. I knew that my father's life, and the reasons for his death, were a secret. A secret that had been sealed away for so many years that it had grown ominous in my imaginings. I feared the truth.

"I want to tell you something about your father I should have told you long ago. But I guess I was and will always remain ashamed that I couldn't save him in the end. Yet he was my friend, son. It's odd, but I met your father in 1939 on the day my younger brother Beaumont was killed in a hunting accident in Maine. And he took much of Beaumont's place in my heart, like a younger brother renewed to life."

"He loved you, I know." I lit a cigarette. "You don't have to tell me anything more, sir. I've lived with not knowing, and I'm not sure . . ."

Ambassador Ransome waved his hand in front of his face like someone impatiently clearing the air of smoke. "The charges were *true*," he stated quickly, and then sank back into the leather cushions.

I shivered and anxiously glanced around the darkened room. "That he was a Communist?" I whispered. And then I felt foolish for my caution. From the time I was a boy, the fear engendered by the secrecy of his life still remained. A Communist—my father? Never stated, but always suspected. Always really understood.

"Yes. He was in the Party in the early Thirties, for about six years as I recall. Hell, a lot of our very best people were. What did it matter? It was about social justice then, before Stalin's show trials."

"He never spoke of it," I said, amazed to be speaking of it even now. "Not once. Is that what brought him down?"

Ransome glanced at me, and then he looked away. "Only partly, son. There was more to it than that. If it had only been the goddamn Party business we could have protected him. But there was more."

He sighed and stopped talking, seeming to wait on my pressing him to continue. And I did.

"More what? I do want to know."

"The rest is classified and not to be repeated, understood? But it's the very reason why he died. In 1946, through the CIA, we were funding and arming anti-Communist guerrillas behind the Iron Curtain. Poland, the Baltic Republics. And for nearly ten years we supplied an anti-Communist army in the Ukraine. I was a special assistant to Truman in those years, as you know, and I had to deal with Stalin and Molotov and those other gangsters. I found out about the Ukraine operations when Stalin broke off negotiations over Austria. He had evidence that we were supplying troops there. I mean *hard* evidence. Captured CIA operatives. And he threw it in my face. When I returned to Washington from Moscow—this was in 1948—I was mad as hell at being caught off-balance, and it was then that Truman secretly brought me into the 'forty committee' that approved covert CIA operations."

"And my father?"

The Ambassador coughed. "He was CIA, as you know. Very brilliant man when it came to planning. He put forth a highly sophisticated plan to mount an anti-Communist resistance operation in Albania, supplying the guerrillas through Yugoslavia, and by sea from Italy. This was after Tito had broken with Stalin . . ."

To the best of my recollection, my father had never once mentioned Albania, or the Balkans, although he had spoken with some freedom to me about his actions with the French Resistance during the war. Albania was a complete surprise. "Why Albania?" I asked.

Ransome laughed. "I asked the same question. Why indeed? Since I'd had a good deal of Russian experience, I was asked to give advice on the operation. I opposed it. I thought it would cost more than it was worth. Given enough commitment of personnel and matériel, we could have taken Albania. But what in hell did Albania have that we wanted? Another base? If we toppled their dictator, Enver Hoxha, it'd only frighten the Yugoslavs and push them back into the arms of the Russian bear, and it would anger the Greeks. So I was against it."

"But it went ahead anyway?"

"Naturally. I nearly stopped it, but the CIA, through British intelligence, received word that Hoxha had granted the Russians the right to a base at Valona, on the Albanian coast. A submarine installation. How the British found that out we'll probably never know, but they're better at intelligence than we'll ever be. So the head of the CIA, with Truman's approval, gave the go-ahead. Your father was placed in charge of the operation.

"He set up a base, with British help, in Malta, which was then in their hands. The CIA and the British SIS trained and equipped guerrilla forces that were either parachuted into Albania or taken in by sea. It went on for a year, and it involved thousands of men. And the most confounded thing happened. Every guerrilla, to the last hapless man, every goddamn one of them was arrested and executed within hours of reaching Albanian soil. We couldn't understand it. They'd land at night and be shot dead on the beach or in the fields. There was a leak somewhere, a mole involved in the operation. And the suspicion fell on your father. Are you following me?" he asked gently.

"Yes."

"Well, in 1950, your father was moved from the CIA to a low-level desk at the State Department. And a year later, the internal hearings at both State and the CIA began. They were trying to beat Joe McCarthy to the wire. You have to understand the politics then, son. The anti-Communist hysteria, and a bureaucracy's natural instinct to protect itself. They had to throw someone to the wolves, and they had to find that person before McCarthy's Senate Committee did. After the fall of China and Eastern Europe, every right-wing lunatic got a hunting license, and we were the game. They went after Dean Acheson, and they went after me. And your unlucky father. All our very brightest and finest people, patriots every one. Both Acheson and I knew your father had been a member of the Party. Hell, the CIA knew it. The OSS knew it when they recruited him. But Senator McCarthy *didn't* know. And that was the crucial point. The game hung on his not finding out. And, by God, did we try to protect your father from their finding out."

Then I understood. "And Michael Garrett blew the whistle."

Ambassador Ransome raised his eyebrows in surprise. "Yes. How did you know?"

I shrugged. "I suspected it. He saw me after my old man's funeral and he told me he meant no harm."

"No harm, huh? Let me tell you, in 1951, late that year, we received word that one of the Senate Committee's staff had made liaison with a former CIA operative—your Michael Garrett who meant no goddamn harm! Horseshit. It was through Garrett that they got wind of the Albanian disaster, and they were about to open public hearings. We knew McCarthy was reading the wind, and he'd start screaming, 'Who lost Albania?' Son, we knew that, willynilly, sooner or later your father would be brought into it and destroyed. The scent led to him. And once that happened, the next question would be 'Who hired the traitor!' and that would lead to me and to Dean Acheson, and through us, to the President himself. It was the start of an election year . . ."

"Was he a traitor?" I blurted out. "Was my father a traitor?" Hadn't I suspected it all along? Hadn't I lived under its insinuation half my life? The resolve it weakened early in me, the shyness it cast over me, the panic it intruded into my life. Betrayal, and the fear the secret would out.

The Ambassador looked at me for a moment, squinting, and pausing as if considering whether the truth was worth the telling. "Your father? Good Lord, *no*! I never believed it for a minute. Not once. And I would have gone up against the wall for him. That's how much I believed in him."

"Then who the hell was the traitor?" I shouted.

Ransome put his finger to his lips. "Let's not rouse the house, son." He sipped his bourbon. "The mole was not your father. The mole was a perfectly charming British drunk named Kim Philby. He was British liaison with the CIA in Washington. I often had lunch with the bounder and, I'm ashamed to admit, even had the traitor to our house in Georgetown. He was well liked in Washington. What fools we are. Regrettably, we didn't learn of the sonofabitch's connection with the Albanian leaks until years later, after Philby defected to the other side. And by then it was much too late to help your father. He had already killed himself to keep his friends safe, to protect State and the CIA from the wolves. To protect *me*."

Ransome stopped speaking. He lowered his head and closed his eyes tight. He gripped his hands together, working to control his emotions.

"Once he died . . ."—he continued, throwing back his head and looking me straight in the eye—"once he was gone the McCarthy committee assumed his death was a confession of guilt, and they went after other victims. So now you know . . ."

"Now I know," I replied softly.

"I regret it, son. I could not protect him. And that fact has eaten away at me all these years."

I nodded. "Could no one have saved my father?"

He shook his head. "Not a one. It was a lethal world we were part of, it's as simple as that. I'm angry and I'm still aghast that it was your father who had to take the fall."

"Drinking, Orin!" snarled Varina, sweeping into the library. "What a disgusting, unrepentant thing to do!"

"We're only having Cokes," I piped up, remembering Ransome's request.

She marched over to his chair and grabbed his glass. She sipped it and made a disagreeable face. "*Coke*, is it?" she said to me, "So now he's got *you* lying for him. Shame on the both of you. Get up to bed, Orin."

"Now, Mama . . ." he said, trying to pacify her.

"Don't Mama me! Are you deliberately trying to kill yourself? Or are you trying to kill me? Get up to bed. This instant!" she commanded, pulling at his sleeves.

"You don't have to pull at me," he groused, getting to his feet. He moved toward the door, Varina following closely behind, giving him a little shove to keep him moving.

Thirty-Four

I WAS UP at six, before the others were awake, dressed hurriedly and tiptoed down the long upstairs hall past the many bedrooms. I could hear Orin Ransome's heavy, irregular breathing, like some kind of antique pump on the blink. Like the heartbeat of Timberton itself.

I walked down the gravel road behind the house, then across a field of clover, wet with dew, to the stables. I saddled a horse and rode out across the fields and over the brook.

I stopped a moment by the iron fence guarding the small plot of carefully tended earth that was the Ransome family cemetery. Simple granite crosses, some tilting in the soil, marked the graves of that tragic but gifted brood. The four dead brothers lying in a row, facing east to Jerusalem and the Second Coming, each cross hung with a brass Confederate flag. Under the flag the name of the place at which they fell. Beaumont, Orin's younger brother, buried to the side by himself. In one corner, the future grave sites of Orin and Varina, their son and heirs and, if I desired, a place for me here under this closely cut Southern grass. And, in a few hours, a place for Pearl, too, as she joined the Ransome clan.

As my horse nibbled at the grass, I considered where I truly belonged. I was not a Ransome, but then I was nothing else. I had no place, no roots, no history worth a fig. No family that I had ever felt a part of, beyond the Ransomes, to whom, at the last, I did not belong.

Pearl, as certainly as these crosses stood, would with her marriage become as much a part of the sinew and blood and continuing saga of this family as Varina was or Abigail Thistle de Lyons whose grave was near the grass my horse was nibbling. There was both comfort and distress in that, and the key to all that was to come in Pearl's young life.

But this I knew: I did not belong, and yet I *longed* to belong.

Pearl did not belong, and yet, although I had twenty years with this family before she ever asked me Hayton's name, she would soon belong more than I ever could in a hundred. And I thought, that's good. The luck of her. For to belong to this family was to belong to America and its story as few Americans did. There's a pecking order in America, degrees of authenticity. Time, and instinct honed in the nation's life, confer legitimacy. I felt illegitimate. I could *believe* my father was a traitor because I could conceive of my own betrayal against my people. Because I had no plot of Southern earth in which to lie, other than as a guest, and therefore nothing finally to stay my hand. And that, I thought, is the trouble with my country. Most of us have no abiding place in her.

I rode on along the bridal path through the woods toward the town. And I thought of my dead father.

And I thought of my son. I didn't even know his name. Think of that.

I had often thought of my little boy since seeing him on that subway. I was lonely for him. I wondered if he was a good child, and happy, and if he'd grow to be a good man, and what the world would do to him, and how long he'd survive, and what I could have taught him that he will never know that might have made some step easier for him, one mistake not made, one hurt not known.

I think a lot about things like that. What it means to be good. And whether I am.

I always wanted—before I had a son—and, having him, couldn't do a damn thing about it—I always wanted a son of mine to go to an Episcopalian boys' school. Not that I am Episcopalian. But I went to one, a military academy, and it was good for me, so when all's said and done it would be good for my son. I'm sure of that.

My father sent me there to get away from Washington when the noose began to tighten around his throat. (I mean that metaphorically; the real noose came a year later.) I believe he did it because he did not want me to see who he really was, his character and therefore his awful destiny, the toxic weakness in him unbuttressed by any passion, even malice.

He loved figures, computation, and silence. He loved clocks, and gadgets, and machinery. He loved what could be weighed and measured. He loved the predictable, the controllable, the rational, what was without surprise. He was at a total loss when it came to human beings.

His life began to fall to pieces in 1951. That's when he was called in for his first departmental hearing at State, and the examiner began to question him about friends whom he had known in New York City but had not seen or thought of for twenty years. Four months later, to forestall what he knew was coming, he resigned from the government. A mistake. They saw it as the beginning of a useful confessional. But of what? I never was told. Until last night.

And my sisters were never told either. They were living with my mother in Santa Barbara. She was divorced from my father at the time. When his end came, they heard it on the radio, which was probably worse than the way I was told.

My sisters. Only Rebecca I loved. A year younger than me. And you must know this now: I loved her more than was proper, and it frightened me, and it made me hurtful to her because I could not seem to control that desire. So I was glad when she was taken to the Coast and the silent nightly groping stopped.

I was informed of my father's death by the headmaster of the Breck School in Saint Paul, Minnesota. It was just before the

Christmas break. I was called in from drill. I stood at attention in the headmaster's oak-paneled study. There was a Christmas tree in the corner. I have always loved Christmas trees. This one was decorated with tiny red velvet bows, the kind that might hold a girl's hair in place. There was an angel on top, holding a tiny gold trumpet to its mouth.

My feet were cold from marching with my cadet regiment in the snow. As I stood there, waiting for the headmaster to acknowledge me, I thought, It's only two weeks to Christmas vacation and then I'll be in Florida with my old man.

The headmaster cleared his throat, then looked up at me. "Michael . . ." he began.

Michael? I knew something bad was coming because the headmaster normally called the boys by their last names.

"These things happen, Michael. We have to be sturdy about it." He paused. He lifted some papers off his desk and began reading them.

I coughed to get his attention.

"Sir, I . . ."

He looked up at me. He sighed, as if he and he alone bore the weight of the world's woe. He seemed annoyed. "You haven't been informed? I assumed the chaplain . . . ?"

"No, sir."

"Well, your father, uh, a widely respected man in certain circles . . . You must be proud of him regardless. He's dead, Michael. May God have mercy on his soul."

"Wha-a-at?"

"Yes. And men don't cry."

I was fifteen at the time. And what of it? I cried anyway.

My old man made a noose with his belt. He stood on a chair and with three penny nails hammered the end of his belt to one of the rafters in the ceiling of our living room, near the bay window of our house in Alexandria. It overlooked the Potomac, and from this window you could see the Lincoln Memorial and the Capitol in the distance when there was no fog. He liked the view.

His belt was made of English leather. Cowhide. He bought it at Selfridge's in London during the war. It was a strong belt; it would do.

He fitted the noose around his neck, and jumped off the chair. It held.

It was in that room where I last saw my father. I had come home from Santa Barbara after spending a week of my summer vacation with my mother and two sisters. I was about to return to school. I did not want to go back.

I asked him why I couldn't go to school in Alexandria. Why I couldn't stay at home with him?

I am now older than he was when he ran out of gas. But he looked like an old man to me. His hands trembled convulsively, and there was the smell of gin about him.

"Because I don't want a pagan for a son," he said. "You can't be literate in the West without knowing something about the ethos of Christian civilization." He talked like Lionel Trilling, a professor at Columbia, where he had studied. "Finish high school, and then you can toss your education aside. But I hope you won't."

It was the first time I knew that my father, though an atheist, was a religious man. He believed in continuum. He believed all that is is process.

He was right, of course.

As I mentioned earlier, I did a script on the Founding Mothers and Fathers of the American nation for the BBC. During the writing, I kept getting memos from the producer. He cut lines like "a widow's mite" and "a good Samaritan" because he had no idea what they meant. He was a pagan. In one scene a character referred to the "Passion" and "rapture" of Jesus. The producer cut it because he thought it had to do with sex. That sort of thing.

He was the type of person, illiterate about the referents of his own culture, that my father did not want me to be.

I wanted to raise my son as his grandfather had raised me. But I never had the chance.

Thirty-Five

HAYTON stumbled over a pile of white trellis on the front lawn moments after he and Binky Rockefeller exited from their limousine. "Jesus, it l-looks like a lumberyard!" Hayton said.

Binky Rockefeller said nothing. He was tall and skinny and slightly stooped in the shoulders, and he looked ten years older than Hayton although they were both the same age.

"Hey Binky, there's Mikey!" Hayton exclaimed, waving to me.

"I see," Rockefeller deadpanned. When he spoke, it was with almost no facial expression. He had the thin, dour face of the Rockefellers, the large nose, the tight-lipped mouth that resembled a slit in stretched canvas. Young, and already there was about him the appearance of dry piety, of duty that was no less binding because it was passionless. He was considered the "fun Rockefeller cousin," liberal in his opinions, tolerant in his ways, yet he had no charm.

I was standing on the front lawn when they arrived, drinking a martini, and observing a crew of workmen hurriedly constructing trellis archways under which the wedding party would pass. They led from the Corinthian colonnade of the veranda to an altar of white roses and camellias, before which the matrimonial vows would be exchanged. I looked at Hayton walking toward me.

"You're tight as a tick," I said, "and your mother is fixing to bust your ass for being late."

"Hell, yes," Hayton replied happily, shaking hands.

Binky Rockefeller followed, walking with his hands clutched behind his back like Prince Philip behind the Queen.

"My bachelor party in New York went the whole b-bloody night. At the Pierre. It didn't end until six. My head feels like a bus drove over it. Where's Pearl?"

"In the house. Secluded like a nun."

"I'll tell her I'm here."

"Not on your wedding day, Hayton. That's bad luck."

"You're right. Forgot. Damn sorry we're late. Bink and I missed the plane. Had to charter one. You know how difficult it is to ch-ch-charter an airplane on short notice?"

"No," I answered, never having had to face the problem.

"It's tough as hell, believe me, old boy," he said expansively. He threw his arm around me. "I say, we had the most fabulous p-piece of ass last night. She came bouncing out of this great cake, raunchy as a cat in heat—little tassels on her titties, nothing anywhere else. Hey, Binky"—Hayton called to Rockefeller who lingered several feet behind, self-protectively, like a hypochondriac fearful of germs —"I'm telling Mikey about the girl inside the cake last night. Must have put Winston back a bundle."

"Choice," Rockefeller allowed, stepping a foot or two nearer. "Appropriately choice," nodding soberly at me, disinterested. Except for his uncle Nelson, none of the Rockefellers were especially warm or demonstrative or even particularly likable. They had blood like ice water, and the demeanor to match.

"Tits like Jayne Mansfield," Hayton enthused. "I think it *was* Jayne Mansfield. Just like old Winston to hire a movie star."

Old Winston was Winston Cabot Sloane, a young lawyer whose money came out of Boston. And he couldn't have hired Jayne Mansfield because she was decapitated a year before in an automobile crash.

"She's dead, Hayton."

"Dead?" He was confused. "You're kidding! Then she came bouncing back to life last night. What bazoos!" He laughed in recall. "Where were you, Mikey? I'd have given you an honest go at her, damned if I wouldn't."

"I was here. I came directly from Los Angeles."

"You're not writing another lousy film?"

"Just hanging out."

True. After Robert Kennedy was shot down I stayed on in a rented cottage at Malibu, feeling paralyzed by the loss and by a future I had no enthusiasm for. I watched the Chicago Democratic Convention on television, the police beating antiwar demonstrators, Mayor Daley giving the finger to the senior senator from Connecticut, who accused the Mayor's police of using "gestapo tactics"; Bill Buckley and Gore Vidal going beyond profanity and nearly coming to blows. It was not the best of seasons: a sadness, a weariness with conflict and death, a sense of defeat and powerlessness. I felt it in my own life, and so I stayed put on the beach reading novels and watching soaps and game shows and sunsets and surf, and getting into a rented Ford a few times a week to drive to Caesar's Harem or another of the massage parlors-cum-brothels that dotted the Hollywood Hills. I kept the phone off the hook. And I was not proud of myself.

"You should've come to my bachelor party, damn it," Hayton said petulantly. "Are you mad because I didn't make you best man at my wedding? That it?" he teased, his arm still draped over my shoulder. Then he whispered, "I *had* to ask Binky to be my best man. Binky went to *Yale*. He was my roomie. You were my roommate, weren't you, Bink?" he asked, as if he thought I doubted his word.

"Certainly, Noodle." Noodle was Hayton's Yale nickname.

"Right. And *you* went to bloody Princeton. I couldn't have a Princeton man as my best man, now could I?"

"Of course not." I couldn't have cared less.

"Is that Jeremiah?" Hayton asked suspiciously, squinting into the sun.

Jeremiah was standing ten yards away, leaning on a rake and gazing sleepily at the workmen.

One night, years ago, when the Ransomes had gone to New Orleans for a party and we were alone in the house, Jeremiah had disciplined Hayton. Hayton had thrown one of his bedtime temper tantrums, and Jeremiah, hearing the boy screaming, had rushed into the house to see Hayton encamped in the china pantry throwing crockery at Aunt Kattie. Jeremiah, not the most artful of dodgers, got hit in the head by a pot. And that was that. Hayton was thrashed and sent to bed. It was deeply humiliating for him—

not the spanking itself, but that it had been suffered at the hands of a Negro man who worked for his father. If it had been a Negro woman, say Aunt Kattie, Hayton would have accepted the punishment. But it was a black male, and that violated a code of Southern behavior, i.e., that a black man never raises a hand against a white child. The Ransomes, when they returned, sent Hayton to his room for two days for breaking the crockery. They also pointedly reprimanded Jeremiah. The assumption, born in slavery, was that black male rage had to be contained at all costs, regardless of how justified its expression, knowing that once it was let loose it could never again be contained.

Hayton never relented in his hate for Jeremiah, and whenever he had the opportunity to hurt him, he did, in petty, spiteful ways. Letting go of grudges was something Hayton Childs Ransome never learned, and it was to cost him dearly in the end.

"Jeremiah!" Hayton shouted angrily, shoving away from me like a boat pushing a dock.

When he was drinking, Hayton often became violent for no discernible reason. In a mind whose muscle had never firmed up was a rage ignited by the most unlikely sparks. It was as though his brain's wiring was frayed and, damp with alcohol, short-circuited in flashes of malice.

"Get your black ass over here and take my bloody bags upstairs!" Hayton swung around and marched toward the house, head lowered like a bull charging a matador's cape. "When Father's dead I'm selling this goddamn w-white elephant and throwing every one of those lazy bastards into the street."

Binky Rockefeller followed behind, bemused contempt on his long face.

Thirty-Six

THE WEDDING was scheduled to begin in two hours. About forty of the guests had already arrived, their expensive cars and limousines filling the tree-shaded parkland along the main driveway.

Most of the guests were gathered to the west of the house by the swimming pool, where they were drinking champagne cocktails and eating tiny, crustless tea sandwiches like the ones they serve at the Palm Court of the Plaza. Negro waiters in white jackets and black trousers circulated through the crowd, offering as well golden caviar and mint juleps in frosty silver goblets. Except for the Mississippians, no one drank the juleps. Most of the guests were from New York, Washington, and abroad, and even if they knew what a mint julep was, they were having none of it.

I wandered over to the flagstone patio by the pool.

The sun was high and hot. Everyone sought the shade under the oaks and cottonwoods, or under the beach umbrellas sprouting like mushrooms from cast-iron tables.

Under one umbrella sat the Governor of Mississippi with the junior senator from that state and their wives. The two were engaged in animated conversation, leaning toward each other conspiratorially like two Anarchists in a Madrid tavern. The women sat on either side, staring listlessly at the pool, waiting with diminishing hope for their husband's notice.

The Governor's face was beet-red. He puffed on a large cigar whose acrid stench reached me on the far side of the pool. Every man present was correctly dressed in formal wear, but not the Governor. The old segregationist was living up to the good ol' boy image that brought him votes. He wore a rumpled brown suit, its jacket open, its armpits stained with sweat. His shirt was unbuttoned at the neck; a narrow tie lay loosely over his considerable belly. His brown, pointed-toed shoes were badly in need of polish. There was arrogance in his disarray. Throughout the day Varina didn't say an impolite word to him, but after tonight he'd no longer be received by the Ransomes. After tonight they would work for his defeat.

Sabina Phips sat at a table by the pool. Beside her was Giorgio Milano, his wife Arlene, and Sir Cecil Chard, who had flown in from London. Cecil would be the man to give Pearl away.

There were other celebrities, Washington politicians, movie actors from Beverly Hills, artists from New York, a director or two; the Ambassador to the United Nations and his wife; the Earl and Countess of Hutchingdon, and so on.

"Darling!" Sabina called upon seeing me. I went over and leaned down to her cheek. "Kissy, kissy," she said. "Into horses, are you? Riding alone at break of dawn? How decadent."

I took a chair opposite her and lit a cigarette.

"We were just talking about you," Sabina informed me. "Dear Arlene tells us that you were the very man who introduced Pearl to Hayton. What a clever matchmaker you are, to find Hayton such a . . . delicious girl." She smiled, her voice laced with sarcasm. "And you never *told* me. Naughty boy."

"Slipped my mind," I said.

"Nothing slips your mind, darling. Your mind has flypaper floors."

I turned to Cecil. "How was the flight from London, Cecil? It was great of you to come. I know Pearl must be happy."

"It was ghaaastly!" he squealed, drawing out the first vowel. Cecil was dressed in a white dinner jacket, and he wore a pure-white panama hat with a huge brim. He loved big hats. "I was dragooned by my travel agent onto a one-class flight—"

"Oh, you poor thing!" Arlene Milano commiserated, "From now on you must use Susan Shiva's travel service at Saks. It's heavenly." Susan Shiva's father owned Universal Pictures, among other things. "Susan would never permit any of us to go second class. She knows we'd simply die."

"It's called tourist class, darling," Sabina intoned slowly. "I fly it all the time. It's cheaper, dear, and just as fast as first."

Arlene Milano was originally from Flatbush, and her father was a pawnbroker, facts that everyone but Sabina was willing to overlook.

"The plane was filled with chaps I love, hippies and students," Cecil said. "One finds them amusing, what? No, no, it was the *food* that was horrid. The poor steward only had wine of a vintage the most depraved wino down on his luck would refuse."

"Don't we *all* prefer private jets?" Arlene asked grandly. "We flew in the Aga Khan's plane to Esmeralda last year, and went on to Niarchos's new development in northern Greece, and it was a swell flight all around. But public transport? Even the Cunard ships have become terribly common, don't you think?"

Arlene glanced around the table, waiting for agreement. When no one joined in she continued on, her voice tight, as if someone were pressing his fingers hard against her larynx.

"When Giorgio and I took the *Q.E. Two* over to France for the spring collections, I was stunned by the commonness of the passengers, and this was first class yet."

The "yet" gave the game away.

"Compared to Flatbush, the *Queen Elizabeth* must be a real ordeal." Sabina again.

"Flatbush?" Arlene parried lamely. "What's that?"

"Leave her alone, Sabina," I said.

In many ways I felt sympathy for Arlene, for all her pathetic embarrassment over where she had come from, her desperate need to pull the wool over the eyes of the wolves in whose Pack she had elected to run. She ran well, having a remarkable eye for what would sell in the rag trade, and a keener sense than most of what fads and trends lay ahead, and that meant profits on Seventh Avenue. Never successful enough, though, she remained formidably insecure, socially and sexually, particularly about her husband Giorgio, whom she had raised from obscurity to the first rank of American designers. Not an easy trick, considering the fact that he was not an American, but an Algerian Moslem who was living in

Paris when she happened upon him twenty years ago. To take a Moslem to Manhattan of all places, a city whose couture houses are largely under Jewish ownership, and there to make him, in the words of the *New York Times,* the "quintessential American designer" wasn't jacks. Now that he was famous she feared to lose him, and that fear heightened her irritability and her foolishness. The fear of losing successful husbands infected the Pack like an incurable virus.

Arlene had greater reason to fear than most. Giorgio, despite the flaccidity of his personality, the oily, too-cautious nature of his charm was, to many women, a sexual prize. Tall, with a receding hairline and dark, somewhat Asiatic features, he was known for his infidelities and his athletic sexual prowess. When, amazed by this fact, one inquired further, one discovered that his success was accounted for by his reputation as a lover with gifts, or rather *a* gift equal to the late Ruby Rubirosa's. Rubirosa made a career of being the lover of and sometimes the husband to a succession of rich women. Large warts on the kazoos of both men gave, it was said, the texture of a French tickler to their equipment.

"I've come to give dear Pearl away to Hayton and up unto a life of unremitting glamour, God help the child," Cecil wheezed. "I was astonished when Varina telephoned me in London. Varina has been making discreet inquiries . . ."

"Oh?" Sabina leaned forward. "What's the dirt?"

"Our Pearl is an orphan. Rather sad, that. Rather brave. But then I'm one myself," he said. "Apparently she lived in a series of foster homes when she was a child."

"And not a dime," Arlene said in surprise. "I don't think you should marry money, I mean millions, unless you have a lot of your own. Otherwise you can really get screwed."

"Speaking of screwing," Sabina began, and then paused, eyeing each of us through her green sunglasses to make certain of our complete attention, a calculated pause that always proceeded the delivery of gossip. "Have you heard about Roxanne's latest?"

"Tell us," Giorgio encouraged. "It's bound to be ripe."

"*Arab*, Giorgio," Sabina smiled, flashing her teeth at him. "Roxanne's having a thing with the nephew of the King of Saudi Arabia."

"It's not possible." Arlene again.

"The entire civilized world knows, Arlene," Sabina said, "where have you been? Roxanne met him through her husband—"

"The senator?"

"The very. The King's nephew keeps a twenty-room suite at the Dorchester, where the Arabs pee on the English carpets and eat off the floor like dogs . . ."

"Roxanne should feel right at home."

Sabina stood up. She smiled vaguely, and pushed her chair away. She gave Cecil one of her touchless kisses, and then did her kissy-kissy routine with Giorgio. She nodded coldly at Arlene. "Darling, we only have an hour or so until the wedding. You'd better hurry and change into something suitable."

Arlene was speechless. She was already dressed.

Sabina nodded at me. "Come walk with me. We have state secrets to discuss."

Thirty-Seven

SABINA and I walked across the eastern lawn and then down a flagstone path for several hundred yards, our destination a stand of poplar and willow trees through which the brook flowed.

When we reached the grove we followed the path as it turned about a small hill, and there before us, suddenly, was a waterfall tumbling into a deep pool dappled with sunlight; at its edges, among the rocks, masses of lily of the valley scented the cool air.

"How lovely," Sabina remarked. "All the times I've been to Timberton, I never knew this was here."

"It was built by Hayton's great-grandfather a century and a half ago," I explained, happy with her delight in the beauty of the place. "He had a brook diverted for the waterfall and the pool laid with limestone rock. He built it for his five sons."

"Extraordinary family, really, when you think about it. I mean, they take their position in such easy stride. Unlike that impossible Arlene Milano. What a phony name. They say she read it on the paper wrapper of the butter patty Giorgio served her when he was a busboy or whatever in Paris when she discovered him. Milano butter, or some such thing. Well, you have to give the bitch credit. People with perfectly good sense in everything else pay a fortune to have that Milano logo on frocks and luggage and on their asses, for all I know."

"He designs well."

"You think so?" She didn't agree.

"I've swum here a lot, when I was younger. I much preferred it to the swimming pool up by the house. I pretended I was Tarzan as I leaped into the water."

Sabina laughed. "You and Hayton. I can picture it, in your birth-day suits, no doubt. You were Tarzan, and who was Hayton, Jane or Boy?"

"Hayton never swam in the pool. He's afraid of the water."

"That's perfect! Do you know where they're going for the honey-moon? An around the world cruise! And you tell me Hayton can't swim? That's one for the books."

"No, he can swim. He just hates doing it."

"The cruise is a disastrous idea, no question about it. I told Varina, my God, the worst possible arrangement is to trap two young people, newly married, who barely know each other, on a French cruise ship for three long months. They'll return loathing each other."

"What did Varina say?" I asked.

"Varina said that Pearl had to learn the French language and French culture and Continental cuisine and acquire some elemental

knowledge of life so she didn't go about embarrassing the Ransomes—that is, Varina—for the next fifty years. You know how
Varina is: Mother Take Charge. She's hired tutors aboard ship to
turn our duckling into a swan. Come to think of it, I've never liked
swans. Filthy, disagreeable birds, if you ask me . . . And Hayton will
be bored to distraction without his daily supply of cocaine and
Russian vodka and whatever else he uses to slide through the day.
But then again, there's always the ship's staff to dally with."

"You're a cynic, Sabina."

"You're goddamn right. But I'm a realist when it comes to matters of the heart and finance. That's why I envy Varina. She married
a man she really loves, even if it was the second time around. And
she made it work. She keeps her son more or less in line, and she's
pulled off what might be a successful marriage for him. And that
means lots of grandchildren and lots of love when you're reduced
to pacemakers, and an aluminum walker for a best friend, and sitting in some wretched overpriced waiting room for death. At least
you'll have that beautiful daughter-in-law and the grandchildren to
live through, and to love. Not bad when you consider the alterna-
tive."

"But you had a good marriage, Sabina."

I thought she had, on balance. It lasted fourteen years and while
childless, seemed contented.

"Ha!" she barked. "How little you know. For someone whom
everyone supposedly tells everything to, you know very little, my
dear. Horace, my husband, had far more interest in the rise and fall
of South African mining stocks and coffee and silver futures than
he ever had in me. It didn't bother me after a while. I soon came to
enjoy the clarity of living with someone whom you knew never listened to a single word you ever said. Horace said I nagged him.
Well, damn it, I'd have to repeat something fifty times until it
caught his attention. It became a game. I once jokingly told him at
dinner that I was dying of lung cancer and that they had, addition-
ally, discovered a fatal tumor on my brain. He made no response.
I finally yelled at him, 'Horace, are you listening to me!' and he
smiled and said, in that addled monotone of his, 'Buy whatever you

like, goddamn it. But don't use your checking account. You're overdrawn again.' I filed for divorce the next day . . . Let's go back to the house, darling. I'm beginning to feel the damp. This place has the smell of a burial ground."

We strolled back.

"Could you do me a favor, darling? I hate to ask."

"Anything," I replied.

"Poor Doris has been hospitalized at Memorial, did you know?" Sabina sighed theatrically.

"I'm sorry." I was.

"Yes. And, of course, I'm worried sick about poor David, who must be impossibly distraught. How crushing it must be for him, and without me at his side to give him the strength to continue his great work in television. Who would have thought Doris would fade so quickly? And David, so devoted, a saint. I presume he's at the hospital by his wife's side day and night. Such is his fidelity."

"You presume?" I wondered if we were talking about the same people. "You mean you haven't talked to him?"

"Don't be unsympathetic, darling. I've always loved dear Doris. I pray, for her sake, that she goes as quickly as possible."

"I bet you do."

"You're being harsh. Death would be a blessing for her now. You have to admit that. And it would free David from the long agony of watching her . . . her slip into the . . . eternal night."

"You're a poetess, Sabina."

She ignored the crack and pushed on. "David hasn't had the *time* to call me. It's only been three weeks since Doris was rushed to Memorial. So I was wondering, darling, do you suppose you could get a small message to David, the merest suggestion that he give me a call?"

I stopped walking and stared at her. "Me?" I said. "I don't even know him, Sabina!"

"Of course you know him," she purred reassuringly, putting her arm through mine as we started to walk again. She wasn't going to let me off the hook that easily.

"Sabina, for heaven's sake, be reasonable. I've only seen David six or seven times in my life, at charity dinners and the like. I mean, I know him, but I don't *know* him, you see?"

"That'll do. Why not call his office at the network? Say you have an absolutely killing idea for a television series and that you cannot talk to anyone about it but the president of the network, that's how valuable your idea is. Make a date for drinks at the Carlyle—he likes the bar there. Or '21.' You're a writer, darling. You can think of something," she said.

"But I don't have any killing idea. If I did my agent would handle it. That's how it's done, Sabina. Through agents."

"Don't be evasive. That's just an excuse. *Truman* doesn't have an agent . . ."

"He has a lawyer. It's the same thing," I said.

"See David, darling, and ask him to call me. *Please.*" She squeezed my arm. "It means the world to me."

"Why not have Varina do it? She and Orin are close to him."

"Because Varina thinks I'm a fool. She thinks David won't marry me when Doris dies. But she doesn't *know* David like I do. She's never seen him *come.* Oh, darling, he loves me. Seven years now. I'd die if we didn't marry."

"*You* should call him then."

She laughed sardonically. "How naïve you are. I've never once been seen in public with David, not in all these years. He's terrified of his wife, and always has been. Dying, and he's still terrified of her. Do you know what it's like to have a man send a company car for you, then have the car pick him up in some godforsaken place that's *safe*, like City Island or Grant's Tomb where *no one* we know would ever be caught *dead*? And then be driven around Manhattan while you fuck in the back seat behind drawn curtains, and arrive at his office and I, the woman he's just fucked, I am not good enough to walk through the door of his goddamn office building in public with him? Because his wife might find out? Well, she's dying. She's finished. She's shot her round, and it's my turn now. I need him all to myself! And I've earned that!"

I looked at Sabina. Behind those green sunglasses I knew there was panic.

"I'll do what I can, Sabina. You know that." I promised with as much convincing gravity as I could muster, knowing there was nothing I would do.

Thirty-Eight

THREE hundred guests sat on folding chairs on the front lawn at Timberton facing the temporary flower-bedecked altar. Over the center aisle, between the blocks of chairs, was the completed trellis arch hung with green ferns and camellias and white roses and lillies. Under the arch, running from the veranda of the house to the altar, was a white linen carpet.

As the service began a small orchestra played "Ah, Sweet Mystery of Life" and other old love songs—"Be My Love," "Some Enchanted Evening." Varina had chosen the music.

I was seated in the front row on the aisle to the left of the altar. Opposite me were Ambassador Ransome and Varina, the Governor and senator and their wives, and the wife of the Episcopal bishop of New York. I could only guess at the ruckus that had preceded the selection of the bishop—Varina was Episcopalian, fiercely so—over the local Baptist preacher. The Ambassador, like all the Ransomes, was a Baptist without strong conviction. Still, it would have been politic in Central Mississippi to go with the flow and hire the Baptist.

Hayton and Binky Rockefeller walked to the altar from the left, Hayton looking somewhat anxious. The bishop smiled at him. I studied his face as he waited for his bride, skin flushed, his forehead dotted with tiny beads of sweat. But I knew he was happy, the lucky bounder.

And the Ambassador? Wearing his public face, dignified, strong, unflappable, commanding. I knew he was happy, too. So it was all right.

And then the brief procession started. A little girl, dressed in a pretty lace dress with lots of crinoline petticoats, walked down the white carpet, and the guests ooh'd and ah'd at her sweetness. She was the daughter of Ambassador Ransome's farm manager, and she carried a small white satin cushion on which rested two gold wedding bands.

The maid of honor followed dressed in pale-pink organdy, and carrying a bouquet of pink tea roses.

"Who's that?" I whispered to Sabina, who stood next to me.

"Susan Vanderlip. Good God, don't you know her? She's a friend of Pearl's. Wants to be a model. Hasn't a prayer."

There was silence that lasted too long. The guests fidgeted and coughed and glanced about expectantly, fearful, as at every wedding, that through some calamity in judgment, the bride might sit it out.

Binky Rockefeller touched Hayton's arm and whispered something in his ear. At last the little orchestra struck up "The Wedding March."

I turned with the others to see Pearl, on the arm of Sir Cecil Chard, moving slowly, regally toward the altar, her face veiled, her Yves Saint Laurent dress, of old satin, shimmering in the speckled light under the archway. The designer was Varina's choice, as were the flowers Pearl carried. Lily of the valley, Varina's favorite.

As Pearl passed slowly by she reached out, eyes ahead, and grazed my hand with her gloved fingers as if in goodbye. It was then I knew with irrevocable conviction that I had lost her. Until that moment, I don't think I believed I really had.

Sabina sat unmoved throughout the preliminaries. She listened coldly to the singing of "I Love You Truly." But when the Episcopal bishop began to read the service—"Dearly Beloved, we are gathered here to join in the state of Holy Matrimony . . ." Sabina clutched my hand and began to weep.

I patted her hand, and looked across the aisle at the Ransomes to see the Ambassador holding both his wife's hands in his. Varina's eyes were wet.

Man and wife, the bishop pronounced. You may kiss the bride.

Hayton lifted her veil, and I saw Mrs. Hayton Childs Ransome's beautiful face and her glistening eyes, and watched as her husband kissed her and, with greater ardor, kissed her once again.

Thirty-Nine

SABINA PHIPS believed in omens and numerology and astrology and the portents to be read in moist tea leaves at the bottom of a bone-china cup. Given that, it was a special day.

She chanced to catch the bridal bouquet that Pearl tossed over her shoulder from the top of the spiral staircase into the group of unmarried women below. Sabina exuberantly leaped for it, and when she discovered the bouquet in her hands she started to cry again.

The party went on for hours. There were drinks on the verandas. There were bars and buffets scattered about the lawns and public rooms. A dance band played in the winter garden. Outside, beyond the open French doors, Hayton danced the first dance with Pearl as the news photographers flashed their cameras.

Later the newlyweds cut the wedding cake, a huge concoction four feet high, Aunt Kattie's proudest creation. For the photographers' convenience they repeated the cake-cutting several times. On the fourth try, as Hayton once again lifted a piece of cake to Pearl's mouth, she bit down too soon and too hard, and Hayton grunted in pain, "Ouch, pumpkin." And they both laughed. The tip of his finger bled a little. He held it up for all to see, like a young hero home from the wars.

That picture, Pearl's teeth on his finger, and his expression of pain and surprise, was published in newspapers around the country and found its way into the *People* section of *Time* magazine. I never forgot the incident, nor did anyone else who witnessed it.

Forty

BEAU!" she cried, and raced toward me across the upstairs parlor. "Oh, Beau, I'm so incredibly happy! What's a body to do?" And Pearl was in my arms, and we stood holding one another, swaying to the music that rose from the band on the veranda below; the breeze through the open jalousies warm and scented with flower and pine and cropland, perfume of the South; the noise of people talking and laughing happily in celebration. I held her for dear life, my face pressed against her hair, fragrant with sandalwood. And for a moment time seemed to stop, and then recede, and memory possessed us, and I was where I first held her and always wanted to be, in a small bed on a hot night in Lower Manhattan when she had nothing in life but Piers and courage and great beauty. Far away and gone, the heat of the night before the future captured her, or my weakness let her go. It was her wedding night and in a short time she would be going to New Orleans to board her honeymoon ship, and so I could not tell her how very sad her leaving made me, and how much I loved her still.

It was after nine. Most of the guests had departed. The few score that remained were clustered on the veranda. Through open blinds I could see the lighted pool, emerald and flatly pale in the darkness of the yard, a jewel set on a black glove. Beyond, in the trees and plantings, masses of fireflies blinked like a great city seen from the air at night. I could hear Hayton's boisterous laughter above the music. I held Pearl. The band began playing "I Can't Stop Loving You," and we began to dance, shuffling tightly together as if we feared to fall; and I, who cannot sing well, slowly sang the words "I Can't Stop Loving You." It was true.

We kissed, deeply, and I felt her hand leave my shoulder and fall down along my body to my crotch. "Oh, Beau!" she giggled, and then pulled her hand away. "You're always up at bat."

"I want you, Pearl."

She kissed me and stepped away. "Not tonight, sweet child."

She was now dressed in slacks and an open blouse with a cashmere cardigan sweater. "I wanted all evening to talk to you, but I couldn't manage to get away from the photographers and the press of the folks."

"You'll get used to it."

"Are you bitter, my dear Beau?" She touched my cheek. "I hope not, honey." She tilted her head and looked gently into my eyes.

"Are you happy?" I asked.

Her hand fluttered to her hair. "Yes, I truly am. And scared."

"If you're happy, that's good enough for me."

She smiled, pleased by my reply. "I knew it. Think of the happy times we'll have, all of us. Hayton loves me, Beau. Really. And I'll be a good wife to him. And Varina and Orin have been just grand. I feel like I got me a home at last. You know how good that feels!"

I remembered then that Cecil had said she was an orphan, and I understood why the marriage was necessary and what the Ransomes and this house meant to her. *I got me a home at last.*

"And Piers?"

"Piers? Why, he's his old self again. I mean to buy him the biggest, fastest fishing boat money can buy. That's what he wants. And when he met Hayton, just for the briefest time, he was a regular gentleman. You'd think, I suppose, that Piers would've been against our marriage. But no, Beau, he thought it right and proper. He wants that boat." She laughed.

"Do you miss him, Pearl?"

"Like sailors miss the sea."

She walked over to the large table in the center of the room and went rummaging through the presents. She hadn't had the time to open them all.

"I'm glad I found you before we all left tonight," she began, "because I wanted to see you alone, and thank you for what you've been to me, and for *this*."

She lifted my present off the table. It was the gold and malachite box she had admired in my apartment.

"I know what it meant to you, Beau. I'll never let it go."

I didn't know what to say. I had little attachment to pricey things. I liked the box, but once emptied of the locket with Rose's hair, I was indifferent to it. So it was an easy gift to give.

"And, Beau?"

"Yes?"

"Don't carry on too much about Piers to Hayton or Varina. Past is past, like they say, and I want them to see a clean slate. Piers, well, there's likely no help for it, not down the line."

"I'll keep mum."

"Now, what on earth was I to fetch? The rocks," she said as she pulled through the pile of gifts. "Hello there," and she held up a large leather jewelry case. When she opened it, lying inside on a yellow velvet cushion was the emerald necklace that Varina wore so often. She had given it to Pearl. I doubted that Pearl valued it overly much, though it was nearly priceless, because she had left it piled among the lesser gifts, like my own.

She held the jewels against her throat. "Ain't bad," she said.

Its stones glittered coldly in the light. There was something sinister in their weight and great size, in the darkness of the green, in the antique, Slavic, brutish character of their extravagant gold settings. An imperial ransom in gems crudely mounted. The necklace was a favorite of the Grand Duchess Xenia's, a birthday gift from her uncle the czar, and it had hung heavily on her tender throat until she was shot dead with Bolshevik bullets. Like so many, she had overstayed her welcome. Like so many, she never knew when it was time to go.

"Kiss me goodbye."

As I was leaving the room, Pearl called out, "I'll miss you, Beau!"

I smiled. "Yeah. And I'll miss you too." She stood by the mound of gifts, looking small and strangely vulnerable, clasping in her hand, almost carelessly, the Russian jewels.

"Listen, baby," I cautioned, "don't fall for all the flattery coming your way."

"I'm no dope."

"In a pinch, run with the emeralds. The rest won't wash."

It wasn't what I meant to say.

Forty-One

WHAT I meant was, *Be careful*. Keep your wits about you, and your eyes open at night. Jump at noises in the dark.

I also meant to tell Pearl that I didn't altogether trust Hayton, even though I believed he loved her. Despite that, he was weak and unstable and full of self-loathing. He hungered for achievement won on his own, without his father's help. It wasn't possible, not for Hayton. He needed achievement to earn his father's respect. But that very absence of respect paralyzed Hayton's will and self-confidence. Without first having his father's respect, he could achieve nothing on his own. He was trapped.

I wanted to tell her that the rich are different, not only because they have lots more money, which is difference enough, but because they are a special race in that they are freed from the consequences of their acts. They are set apart, under a set of laws where cause and effect aren't absolute. They are not required to make answer;

they don't really have to give a good goddamn. A few do, but they are the proverbial exceptions that prove the rule.

What alone would protect Pearl was memory, and memory was usually the first thing to get the boot. It was quickly cheapened and sentimentalized and falsified, and then dismissed as unreliable. Too many fine meals and too much loose change and too much comfort in too many rooms will do that. Pearl would be all right as long as she didn't forget she wasn't one of them. She was a visitor on a visa that could always be revoked. I knew that when in the future she forgot that—on that day, they'd bring her down.

One of the clichés that Hortense de Vincennes liked to cite was, surprisingly, true. "Don't you know, darling, the rich can buy their way out of any fucking thing, except the webs they spin themselves. From that you can't buy passage."

That's what I meant to tell Pearl. From some things you can't buy your way out.

Part IV

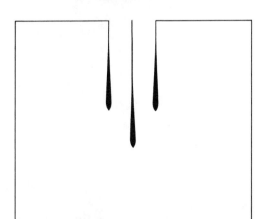

A Marriage

Forty-Two

THEIR marriage worked well in the beginning, which surprised me, although it probably shouldn't have. From the time they began their honeymoon I regularly received post cards and letters from Pearl informing me of their progress, the letters written in her tiny script on ship's stationery and later, after they settled in Paris, on pale-blue Cartier papers printed with their Left Bank address, No. 10, Rue Bixio.

The first few months the tone of her correspondence was one of wonderment and joy, accented with underlinings and exclamation points, elation and awe, indeed disbelief, over what she was experiencing, which was, after all, the world. Or that part of it that a lot of money and family clout purchased entry to. And there was plenty of money. Hayton already benefited from trusts worth just under a hundred million, and there was more to come when the Ambassador died.

Gradually though, the tone of her letters began to change, and a patina of cynicism and ennui overlay her sense of sailing on a sea grown too placid and shallow. She suspected a fundamental unreality and disconnectedness in the world she now so comfortably surveyed. There was no center she could find.

On their honeymoon they sailed through the Panama Canal to visit Honolulu, Fiji, Wellington, and Sidney, and went through the Arafura Sea past the island of New Guinea and through the Indonesian archipelago, stopping for a day in Jakarta and then on to Manila. They toured Corregidor in Manila Bay, and later dined at the presidential palace with First Lady Imelda Marcos.

"The poverty is terrible, Beau! And Hayton says Manila is one of the cleaner cities. Beggars everywhere! Little *kids* selling their bodies! It's heartbreaking. You wonder where their mamas are. Little boys and girls selling themselves on the steps of the Hilton! For a few dollars! Honey, I'll never again complain about having been poor. We went to the palace for dinner with the President's wife, and a lot of local fat cats. The men only wear white shirts and trousers to dinner, no jackets, like it was Bowling Night in Dixie! Mrs. Marcos had tons of jewels on. I should have worn the emeralds and shown her up! She's very strange and stuck-up, Beau, and evil in her way. Made me very nervous. She's tall for a Filipino, and grasping and sly as a fox, and she stared at me *constantly*, and not in a decent way, if you know what I mean? Hayton says there's money to be made here . . . I wish he was stronger. He always seems to be waiting for someone to tell him what to do. He's too much like a patsy sometimes."

From the Philippines they sailed to Hong Kong, where Pearl wrote that they bought silk shirts and dresses and gold. It had been three months since they left Timberton.

At Hong Kong they left the cruise, deciding to continue the rest of the tour by air. They were bored on ship, and Hayton decided they ought to see Red China, since they stood at its gates.

"The cruise was too much, dear heart. When the ship stopped at ports it was fun, but in-between stops there was nothing to do but play shuffleboard and watch burials at sea! Oh, and I took French lessons, if you want to tell Varina . . . we stayed in Hong Kong for a *week* trying to get into China. Hayton even telexed Orin for help. It didn't work, honey. At last I found *something* a Ransome couldn't arrange!"

They continued by air to India. They toured the major cities, and again the poverty and hunger shocked her, as it had in the Philippines, but not as much. She was learning to accept evil as inevitable. She wrote that in Calcutta Hayton insisted upon seeing the red-light district. He thought it amusing, but for days Pearl could not stop thinking of the young women, and boys dressed as women, perched in wicker cages hanging above the street, calling out and cooing as they passed below. A nickel or two, and the cages would be swung by the pimp to the second-floor window where the young whore would enter the house to be taken. For five cents.

With one letter I received a snapshot of Hayton and Pearl standing in front of the Taj Mahal. They were both tanned, and they were smiling and holding hands. Pearl was wearing a white frock and a big straw sunbonnet. Hayton wore a pith helmet and some kind of safari outfit that must have gone out of style with the last British Raj.

On the back of the snapshot, Pearl wrote, "We're house hunting!"

In Maharashtra, near Poona, Hayton went big-game hunting, and that excursion provoked the first major quarrel of their trip. Pearl was terrified of guns and hated killing. "I told him," Pearl wrote, "It's either them guns or me. Can't have both. Why, the *sight* of a gun makes me feel like passing flat out. And the poor animals!"

From India they traveled to the Middle East and there, as elsewhere, Ambassador Ransome's political and financial contacts opened most doors to them. Golda Meir received them in Tel Aviv, and later they were allowed to motor across the Allenby Bridge into Jordan. They visited the King at the palace in Amman, and the following day Hayton went falconing with tribesmen in the desert. He loved to hunt, although he preferred killing by bullet to killing by bird. He was an excellent shot.

They spent four days in Cairo, and then took a boat up the Nile. The heat was overwhelming, and Hayton fell ill as they trudged through the Valley of the Kings. Food poisoning from river eels, which Pearl had refused to eat. They returned to Cairo, where Hayton recovered. While sick, he never let her leave their suite. He was like a child, she wrote, like a baby needing his mother, terrified in his fever that if she left him for but a moment he would die.

In Rome they stayed at the Eden Hotel near the Piazza di Spagna. Pearl hated the traffic and the Roman confusion and noise, and so they made their way to Venice, Hayton still weakened by his recent illness and grown strangely dependent on her.

"He's better, but he seems frightened when I'm not with him. And our sex has changed. It's like the sex of kids, Beau. Very shy and cautious, like he thinks I'm going to yell bloody murder and bring the hotel detectives running. I never knew till now that he had trouble that way, poor baby."

They remained in Venice nearly a month at the Hotel Cipriani, and each day they rode the *motoscafo* across the water to the Piazza San Marco. Hayton seemed despondent, as if the very beauty of Venice, the humidity, the glorious sunsets gilding the ancient buildings, the handsomeness of its people, the city made him captive to depression and remorse without an object. He responded by encouraging Pearl to spend money, to squander it on antiques and gold and malachite pieces, on more jewelry and clothes which were shipped, at great expense, to Paris, where they hoped to settle. He appeared to feel that he had let her down, that he wasn't good enough or manly enough for her. That she could have done so much better.

And she responded to his melancholy with forced hilarity, with unusually high spirits by which she hoped to bring him back to the delight that was so curiously drained away in the fever of Egypt. But under the laughter was stress and fear, and irritation with her husband. He had become bad company.

One afternoon, while touring the Palace of the Doges, Pearl was followed by a handsome young Italian who made his intentions quite apparent. "Hayton went up, big as can be, and talked to him in broken Italian and arranged for him to come back to the hotel. I couldn't *believe* it! I don't know what Hayton expected, but I refused. We argued, Beau, something awful. He made me feel so *cheap*. And so damn sad, so sad. My poor baby feels so inadequate, honey, like he's not enough for me. What am I to do?"

They lunched on Charles Revson's yacht, the *Ultima II*. Among the guests was David Spane, the movie star. Spane's own yacht was anchored in the harbor, and the next afternoon Pearl lunched alone with him there, Hayton begging off with a headache.

The evening before they left Venice for good, Pearl and Hayton were invited to a dinner party at the Venetian house of Prince Carlo Frandolini. The prince was an acquaintance of Varina's. It was at his dinner that they met the Duke and Duchess of Windsor.

"Everyone there was very old," wrote Pearl, "especially the Windsors, who are even *smaller* than King Hussein! They both looked *waxy*, Beau, and sickly, like they don't eat right. They could use some collard greens and grits and watermelon. Lordy, how hungry I am for *real* food! When we get to Paris I'm going to hire me a real Southern colored cook and eat proper . . . I felt real sorry for the Windsors. They're like old leftovers from some long-ago time, and they *know* it, that's the truth.

"The duchess said to me, 'How lucky for you *Americans* to have as your first President a man with a name as wonderfully American as *George Washington!*' Now don't that strike you as plum *crazy*?

"Later at dinner she asked Hayton who the strange man was who sat at her left. The duchess was mighty suspicious of him, like he was a gate-crasher carrying a bomb. Hayton told the duchess that he was their host, Prince Frandolini. And she said, 'I never saw him before in my life!' Poor thing, she's only known the prince for forty years!

"About eleven o'clock, hours after dinner, the duchess suddenly asked me when did I suppose they were going to serve dinner! She'd forgotten we'd already dined. Don't that beat all? And later, when they left—they're *always* the *first* to leave, with the royals you got to stick it out until they're up and ready to scamper out, even if it's not till the *cows* come home!!—the duke shook Hayton's hand

and told him, 'I always liked your father, the Ambassador. It's a bloody shame Roosevelt recalled him. Joe was a right sort!' Joe *Kennedy*!!! My Lord, Beau, the old duke thought *we* were the *Kennedys*!! It's no wonder they kicked him off the throne."

From time to time I read in the newspapers, usually the Women's Page of the *Times* or in Suzy's column, of their being at one party or another as Pearl and Hayton traveled about. I read of their house-guesting with the Agnellis in Milan, and their giving a huge party at the Continental on Via Manzoni near La Scala, where Pearl was photographed sitting on the floor sharing quiche with Cary Grant. In Monte Carlo they were mentioned as attending the Red Cross Ball, where Frank Sinatra performed, and in Saint Moritz they were, with the young Churchills and Ava Gardner, among the guests of the David Nivens. By increments of appearance and publicity, they were becoming a hot ticket: the Beautiful Couple, young and rich and handsome and chic, with the knack of knowing how to spend money like it was going out of style.

I was astonished when they appeared twice in one month in the People sections of both *Newsweek* and *Time* magazines. I finally asked Varina if they had hired Earl Blackwell or some other Society public relations man. There was simply too much of it in too short a time.

"We Ransomes," Varina replied, a bit too imperiously, "hire flacks to keep us *out* of the popular press, not to put us *in*. My son and daughter are not cabaret performers trying to purchase reviews!"

I wasn't so sure.

They had been gone for over a year when Pearl wrote from the Greek island of Hydra to tell me that she was pregnant, and very happy. I felt ambivalent about the news. I was glad that being with child made her feel fulfilled and secure; it certainly solidified her position with the Ransomes. But I can't deny resenting the permanence within the family that a child promised. Even now I had difficulty letting Pearl go. Some love is always there, in sight and just out of reach. So it was with her. I shared vicariously in her life; I envied Hayton; and I waited. For what? if not for things to come apart.

"We're going to name the baby Philip Orin Ransome, if he's a boy; Samantha Varina Ransome, if she's a girl. I always did imagine my *real* mother's name was Samantha. I swear I don't rightly know why."

And then she wrote, "Oh Beau, darling, would you be the godfather?"

Within a month they were living in Paris in the Ransome house. Two weeks later Varina flew to Paris and spent a month with them. She returned to tell me that Pearl had lost the child.

"There was a loose carpet tack," Varina explained. We were lunching at the Four Seasons by the pool, and she was reluctantly telling me about the miscarriage. "Can you imagine? A loose carpet tack, and the poor girl toppled down the stairs. It was the day before I arrived. We were all quite horrified, of course, especially Hayton, who wanted the baby so. But Pearl's still very young, and there'll be others."

I asked Varina if Hayton was drinking.

"What an impertinent question!" she snapped. "No more than normally. Did you ever know a Southerner who didn't like to drink? It's unthinkable. I wouldn't trust a man who *didn't* drink. Even Orin keeps sneaking his bourbon when he knows it's poison for his heart. It can't be easy for Hayton, a young father having his first child miscarried, now can it?"

"I suppose not."

"Exactly. And he's still trying to find himself. Both his father and I think he should try investment banking. We own shares in one of the better private banks in Paris, and he would be happy there. But, my God, he has to do *something*. I think his moping about is quite unhealthy for him and for the marriage. It's a difficult time, the early years."

"It is," I agreed. And then I realized, in my marriage it was the early years that were the most blissful.

I considered Hayton's erratic behavior over the years, his drunken rages, his blackouts. The drugs. I remembered his arrest, that the Ambassador later suppressed, in New Orleans during Easter vacation from Ol' Miss, when he slugged a prostitute and broke her nose in his room at the Royal Orleans Hotel. "I thought she was a decent girl," he explained to the police, "and then she demanded ten bucks."

Varina said Pearl fell down a flight of stairs in the Paris house. A carpet tack, she said. I have been in that house many times. There is no carpeting on the stairs.

Forty-Three

I DIDN'T hear from Pearl for several months. And then she began writing to me again, although her letters were less frequent and more subdued and told me little. Even her complaints were unremarkable. "I need to work . . . I'm tired of no purpose . . . I'm tired of hotsy-totsy parties . . . The French really *hate* Americans . . . I have to get out . . . I wish I hadn't lost my baby . . . Why do I have to make *all* the decisions? Hayton just drinks and gets stoned. He's bored. I'm bored. All of *Paris* is bored, and it *should* be!"

Three years after they were married they returned to New York. Appropriately, that month Pearl was on the cover of *Town and Country*. The entire magazine was devoted to young Americans in Paris and their smart and glamorous lives. The main feature article was about the "delicious, delightful, deliriously happy Mr. and Mrs. Hayton Childs Ransome." There were photographs of their house, pictures of Pearl seated between Princess Grace and Elizabeth Taylor at Dior's spring show; a party at the palace of Versailles, where she was shown talking with John D. Rockefeller III— "Mrs. Ransome, like all the concerned American colony, is passionately interested in the restoration of French architectural treasures and has given generously to the Versailles Fund"; her hosting an "intimate dinner" for the new American ambassador to France, the caption praising her intense and lively ardor for fostering peace among the nations; lunching at the Ritz with Jan Cushing, Sabina Phips, and Merle Oberon, where we were told they discussed the plight of the children of foreign workers in France.

Reading through it I wondered about Hayton and why there was only one picture of him, and nothing in the text but a brief note concerning his distinguished family and his plans for entering the world of investment banking. It was all about Pearl, which must have been galling to him, given his insecurities.

"Banking?" Sabina Phips exclaimed, when I saw her on her return to New York from Paris. "Hayton can't keep his *checkbook* in balance. If anyone should go into banking, it's Pearl. Now *there's* an executive. She's got a ring through Hayton's nose, and he seems to enjoy it when she pulls hard on the leash. Would you have thought he could be so weak?"

I wondered about his weakness. And I wondered about the carpet tack.

Forty-Four

ONE MORNING, during the week I expected them to return to New York, Hayton called and asked me to come and see their new apartment on Fifth Avenue.

I arrived shortly before noon. A maid opened the door and ushered me through an enormous and quite empty vestibule into the large living room and through it to a small bar.

Hayton sat on one of the four stools. The bar was a strange room to find in a Fifth Avenue apartment, and very unlike the rest of the place. An L-shaped leather sofa built into one wall, which reminded me of a banquette in a roadhouse; a large ceiling fan; bamboo-papered walls; potted palms and cacti; an upright piano; and in one corner an old-fashioned jukebox. There were calico curtains on the windows overlooking Central Park. The floor was sanded, unvarnished oak planks. And there was a brass spittoon by the door, and a large Confederate flag over the bar.

"I know," Hayton ruefully remarked, "it's utterly out of k-keeping with the rest of the d-dump, but Pearl wanted one room that reminded her of the South. So we have our very own, if tiny, saloon."

I laughed at his tone of despair.

"Drink?"

"Sure. Whatever you're drinking."

"I'm on Bloodies. Straight up. You take lime, right? Hot? Just a touch, then."

Hayton came from behind the bar and handed me my drink.

"Sorry, old man. Pearl's delayed in Paris. Movie business, you know. Going to be a big star. I'll be know henceforth as Mr. Pearl Ransome. What do you think of that turn of events?"

I wasn't sure what I thought.

"Hell, why not? She's bored sitting on her butt. See this?" He slapped the jukebox. "Bought it in Paris, of all places, while Pearl was out buying every malachite doodad she could lay her pretty hands on. The thing was built in Marseilles. All the records are genuine American cornball. That's as far as Pearl's musical tastes are ever likely to progress. She claims to love classical m-m-music now, ever since she met Leonard Bernstein in Milan. Even knows how to spell Stravinsky, but all her ears hear is Hank Williams and Ernie Tubb. What the fuck? Who cares? Want a tour of the d-dump? Haven't seen all of it myself."

We walked through its ten rooms, most of them completely furnished, but a few, like the "baby's room," empty.

"Varina flew to Paris a few times with blueprints, carpet swatches. She and Pearl picked the decorators and I paid the bills." He laughed. "M-Mother sold my Beekman Place house, did you know? Hell, she owned it, but I used to live there. She moved my stuff out, sold the place, and didn't bother to tell me. Now she's got the house in Georgetown on the block. Ought to go for a bundle. Economizing, she calls it. Hell, if it's economy she's worried about, why don't they sell Timberton? I wish the hell they would. What a d-drain that is, about two hundred thousand a year."

"They'll never sell Timberton, Hayton. God Almighty, Southern blood and soil and the Stars and Bars!"

"Maybe. Certainly not while the old man's around. But Father isn't doing too hot. They're out in East Hampton now. Been there all summer. They rented an estate there. It had to be an estate, you know, it c-couldn't just be a fucking summer house! No, it had to be two hundred acres on the beach and a twenty-room house and pool and tennis courts for a mere fifty thousand for the season! Fuck."

I searched his face. His dismay was real.

"What's it matter?" I asked. "They've earned it."

"I know. But every dime they spend is one more dime I'm not going to get. *Comprende*?"

"How bad is your father's health?"

"Comes and goes. Sometimes I think he'll never die, and then it scares the shit out of me he might." Hayton shrugged, and we started back toward the bar.

As we passed through the living room, he asked if I liked the paintings. They were Surrealist, except for two by Léger and a Rouault.

"Pearl picked them up in Paris. Alexander Iolas and Brooks Jackson, the dealers, know them?"

"Think so."

"Well, we just about bought them out. If their shoes had been Surrealist, Pearl would have wanted the shoes. Don't like the school, though. The Surrealist stuff makes P-Pearl think of dreams, and for some goddamn reason she finds that comforting. Myself, I like Léger best."

"So do I. He was my father's favorite. We never owned a Léger, but we owned prints and books of his work. My father liked the control and colors and the way his paintings celebrated the machine."

"Yeah. Léger and Rouault. The rest are bloody pikers. Still, the Surrealists are a good investment, if you want to look at it that way. I p-put my foot down when it came to Dali, though. Think he's second-rate."

Hayton asked if I wanted another Bloody Mary. I said no, it was too early in the day. He snorted, poured himself a shot of vodka, and gulped it down.

"Got time to jog?" he asked.

"Now?"

"Sure. Come on. I'll lend you some shorts and shoes. We'll go around the Reservoir for a while, and then take lunch."

I hesitated.

He looked at me and, anticipating rejection, he said, "Please, old man. I don't feel like running alone."

Forty-Five

WE JOGGED three times around the Reservoir and then ran south along the east side of Central Park until I became too winded to continue. I was amazed by Hayton's stamina. He had a strong, muscular body like a man who regularly worked out. For all his drinking, he had firm buttocks and a flat belly, and when he jogged he displayed a physical confidence and grace little apparent elsewhere in his life. I noticed, too, that as he had grown older he had become handsomer, his features mature and defined.

We had lunch at an outdoor café on Third Avenue, hamburgers and Bloody Marys. It was a sunny, balmy day in New York. The avenue was thick with traffic, the sidewalks filled with people. It was pleasant and easy to sit and watch them parade by as we made comments about the girls, indecent remarks mostly. I began to feel a relaxed closeness to him. In part it was the booze and the shared sexual epithets, devices males always seem to use to create bonding. I thought I had been wrong about him, that I should have been a better friend. I was, after all, the closest person Hayton had to a brother, and I had not honored that.

"What's the movie Pearl's going to do?" I asked.

He laughed. "A thriller. She plays a gun moll. Can you see it? Movie's about a bank robber in the Southwest during the Depression who holds up some two-bit bank in Arizona. Pearl plays one of the bank tellers, and the crook takes her as a hostage. She falls in love with the sonofabitch, and goes on a bank-robbing spree with him. They both end up as dead as Prohibition! You know who's starring in it?"

"Let me guess? Jon Voight?"

"Fuck. This guy's a *big* star."

"Paul Newman?"

"Too old. Come on, old man, *think!*" He hit me playfully on the arm. He was enjoying the game.

"Hell, you got me. Who's the actor?"

"Finish your drink first. Wa-waiter!" he called. "Another round!"

He wouldn't tell me who the actor was until after we were served. Then he said, *"David Spane!"* And he laughed. "Do you fucking believe it? I mean, he's the biggest box-office star there is! I met the sonofabitch in Venice. He floated in on this huge rented yacht, it l-looked like a bloody battleship, for God's sake. Now he's in Paris going over the script or whatever. Mister Body Beautiful with a face that makes women wet. He's p-probably screwing my wife even as we . . . even as we speak."

I stared. It was an extraordinary thing to say, and he said it with perverse pride, as if Pearl's sexual conquests implied something positive about himself. In fact, he *smiled* when he said it.

"Come off it. You don't believe that," I said.

He narrowed his eyes and leaned back in his chair. It was in that intense expression of his eyes, the dislike of being doubted, that he most resembled his father.

"You think I'm k-kidding? David Spane's fucked every star who ever played opposite him, and half the ones who didn't. His career's built on that. So it follows, right? Pearl thinks he's the coolest thing since dry ice." And he gave me that curious prideful look.

"Still . . ."

"You think my wife isn't beautiful enough to ball with Spane? Hell, she's the hottest piece of ass on two continents."

"Why is she doing the picture? Is it the money?"

"Hell, no. I give her anything she wants. But she's *bored*. She wants her own identity. Being my wife isn't enough, obviously. Women's lib. And she's flattered, I think. She's had movie offers before, but David Spane's been pursuing her like mad. And, too, the baby . . ."

"Oh, yes."

"She wanted that baby badly, and now she thinks we . . . you know."

I knew. I'd been there.

"What's Spane like?"

"What you'd expect," Hayton replied, his voice edged with contempt. "A d-dummy. A stud. He thinks he's John Barrymore and Norman Mailer rolled into one hunk of meat. He's got an ego bigger than God's . . ."

"Sounds fun."

"Doesn't he? Spane lives in a cabana at the Beverly Hills Hotel, and he subscribes to every lousy intellectual rag published this side of Outer Mongolia, and then he sits in the Polo Lounge with a *dictionary*, for Christ's sake, and a secretary to take down his critique as he reads the latest hare-brained theories of the old and new Left. He lives in a thousand-dollar-a-week cabana, not including room service, and he considers himself Hollywood's leading *socialist*. You figure it out."

I laughed. It was the first time I realized that Hayton had a sense of humor. And a sense of the absurd.

"And my wife, who doesn't know the difference between eczema and existentialism, thinks Spane is Sartre playing Don Juan! It's enough to make you weep."

"How long are you going to be in town?" I asked.

"I leave tomorrow for East Hampton."

"To swim?" I asked, and then remembered he hated to swim.

"Are you crazy? Fish shit in that water. No, I'm going to shoot rabbits and whatever else trespasses on Momsy's rented digs. You know the Bois de Boulogne?"

"The park in Paris?"

"You know where the whores solicit the cars?" he asked.

"Not exactly."

"Well, a mile from there is a rifle range. I took Pearl to learn to shoot. Hopeless. She kept dropping her gun. The noise t-terrified her. She complained the gunfire made her ears ring for days. A Southern girl, and she couldn't hit the side of a tobacco barn. And now she's going to play a pistol-packing, gun-slinging bank robber in Spane's latest turkey. When the first shot's fired on the set, Pearl will pee in her panties, and they'll never finish the bloody picture!" Hayton laughed. He was feeling good.

"You're probably right."

"Do you remember Susan Vanderlip?"

"She was Pearl's bridesmaid."

"Right. The Maid of Dishonor. She comes from a very old New York f-family, and hasn't a dime, not really . . ."

I glanced at my watch. It was after four. "I've got to go, Hayton."

"Stay a minute, huh? I haven't seen you in years." He sounded lonely, and it troubled me.

"You miss Pearl, don't you?"

He didn't answer. Instead he ordered another round of drinks. I lit a cigarette. He looked at me for a moment, a half-smile on his face, wistful, as if his thoughts were elsewhere.

"I'd die without her," he quietly said.

"Pardon?"

"I said . . ."—Hayton looked away, pretending to hunt for the waiter who was moving toward the table with our drinks—"I said, Do you know why I brought up Susan Vanderlip?"

I let it go by.

"Because you're pimping for her?"

That broke him up. "Wish I were, old man! I'd be richer than Father. You know what they say about Susan: if you had a nickel for every inch of man that's been inside her you'd be a millionaire!" He laughed again. He was getting drunk. "No, actually, the reason wh-why I bring her name to your attention is because my wife wants you to bring Susan to our housewarming. As your date. They're old pals. They were at the same modeling agency. That sort of thing. She wants you two to become an item."

I thought about it, and then I grinned. "Sure, I'd love to bring her."

"Since I'm married, give it to old Susan for me, okay?" He smiled, but his overture was serious. And it suddenly struck me what was essential to his nature, and plain as day, and I had never noticed it before: he was both a voyeur and a masochist. He enjoyed indirect involvement in the sex lives of others. I'm certain he got a vicarious kick out of his wife's sexual infidelity, that he may even have urged her to it. The idea of handsome men being intimate with her pleased him at the same time it demeaned him. And I thought, there must be something homosexual lurking there, too. Pearl was going to bed with men on Hayton's behalf that he himself was attracted to but for some reason could not proposition himself. Perhaps that was too simple. I remembered Sabina telling me at Quo Vadis that Pearl had been to bed with Rupert von Tallenberg, and that for a time Hayton had watched. I hadn't believed it then. Now I wasn't so sure.

Anyway, I saw that that insight into his character, voyeur and masochist, was true. What I didn't know was what his rules were, and without knowing them I was bound, sooner or later, to violate them. And that was dangerous because masochism is rooted in profound self-loathing. And hatred of the self can easily, like the flicking of a switch, be turned outward in rage against others. The more I thought of Hayton, the more complicated he seemed, and the more psychologically and sexually snarled his relationship with Pearl, like clockwork gone mad.

He called for the check. As we waited I told him I'd read the article on them in *Town and Country*. He grimaced.

"Do you know what your mother said when she read it?" I asked. " 'Water finds its own level.' "

"And what did you say?"

"I said, 'And cream always rises to the top.' "

"Yeah," he agreed, "but so does shit."

Forty-Six

WE LEFT the café and strolled over to Madison Avenue, where every so often we entered a shop and browsed about. It was obvious that Hayton did not want to go home, and I couldn't blame him, since he was alone in that enormous apartment with the servants. So he dallied in the boutiques, stretching out the time.

"I met Susan through her brother Rick," he began out of nowhere. I thought he had dropped the subject of the Vanderlips. "Nice kid. I met him at Hortense Vincennes', remember her?"

"Yeah. Pity about her . . ."

"All of us have to die, old man. If it's n-not c-c-cancer that gets us, we choke on a piece of steak or get hit by a bus. What's it matter in the end? The pity's that Hortense had to linger on in the cancer ward so long. Bad deal, that. When I go I want to go fast, in a flash. I don't want to know what hit me. I want to go like Rick did."

"Susan Vanderlip's brother?" I was getting confused.

"The same. Killed himself, five or six years ago. Worked for a time on Warhol's magazine. He died on a day like this, when death's the last thing you'd expect, and there it is reaching for you. It's always there, I s-suppose, like the common cold. You just invite it in. It was just before I met Pearl, or about that time, yes, about that time when he died." Hayton sucked in his lower lip, and he seemed bereaved by the remembrance. And I thought of my father, and my daughter Rose, and I shoved the thoughts aside. Where is the profit in such memory? There's just the sting.

"Day like this . . ." He began again, as we slowly walked along Madison Avenue. "Candy Kisses, did you ever meet her?"

"Never had the pleasure." But I knew who she was. An underground Superstar who made films, like those Warhol did in the Sixties but not as good.

"Candy was making a film in someone's room at the Chelsea Hotel, down on Twenty-third Street. That's where Rick lived. They were doing a bubble-bath scene, and they ran out of bubbles. So Candy Kisses called Ricky and asked to borrow twenty dollars to buy more soap. In exchange for the money she gave him a needle and a vial of pure liquid amphetamine. He had never taken speed in his life, but he was game to try it. He was game for anything, that's why everyone loved him. That, and his sweetness. He shot the speed into his arm and he was dead ten seconds later. Bang! Like that. It stopped his heart. For some lousy bubbles."

We entered a bookstore and browsed around, looking out of place in our running clothes. I stopped and paged through picture books, trying to take my mind off of Hayton's harrowing story about young Rick Vanderlip's dying senselessly, and the memory of my last visit to Countess Hortense de Vincennes at Memorial Hospital. In the terminal ward there, trying to talk to her as she lay virtually denuded of muscles; skin and bones, like a corpse, her face heavily rouged and painted to give it some semblance of health. Grotesque is how she looked, and brave. I had to lean down to hear her weak voice rasp out silly anecdotes about socialites and celebrities she had numbered among her friends, not one of whom visited her deathbed. Only Varina Ransome and Sabina Phips had bothered.

Hortense asked about the annual show at the Whitney, and about a huge party Drue Heinz had given, and if I had seen the Larry Rivers show at the Marlborough, and the Copley at the Iolas Jackson Gallery. She had little hair left, and she no longer wore a snood. As I stood to leave—the groaning of the other dying patients in the ward becoming intolerable to me, low, rumbling, gasping, anonymous cries of the cancer-ridden behind beige hospital screens— as I stood to leave, Hortense said, "Remember all the fine laughs we had, dear one." And she laughed, or rather tried to laugh, her hearty staccato gone for good. And she moved her hand to her head, and gently, easily, like someone smoothing windblown hair, she ran her withered hand over her scalp and like someone pulling wisps of cotton from a boll, drew a handful of hair from her head, and handed it to me. "It's all I have left to give," she explained, smiling. For a moment I thought she was kidding.

I discarded her hair as soon as I left the room. And when I returned home I threw out the lock of baby Rose's hair. There is too much death in life. Even as they are dying, even dead, they won't let go.

In the bookstore I found a picture book on the Hollywood stars. In it was a large spread on David Spane. In fact, he accounted for more pages than Robert Redford, or Warren Beatty, or even Brando. I bought the book and gave it to Hayton.

"Ah." He laughed. "Something to wipe my ass with."

We left the bookstore and walked west to Fifth Avenue. The wind was up and the air cool off the park. Dusk was beginning to settle over Manhattan. The lights were going on in apartment houses across Central Park and people were hurrying home. It was a special time in New York and in all places where men build cities, when your steps quicken as you leave a wider world at the close of the day to go back to your place and people. And if you have no people, it is especially lonely at that hour, which is why Americans, with their talent for turning a profit on all human sentiment, invented the Cocktail Hour at twilight. The Happy Hour.

I was horny and impatient to get home. Through my mind went an index of women I would call as soon as I left Hayton. It wasn't sex so much as intimacy I wanted. I hadn't been with a woman in two weeks, and I needed to be with one tonight. Hayton was right. Death is always there, hanging around waiting to be invited in. And women, if you are straight and maybe even if you are not, women, when they're good, are one of the few reasons you don't invite it in.

"I need a drink," Hayton declared as we stepped into his apartment. It was dark inside, and he felt along the walls for the light switch. We walked through the apartment toward the bar, and as we went Hayton began pulling off his clothes and tossing them on the floor, something I remembered him doing as a child, to the perpetual consternation of Aunt Kattie.

By the time we reached the bar he was down to his jock strap. He made us martinis, and the telephone rang. It was Pearl calling from Paris.

"Talk louder, love. Bad connection," Hayton shouted into the phone. "Right . . . not till then? Ah, hell, honey, I'm lonely . . . you drunk? . . . What? . . . No, Mikey's here with me . . . What? . . . Next week, then . . . Ginger Snaps, baby. Ginger Snaps. Bye-bye."

"Pearl?"

"She sends you her love. Won't be coming in from P-Paris for another week. Hell."

"Sorry."

Hayton shrugged.

He showered first, and then I did. He remained in the bathroom, shouting to me over the noise of the water.

"Susan Vanderlip balled David Spane, did you know that?"

"No," I shouted back. "And I don't give a damn. Where's the shampoo?"

"Don't have any yet . . . Listen, ask Susan about Spane! It's a good yarn," he shouted back. "Spane can keep it up for hours. There's got to be a trick to it. I mean, his dick never gets soft. Like Nixon's heart."

I came out of the shower. Hayton was leaning with his bottom against the rim of the wash basin.

"You should get dressed, don't you think?" I suggested.

"I have to ask you something." His voice was soft, almost shy.

"What is it? I don't have much time, Hayton."

"It's serious."

"Shoot."

"Are you ever impotent?"

I was taken aback by the question, and by the painful difficulty he had in asking it.

"Every man is, Hayton. It comes with the territory. Why do you ask?"

He looked at me, and then in embarrassment he looked away. When he spoke his voice was low and quiet, either from shame or fear, I don't know which.

And then he said, softly but in a rush, like a child trying to announce bad news before you have time to smack him for it. "I can't get it up anymore. Not with Pearl."

I was saddened by that, and a little alarmed. It came so totally out of left field that I was speechless.

"Not with my wife," he repeated, more to himself than to me.

I touched his shoulder and squeezed it. It was like the time he was suspended from school and told me first because he was afraid to face his father. The same dejection, the same sense of defeat.

"It's a phase, Hayton. It'll come back. Give it time." Even as I spoke I thought it probably wasn't true. But I knew that occasional impotence was caused by drink or anxiety or fatigue and that you dealt with it by ignoring it, although that was more easily said than done. "Don't dwell on it. Don't force it," I continued, beginning to feel superior in manhood to him, and rather liking the idea. "Put more adventure into it, and for God's sake, don't drink before you do it. And stay away from drugs for a while. Booze and pills will deflate it faster than anything. You'll see," I confidently advised, "you and Pearl will be at it like bunnies again. If there's one thing Pearl loves it's sex—" The second I said the words I regretted them.

Hayton jerked his shoulder away from my hand. He rubbed his eyes with his hands, and then faced me, taking a deep breath. There was no anger there, no righteous assault. There was only defeat grown too familiar, and sadness, too, and the wary vulnerability of a man who no longer trusted his body. I felt sorry for him, but I was powerless to comfort or make right.

He stared at the floor now, and ran his hands through his hair. "Were you . . . were you," he began haltingly, "were you ever im-*imp*otent with my wife?"

I made no reply. There was none to make but falsehood. In the silence he grunted. And then he left the room.

Forty-Seven

"DON'T STAY in the sun too long, Orin," Varina said, as she and Pearl approached the swimming pool at the Ransomes' rented estate in East Hampton. I was standing in the pool. Ambassador Ransome lay on his back in the water as I supported him underneath. He floated there, paddling his arms and legs slowly. He could no longer swim unattended. His heart had become unreliable.

"I'll stay in the sunshine until I'm good and ready to go in, Caroline, and not a minute before. Leave me be!"

Varina stiffened at the mistake.

"Have it your way, dearest," Varina said icily. "But if you get as red as Georgia clay don't come crying to me. Let's go, Pearl."

"In a minute." Pearl walked over to the side of the pool and squatted down. "I want to kiss the men goodbye."

I felt the Ambassador chuckle as I floated him over to the side of the pool, where Pearl kissed him. And then she kissed me. I smelled sandalwood.

"Where you off to, child?"

"We're having lunch at the Maidstone with Sabina and Helen . . .?" Pearl stood up. "What's Helen's last name again? I plum forgot."

"Mellon. Helen Mellon," Varina replied, exasperated. She glanced at her wristwatch. "Come, Pearl, the car's waiting."

"Helen Mellon," Pearl repeated, as if she were trying to remember the name.

"It rhymes," I said.

"Right. It rhymes with money!" And Pearl laughed, and waved, and they left.

The Maidstone is a country club about a mile from the estate the Ransomes rented that summer and would later buy. The club, like many others, did not knowingly accept Jews, nor did it accept a lot of other groups, although of course the discriminatory policy was never publicly stated. For that reason Ambassador Ransome, being an incorrigible liberal of the old school, refused to set foot inside the club. "I won't go where Jesus couldn't buy a drink," he said, and he meant it.

The Ransomes' swimming pool was about fifty yards from the main house, on a vast lawn that spread between the house and the ocean dunes. Closest to the dunes were two guest cottages that overlooked the wide white beach. Sabina Phips occupied one, and I the other. Hayton and Pearl stayed in the main house with Orin and Varina.

The pool was heated. It was kept at 85 degrees for the Ambassador's comfort and because of the temperature everyone but the Ambassador swam in the ocean. He'd always loved ocean swimming, but he could no longer safely withstand the surf and the undertow.

We heard the pop-pop of an air gun firing twice.

"There he goes again, the nitwit. You know, that boy's illegally slaughtered nearly a hundred jack rabbits and God knows how many birds and foxes just this week alone? He brings them home, where they rot until Varina has one of the groundsmen dig a hole and dump them in. That doesn't make much sense, now does it?"

Every afternoon after lunch Hayton was in the habit of stomping the woods and fields of the estate shooting at whatever moved. He enjoyed it, but I think he enjoyed even more Pearl's sputtering horror at the killings. I had been with them for three days, and I had come to understand something of the war of nerves they waged against each other, the constant testing of each other's limits, their marriage a tangle of resentments and affection, a kind of woolly romanticism overlying a mutually unacknowledged hostility that seemed to excite them both. There were sadistic and masochistic elements there, and there were dirty secrets, too. One concerned the loss of the baby. Another, the strange enjoyment Hayton derived from Pearl's infidelity. It was never Pearl who brought up her faithlessness. She seemed deeply embarrassed by Hayton's accusations, most of which I was certain were not true. And yet her very discomfort seemed to egg him on to make them, and to make them in front of people who were not close friends. It was an unhappy business all around. And I kept recalling Lionel Trilling's observation that "often the very things that make a marriage unbearable also make it unbreakable."

Both Pearl and Hayton were keeping score, I felt that instinctively. And neither one would leave off until the game was called in their favor. Punishment paid with punishment, and still an undeniable love existed in the thicket of abuse and challenge.

"Damn that Nixon," the Ambassador said as he paddled his arms in the water. "He asked Harriman to see the Vietnamese. Nixon's always wanting Harriman to go here and go there. Hell, Harriman's got to be ten years older than *I*, and he hasn't got sense enough to come in out of the rain anymore."

It was a surprising declaration of hurt vanity, and I found it moving. He had been harping about the Nixon-Harriman axis ever since I arrived for the weekend. What it said to me was that the Ambassador, being in poor health, resented being left out of affairs of state. Part of that resentment was directed against Harriman, and part was aimed at Hayton, who, unlike Joe Kennedy's sons, did not enjoy a public life through which his father could indulge his love of power.

"It's your health," I said. "A year from now everything will be different."

He splashed water in my face. "You're as dumb as Harriman," he groused.

"Thanks."

"My health be damned. When Nixon first came to the Oval Office—and how he managed that only God can explain—he called me to Washington. He had his foreign-policy people there, a lot of new faces except for Bill Rogers, who should have kept to corporate law. Bill was never any match for Kissinger, or even Nixon, when it comes to that. We talked about Vietnam and Cambodia, and the rest of it. I don't know what the hell there is about Dick Nixon, but something in his makeup always makes me want to lecture him. Something half-educated about him. Bright enough chap, but unclean. He hasn't changed or grown an inch since the Fifties. Nothing but spite and small change, if you want to know the truth of it . . ." The Ambassador started to cough. I felt his body contort as he hacked out hoarse, ragged sound. "Help me out of here," he said.

We struggled out of the pool and he dropped onto a chaise longue, where I covered him with towels.

He was quiet for a few minutes, his breathing heavy and somewhat irregular. His eyes were closed, and he seemed to be sleeping.

"I'll miss the sunlight when I'm under the sod. How I'll miss the sunlight," he said, and coughed again.

I sat for a few minutes on the end of his chaise, gently massaging his lower legs, and then stood to leave.

"Where you off to, son?" he asked, his eyes still closed.

"To get a hat for you," I lied.

"Hat? I haven't worn a *hat* since Harry Truman. Now, there was a President. I keep meaning to call him. What was I going on about in the water?"

"President Nixon."

"Yes. Altogether shiftless and shifty, if you ask me. The war. That's what he inquired about. The war over there in Indochina. So I told him about war, about Sherman's goddamn march through Georgia and the Carolinas, about Varina's family house burning in Atlanta, and their plantation burned in the east country. I told him about the destruction of Columbia, and Savannah, and Orangeburg, and the rest of it. The first total war. The atrocities against our own people, against women and little children, the Yankee killing and pillage and rape, and Sherman's pernicious, devilish bummers. And I said to Nixon—I had one hell of a time calling that skunk Mr. President, but, by God, I got the words out—I said what you are doing across the seas in Indochina to those yellow people is what Sherman did to us, and it led to seventy years of fiery hatred, resistance, and sorrow. It led to deadly backlash. I said, the Orientals will despise our name for a century if we don't act fairly and justly now . . . And, hell, I can't remember what else I said but it was mighty fine stuff."

"What did President Nixon say?"

"Say? Nixon? He didn't say a damn thing. He looked at me like he once looked at Alger Hiss. He saw a pinko. A Communist. So Harriman got the job. Harriman just stands and mumbles and chews on his tongue. So he gets the jobs."

"The sonofabitch!"

"Sherman?"

"No, *Nixon*." I laughed.

"Why, Nixon couldn't hold a candle to Uncle Billy Sherman. He may have burned us out, son, but after the War Between the States they broke his ass, Stanton and the other carpetbagging Radicals, because Sherman wanted to treat the South with a modicum of human decency. If Nixon is Sherman, which I heartily doubt, then Kissinger's his Stanton, although he wears the feathers of a dove."

He opened his eyes and grinned. "I'm not senile yet, Michael." He laughed and patted my hand. "Now, get the old man a drink before Varina returns. And if she asks—"

"I'll say we're drinking Cokes."

"Good boy."

When I returned, he talked a bit about Timberton, which he had decided to will to Hayton's children, if Hayton ever had any. If there were none, it would be given to the National Trust. "They aren't going to build ticky-tacky development housing around *my* grave, goddamn it. A brothel I might fancy, or even a roadhouse. But short of that . . ."

He drifted off again, and seemed to sleep. I sipped my drink and watched the waves break on the beach far below us. It was good being with him. I thought he looked in better health than I had seen him in some time, although he had suffered two small heart attacks the year before. He had good color, and while he seemed more easily annoyed by little things, and his memory of recent events was not as acute as it had once been, on the whole I thought he was far from dying. In the past year or two, his physical frailty and his unsteady memory had given him a childlike quality, the irritable nature of a child overtired and snappish and petulant as a result. He enjoyed being indulged now, and he enjoyed being pampered, even though he complained loudly when it was done. Still in all, the attention reassured his aging vanity.

"Where the hell's Varina?" he asked, holding his hand above his eyes to guard against the sun. "Off conspiring somewhere?"

"She's at lunch."

"But we *had* lunch, didn't we? Or *did* we?"

"We did. But Varina and Pearl went to the Maidstone Club."

"Bunch of phonies at that damn club. Hate the Jews, don't you know. That's the first sign of a dangerous fool. Hand me my drink."

He sipped it, put it down, and then tried to lean forward to sit up. I stood and lifted the back of the chaise.

"Don't do that! I'm not an invalid yet, son."

I sat down again.

"Will you tell me something, Michael, and not hold back?" His chin was down against his throat, his eyes staring intently at me, his silver-gray hair dry and blown in the sea breeze so that he looked patriarchal, Biblical.

"Yes, sir."

"Why the hell did Pearl ever marry Hayton?" he asked. He lifted up his head and shook it slowly from side to side. "Not for money, certainly. She could've married many other men for money. Why on God's green earth did she pick my son?"

"Because she loves him," I replied, and I believed it.

"But in what *way*?" he asked, his gaze piercing and direct. He wanted the truth, and I knew he didn't believe he'd gotten it. There are occasions when people require the truth from you and you tell

it, and yet you suspect that they believe you are holding back because you do not know enough to make the truth convincing.
Truth has been reduced to a good hunch, and little more.

"She loves him as a wife would, in that way," I said.

The Ambassador grunted. He sipped his drink. "And *Piers*?" he
asked. "Where does Piers Goodpasture figure in all this?"

"Why do you ask?" I lamely replied, trying to buy time to quickly
surmise how Piers's name had come to Ambassador Ransome's
notice. I had not thought about Piers in years. I sensed there was
danger in the waters the Ambassador was asking me to swim, but
I had no idea of the nature of that danger. My instinct was to protect Pearl in any way I could, for the danger was to her.

I lit a cigarette.

"Tell me what you know about Piers, son." His voice was
steady and neutral in tone, like he might use in questioning an
employee.

I told him what I knew, how I met Pearl and then Piers, about
the trunk we moved, but I didn't mention Maurice, or Piers's nocturnal visits to Maurice's door.

"He's her oldest friend," I explained, "They were quite close
once."

The Ambassador stared directly into my eyes, coldly as if un-
certain of belief. Then he grunted, and slumped back in the chair.

"Piers is a drug smuggler, did you know?" he asked.

"No, sir. I didn't know."

He closed his eyes. "Take my drink away, son. I'm tuckered out."

I sat with him for ten minutes or so, and then I decided to go
down to the beach and swim.

"I ought to call old Harry Truman tomorrow," he mumbled,
"and see how he's getting along."

Harry Truman had been dead for several months.

Forty-Eight

WE HAD an early dinner, and around ten o'clock Varina and the Ambassador went up to bed. Hayton, Pearl, Sabina, and I stayed on in the library and played poker for several hours. Pearl was a very serious, very sharp player. She won most of the hands. We were all drinking too much, particularly Hayton. And as he drank he became nasty. Finally he threw his cards on the table.

"What's wrong, honey?" Pearl was startled.

"You know what's wrong, bitch. You cheat."

"I *don't* cheat. Why, you're just a bad player. You don't concentrate, so you lose." She was right.

"You cheat everywhere. In bed and out of bed. You're a fucking whore!"

"Is there any other kind?" Sabina laughed. "Now, calm down, Hayton. You're being a poor loser."

"Fuck it." He stood. "Fuck all of you." He stomped out of the room.

"Pleasant man when he drinks," Sabina drawled. "Fun company at cards. Oh, why don't you get rid of him?"

"Because he's my husband, and I love him," she admitted quietly.

Sabina raised her eyebrows above her green glasses in mock disbelief. "Well, you know, darling, it is a subject of great interest to hoards of people why you two stick together. Your rows in Paris weren't exactly the most private of spats." Sabina turned to me. "You weren't in Paris with them. I *was*. And I tell you, I feared for Pearl's safety. I really did, Pearl."

"He doesn't mean it. It's the liquor talking."

"Liquor may talk. But it doesn't throw punches."

"Has that sonofabitch hit you?" I asked.

"Not really," Pearl said. "He talks bad, and then the next day he feels miserable. He doesn't mean it." She touched my hand. "Don't worry about it, I can take care of myself."

"If he ever strikes you . . ." I was still angry.

"If it gets too much, I'll end it. Once he starts work at the bank, he'll be all right. He needs self-esteem, that's all."

"Whose deal is it?" Sabina asked, collecting the cards.

"Let's not play anymore."

"Why, Pearl? Quit when you're ahead?" Sabina laughed. "Personally, I *enjoy* losing."

"Let's get some air," I said.

As we walked out to the patio, we heard the squeal of tires in the driveway.

"What a twit when he's drunk," Sabina remarked. "Where do you suppose he's going at this hour?"

"To a bar," Pearl replied. "Once he starts drinking he can't seem to stop until he falls down. He tries to stop, but he can't."

"You ought to send Hayton to Smithers or Silver Hill, darling. They'd dry him out fast. God, just thinking of Hayton makes me thirsty." Sabina walked over to the outside bar. "Ah, *ice*! What novelty!" she exclaimed, opening the bucket on the bar. "Drinkie, anyone?"

"Is there some bourbon?" Pearl wanted to know. "I do so get tired of wine."

Sabina made Pearl's drink, and then gave me a vodka and water.

"To the wages of sin!" Sabina saluted, raising her glass. "I think we've all earned overtime."

We sat on stuffed chairs near the bar by the lighted pool. The weather had cooled. An ocean breeze from across the dunes caused the heated pool to steam like a boiling pot. We watched it rise pearl-white above the smooth, blue surface of the water, mysterious against the blackness of the sky and ocean.

"It looks like ghosts gathered above the water. You can't hardly see the pool for the cloud," Pearl observed.

"Ghosts?" Sabina laughed. "It looks like Hell to me. One of the better neighborhoods of Hell . . ."

"Sabina," I began, "I've always meant to ask you how you can see a damn thing behind those green sunglasses. How ever do you get around at night?"

"I *feel* my way, darling. More excitement that way . . . Bye the bye, how do you think Orin looks these days?"

"What do you mean?"

"Don't you think he's getting a little, well, *slow*? Sad, really."

"He's like the Duchess of Windsor—" Pearl began.

"The *what*?" Sabina blurted. "Good Lord!"

"I mean the way he forgets things. The duchess forgets too."

"Bully for her. I was about to ask if either of you noticed how often he calls Varina *Caroline* by mistake? And she never bats an eye. I'd slap Orin's face if he did that to me."

"Who's Caroline?" Pearl asked.

"A ghost of his."

"No, seriously."

"Don't you know? Whatever do you and Hayton talk about in bed? I'd have thought he'd have told you some of the Ransome family secrets by now. What else are secrets for? Caroline Farr was a woman Orin was madly, and I do mean madly, in love with about ten or twelve years ago. It nearly shattered the marriage."

"Do you think he still loves her?"

"Probably. Why else would he confuse Varina with her? Do you know who that bitch, and Caroline is a bitch, went on to marry last year?"

"David—" I said.

"I was asking *Pearl*!" Sabina snapped. "Yes, my David. Oh, the scheming golddigger. My only consolation is that that's one marriage that won't last."

David, the television executive, had broken Sabina's heart, or what passed for her heart, with his marriage to Caroline Farr. The marriage, which occurred less than three months after the death of his wife Doris, struck most people as appropriate. Caroline was still a handsome woman. And she was a splendid hostess, something David thought he required in his line of work. But years after the wedding, Sabina Phips was still unresigned to it. It had cut too deeply into her pride, and I knew, looking at her, that she would not cease to plot until the marriage was ruined.

"And you know, that slut had the temerity to invite me to their wedding!"

"Have another drink and forget about it. You're probably lucky you didn't marry him," I said.

"Lucky? How little you know." She laughed hollowly. "I'm off to bed." She stood up. "I thought the race was won when poor Doris kicked the bucket. I was wrong. What a bastard David turned out to be. But then, we're all bastards in the clinch."

Forty-Nine

AFTER Sabina retired, Pearl and I sat together on a chaise by the pool. It was wonderful holding her again, feeling the warmth of her body, smelling her scented hair.

"I want a baby so bad."

I kissed her. "I'll give you a baby."

"That'd be right kindly of you. But it wouldn't be a Ransome!" She laughed. "I want my baby to have everything I never did have. Everything Piers never had. Oh, I want my baby to be a prince. And only Hayton can make that possible. Do you know what he'll be worth in time?"

"Millions."

"Right. Hayton told me. When I was pregnant, before I lost my baby, he got all these papers together and sat me down and went through the whole damn thing. It's all on computer tapes, what the family owns. It's very confusing. Stock in hundreds of companies.

Banks and cattle and land. They have thousands and thousands of acres in Argentina and Brazil, and acres and acres in Mississippi, and oil lands in Louisiana. And then there's the office buildings in New York, and mines in the West. They even own hotels in Europe. I don't know what all. And I don't rightly believe even *they* know the whole of it . . ."

"And Hayton gets it all?"

"The whole shebang."

"And you want that?"

"No. I want my baby to have that. We'll try again, when Hayton feels more confident. Once he begins to work and all. I feel so sorry for him. I know he loves me, and when it doesn't work for him he hates himself so. It drives him crazy, he feels so low-down. But we'll work it out because we have to work it out. I ain't going to let him quit on me." Pearl got up from the chaise. "Come on. Let's swim naked!" She giggled.

"But if Hayton returns?"

She tugged on my arm. "Come on, don't be shy. Hayton's bound to be passed out drunk at the side of the road. That's his way, don't you know. He gets in the car, and passes out."

Pearl was wearing a blue and white silk caftan. She pulled it off, and then slipped out of her sandals. She undid her bra, and pulled down her panties.

"Are you going to swim?" she asked.

"Hell, yes." I started pulling off my clothes. "I was just watching you undress, just drinking it in, baby."

She dived into the pool, and I followed. The water was warm, and the steam above it was thick. Because of the pool lights and the mist one felt hidden away in another world, and safe. It was enormously sensuous, swimming beside her. She was a powerful swimmer, and it took real effort for me to keep pace with her.

We swam fifteen laps or so, and then we rested in the shallow end of the pool, sitting on the bottom with our backs against the tiled wall.

"I declare, I'd love a house with a pool."

"Get Hayton to buy one."

"No, sir. I want to buy it myself. So he could never take it away from me, whatever happens. Everybody's got to have some place of their own where they can tell anyone, even their husband, to get the hell away. Maybe if the movie makes money, maybe then."

"You're going to do the movie, then?"

"Yes. Could use the money, don't you know, maybe to buy a pretty house with a pool like this."

We left the pool. On the patio she paused and stretched her body, her arms thrown wide, her hands clutched, her head thrown back, her breasts thrust forward, their nipples dark and erect, her skin glistening in the artificial light. I shivered at the sight of her naked body, lithe and youthful, full of strength and play.

"Ummmm," she exhaled. "I ain't felt so good since Sherman left Dixie!" She cocked her head to one side, and looked at me. "And you, Beau. How about you?"

I just smiled big.

"Come on, tough guy," she said in a gruff baritone, trying to sound butch and swaggering, "Let's fuck, sailor." And she punched my arm.

We gathered our clothes and ran to the cottage where I was staying. As we entered, Pearl touched my bobbing erection.

"Don't it never get soft?" she giggled tipsily.

"Not around you, Mama."

Now, I don't know why I called her Mama, something a man might call his wife, but Pearl responded by calling me Dad, and as we made love we used those terms with each other, like an old married couple with too many kids whose familial roles had become their pet names. We giggled as we played Mama and Dad.

"French-kiss me, Dad," she said gruffly as we lay on the bed, the sheets damp from our wet bodies. "Come on, Dad," she giggled. "Give me that hot tongue." We kissed, facing each other, the lights on. We ran our hands over each other's bodies, becoming acquainted again with what we both had missed. "Your ass is bigger, Mama." "Thanks, Dad. But so's yours." She laughed and gave it a slap. "And your hair's turning gray at the sides, but Mama likes that." She kissed my ear gently, and then tongued it, making a buzzing hiss that tickled and made me laugh. "You got beautiful tits, Mama." "Then suck on 'em, Dad." And I did, and she groaned with pleasure. I was hungry for her, and I ached in memory of the years we had been apart, at the waste of it.

Pearl was the most sensual woman I have ever known. Completely at ease, and wanton. Men often suspect that women don't really want sex, and that's because they withhold it as punishment, use it to manipulate, grant it as reward. One frequently suspects they are dissembling passion, more faker than lover. It was never that way with Pearl. I don't think it ever occurred to her that sex might be a means to something else. The means and the end were the same with her. Everyone she was sexually with, whether her husband or Piers or me or God knows who else, she was with completely. Only you existed. You were for her what pleasure was, what love was made to celebrate. She was a great lover, it was as simple and extraordinary and blessed as that.

When I fondled her breasts, when I drew my mouth down her thin body, feeling her muscles tremble harmonically with the movement of my tongue, when I tasted her sex with its soft and impossibly straight pubic hair, its heavy moist lips, and later, when I kissed her mouth, coupled there as I thrust into her body, she seemed to love every gift of touch, to want to prolong it, to move slowly, to linger luxuriant in movement like someone who had been empty too long, and had been unloved or wrongly loved. We both knew that our being together was rare. It would always be. There was no help for it but to seize what we had now and to remember it. She was ardent for love because of her early life, the orphanages and foster homes, being shuttled about as a child like a package forever misaddressed. It was because of the poverty of those years, both material and emotional, that she now clung in craving, as if in loving her you were depositing affection against a childhood in which it was withheld.

"Do it, Dad! Do it, do it!" Her body rocked with mine, her legs up and wide, her arms around my back where she gripped the flesh, kneading it hard. "Do it!"

Fifty

Do YOU know why I love you and Hayton?" Pearl asked. We were lying together on the bed, her head on my chest, one leg sprawled lazily over my thigh. I gently rubbed her sex, with featherlike tenderness, amazed at the freedom to touch her there.

"Why, baby?"

"Because, except for Piers, I never thought anybody could love me and be so nice to me. Like you were, honey. And like Hayton's been, for all his anger and drunkard ways. I'm happy, Dad. Are you?"

"I've never been happier." I lifted her hand to my lips and kissed the palm.

"You have the softest lips," she said, "like Piers."

I remembered the Ambassador asking me about Piers, and I decided she should know.

"Orin asked about Piers this afternoon."

"Oh?" Pearl said. I felt her body tighten. "What did you tell him?"

"How we met. That you and Piers were once good friends."

"That all, honey?"

"Yes."

She relaxed. "Piers got himself arrested sometime back. They seized his boat in Gulfport, the boat I bought him."

"So you did buy him a boat?"

"Yup. Hayton gave me the money. He knew it was for Piers."

"That was generous of him." And, I thought, strange.

"I promised I wouldn't see Piers again if Hayton bought him a boat. Hayton was crazy jealous of Piers. You can't even mention that boy's name around him or he goes wild."

"Have you kept your promise?"

She laughed. "More or less."

"So now he's in jail."

"Not anymore. Do you have a cigarette?" She sat up in bed.

I lit hers and then lit one for myself.

"The state police in Mississippi," she continued, "searched Piers's boat and they found cocaine on it. A lot of cocaine. Piers didn't know a thing about it, I swear . . ."

"I hope to hell he's got a good lawyer."

"It was the other boys, hippies who worked for Piers on the boat, it was that trash who smuggled the coke aboard when they docked in San Juan. Piers was innocent as the Baby Jesus. He may not be the best boy in Sunday school, but he isn't dumb. Not *that* dumb."

"Is that what the judge said? Dumb but clean?"

"No, that's what *I* said. Piers's lawyer called me from Gulfport. I was in Paris, and the only soul I knew who could help Piers out of that corner was Orin. Hell, Beau, don't you know, the Ransomes practically *own* the State of Mississippi, lock, stock, and barrel. And since I am a Ransome myself now, I figured Orin would be willing to lend a hand with the police. He was at Timberton then— this was a couple months past—and I flew there. Nobody knew about it, not even Varina, who was in Palm Beach. I told Hayton I had to go to California on movie business. I saw Orin and told him about it, and how very important a matter it was to me. I told him I couldn't ever turn my back on Piers, whatever the cost, and if he wouldn't help me I'd go to Gulfport alone and fight the good fight myself, even if it did get into the newspapers . . ."

"And how did Ambassador Ransome respond to that threat?" I asked. I would not have the guts to speak to Orin Ransome in that manner, and I don't know anyone else who would either.

"Well, he kinda laughed. And he kissed me, and called me a good ol' girl. He said he liked balls on anybody, man or woman, and I had me enough for pocket pool. He said he respected one virtue above all others, and that was loyalty."

"You got him down pat, baby. Congratulations."

"Thank you kindly. So anyway, Orin talked about his ancestors who'd been smugglers in the Gulf and such, and then he called the Governor of Mississippi at home. He said he carried the Governor's balls, along with his future, in his pants' pocket. The Governor was obliged to call the District Attorney of the State of Mississippi and, with one thing and another, the charges against Piers were dropped. Only thing, though, they wouldn't give Piers his boat back. Now, that isn't hardly fair."

"Fair?" I had to laugh. "Are you nuts? He's damn lucky."

"Really?" she asked, when she knew he was. "Well, I went to Gulfport—there isn't a decent hotel in that town—and I saw Piers the day they let him out of the pokey. We flew on to Key West— that's where he's living now . . ."

"I thought he couldn't go back to Florida because the police wanted him there."

"You did?" she said. And stopped and thought a moment. "Oh, *that*. Why, that was years ago, over that killing in Panama City. They closed that case down. Piers had nothing whatever to do with that. He wasn't even *in* Panama City at the time. He was in New Orleans with me."

"That's comforting to know," I said. I really did not believe her, and I really didn't care. What was Piers to me? Someone she loved whom I had met years before, a sick, pretty boy who sold his ass to a black saloon owner long ago. What did it matter to me what was true or false, whether he had killed in Florida or killed Paco in New York or smuggled cocaine? It was too remote. He was something Pearl loved to talk about, a reality that had little consequence in my life at that time.

"Piers can't ever go back to Mississippi—that's part of the deal Orin made. I love Piers so darn much."

"I wish you'd quit telling me that."

"I'm sorry, honey. I know it's wrong to love him. It's a cursed thing. If people knew the half of it they'd ride me out of town on a rail. But I can't rightly help myself!" she said, hitting her fists against her thighs in frustration. "So I bought him another boat."

"You didn't."

"I surely did. He has to have a gainful livelihood, now you know that. And he does so love the sea and being a fisherman and all. Cost me a hundred thousand dollars, and the damn boat wasn't even *new*."

"A hun . . . Where'd you get the money, Pearl?" I couldn't conceive of even Pearl having the moxie to hit Hayton for another boat for Piers.

"I hocked the emeralds."

"The ones Varina gave you?"

"What else was I to do? I couldn't ask Hayton!"

"My God, Pearl, Varina will boil you in oil when she finds out."

Pearl laughed. "No she won't," she said slyly. "Because she won't find out."

"No?"

"Not unless you tell her."

"I'm not going to tell her."

"I had a set of fakes made," she declared proudly. "You can't tell the difference. Hayton's seen the fake necklace, and he thinks it's the real McCoy. Anyway, I'm set to get two hundred thousand Yankee dollars when I do David Spane's dumb movie."

"That's a heap of money for someone who's never said a line before a camera."

"I know it is," she giggled. "And when I get the money I'll redeem the emeralds and nobody'll be the wiser. Easy as pie."

I laughed at her designs. She'd redeem the emeralds. Hayton would give her a baby. Everything would go to the baby. Piers would stay out of trouble. She could love whom she wished and somehow it'd all work out in the end, easy as pie. She was new to the game, at least as it was played by the Ransomes and the other high rollers. She was betting with other people's money, and she was blithely convinced that she would win big without anyone's getting hurt. The rabbit would always be sitting in the hat when she grabbed for it.

"You're going to have your cake and eat it, too, right, Mama?"

"*Cakes*," she said jokingly. "I'm going to have my *cakes* and eat *them* too . . . Come on, Dad. Let's swim one more time."

We went back to the pool. She carried her clothes. I left mine behind in the cottage. We swam ten laps in the water, and we splashed around and laughed like there was no Judgment because there was no tomorrow. Not for Pearl. Just one long Happy Hour.

As I climbed out of the water, following her up the ladder and glancing toward the darkened house, Hayton was standing by the glass doors off the patio. He watched us for a few minutes as we stood naked and dripping wet. He said nothing, merely looked at us with a curious half-smile, as if he were both saddened and oddly pleased by what he witnessed. And then he turned and drunkenly staggered into the house.

"There goes your husband," I said. "Now the shit will really hit the fan."

"No it won't, Beau. Hayton won't remember a damn thing in the morning. He's too drunk."

She was wrong.

Fifty-One

I LEFT East Hampton the following afternoon for New York. I'd slept late, and by the time I awoke Hayton was off in the fields shooting small game.

Pearl returned to Manhattan the next week, and we spent some time together. She was busy finishing the apartment for her party. It was to be an important affair, officially hosted by Ambassador and Mrs. Ransome as a housewarming for Hayton and Pearl, but in fact it was a coming-out party. Five hundred guests were expected for cocktails, crêpes and salad, and strawberry mousse, followed by late-night dancing.

Pearl had a week to pull the loose ends together—dealing with caterers, florists, and newly hired servants, buying household supplies, selecting linen, and choosing a dress for the party. The last proved more difficult than I thought possible. In the end she purchased six dresses, two by Oscar de la Renta, one Giorgio Milano, and three Halstons. She ended up wearing the Milano. It was Varina's choice.

Twice we lunched and went shopping in midtown together. It was fun for both of us. The weather was balmy, with just a hint of autumn in the air, and we both enjoyed walking, something Manhattan was designed for. Pearl loved spending money, and I liked watching her do it. The city had become one giant F.A.O. Schwarz toy store and she was six years old.

At La Vieille Russie she found a tiny malachite-and-gold picture frame edged in seed pearls. It had been made by Fabergé for the czarina, and had once contained a hand-painted porcelain miniature of her son, the czarevitch Alexis. The miniature, like the czarevitch, was now lost to history.

Pearl looked at it, thought about it for a day, and then bought it. It cost nine thousand dollars, which I thought excessive for an object you could easily fit inside a vest pocket.

"The baby'll need a picture frame, and this will be perfect," she explained when I informed her the price was exorbitant. "I'll never find another as precious."

"Why don't you wait until you're actually pregnant? Aren't you pushing things a bit?"

"I'll be pregnant in seven months, as soon as I complete shooting the movie."

"Seven months, huh?"

"You want to bet?" she challenged, ending the discussion. She was a hell of a lot more confident of Hayton's ability to get it up on cue than either he or I was.

She had the bill for the Fabergé frame sent to the legal firm that managed the Ransome family's trusts and investments. Like most of the very rich, Pearl never saw a bill or dunning letter or a creditor's summons. She signed for whatever she wanted. She had only the vaguest idea of how much money she spent in a month, and she didn't care how much it was. And Hayton liked her not caring. He understood that part of what held her to him was her being able not to care.

"Why didn't you have the bill for Piers's new boat sent to your lawyers? Why hock the emeralds?"

"Hayton would have found out. Anything over a certain amount, I think it's ten thousand, they call him before it's paid."

And for all that, Pearl never seemed to have any cash on her, another characteristic of the very rich, especially the old rich. It never occurs to them. So Pearl was incessantly borrowing taxi money from me that she never remembered to repay.

"Why don't you carry a couple hundred in your purse?" I asked her.

"Why?"

"In case you need it."

She thought a moment. "Because it means I have to send the maid to the bank in the morning to cash a check. And it takes her hours. And when she gets back she's grouchy all day. I'd rather sign."

So much for that.

The day before the party I went with Pearl to Andy Warhol's Factory on Union Square. She posed for hundreds of Polaroid snapshots that Warhol and his assistants took. He would use them to do her portrait. She was having it painted as a birthday present for Hayton's birthday eight months away.

As we got into a taxi on Union Square after the Warhol sitting, I asked Pearl how much the painting would cost.

She gave me a look of shocked disapproval. "Don't be vulgar, Beau," she said, refusing to answer.

The housewarming party was scheduled to begin at nine o'clock on Thursday, that being the chic-est night to have a party in New York. I once asked Sabina Phips why no one had parties on weekends anymore. She replied, "Don't be a twit. *Everyone* is at his country place or south on weekends!" Another reason was that Saturday used to be the best night until it dawned on the rich that

Saturday night was when the middle class and the working people had *their* parties. Because any other night they were tired from work or had to go to work the next morning. Saturday night parties implied *your guests had to work for a living.* No, the fashionable parties had to be midweek, preferably Thursdays.

Fifty-Two

YOU'RE my date?" Susan Vanderlip yelled through the door of her fourth-floor walk-up off Gramercy Park.

"Yes!"

"You're early!" she shouted, and began unlocking the four bolt locks and undoing the chain leash. Finally it opened.

"Don't you hate these locks?" she said. "We all live in cages now, like a tribe of fucking baboons. What time is it?"

"Nine o'clock."

"Nine? Shit, I overslept. Come on in."

Susan was wearing a white terry-cloth bathtowel. Her hair was tied around enormous plastic curlers. "You want a drink? An upper or downer? You better have a drink. I don't know how long the beauty overhaul's going to take. Nine o'clock," she repeated, blearily. "Must have overslept. It's the ludes. I just don't hear the alarm when I drop pills in the P.M."

I followed her into the kitchen. It was, like the rest of the one-bedroom apartment, cluttered and dirty. The bright-yellow wall-paper was stained with grease and was peeling. Dirty dishes were piled in the sink and on the counter. Garbage overflowed the trash can. The place looked like a college dorm after a panty raid.

"My cleaning lady quit, the uppity bitch. Wanted more money. Combat pay." Susan laughed, rifling through the mess in search of a corkscrew to open a bottle of white wine. "Eureka!" She found it.

We went into the living room. She shoved old newspapers and magazines off the couch. "Sit down. Can you open this?"

I opened the bottle.

"Pearl tells me you're not married," she went on, "And you're straight. Jesus, you're as rare as hen's teeth in this town. What's wrong with you? You have a terminal disease or something?"

"I'm divorced."

"Lucky me. Wait here. I'll just be a minute." And she ran into the bathroom.

I sat and drank my wine and listened to the toilet flush, the water run in the shower, a hair dryer purr.

"I'll only be a few seconds more!" she called from the hall. "There's some peanuts in the cigarette box on the coffee table if you're hungry. They're pretty stale, though." She disappeared into the bedroom.

A few minutes later Susan walked into the living room and shouted "*Voilà!*"

She was wearing a very tight, pale-green cocktail dress that was at least ten years out of style, high-heel shoes, and nylon stockings with sequins sewn on the legs. Her hair, which was dark brown, was tightly curled and piled in a loose bundle on top of her head. From her ears dangled gold hoops, and she wore fifteen or twenty gold and silver bangles on each arm. They tinkled and chimed as she moved. She looked like a gypsy streetwalker in Naples, and sounded like a chain gang.

"Don't you look pretty," I remarked as I stood up.

"Is that a question?" she cracked. "Don't you love my jewelry?" She twirled around and shook her arms, rattling the bracelets. "It was my mother's junk. It's the real shit, eighteen carat. Can't leave the damn stuff in the apartment or the spades will get it. You know spades, they smell gold a mile away, and they can eat their way through concrete walls. So you like my dress? I found it in a thrift shop on Third. Makes my boobies look big." She laughed. "Listen, pal, I usually don't go this far on a first date, but why don't we skip the party and get married instead?"

"Not tonight."

"Never hurts to ask. My rent's due."

I smiled. "I thought you did well as a model."

"You putting me on? I worked at it for three years, and nothing. And one day Pearl comes into the agency with Cecil Chard, and in two months she's the hottest model in New York. Me? The cheap look never came in."

She went to the hall closet and pulled out a ratty Persian lamb stole. No one had worn fur stoles since Mamie Eisenhower was First Lady. "Here." She threw the stole at me. "Carry it, will you? It used to belong to my mother before she drank herself to death out of sheer spite . . ."

"Sorry."

"About what?"

"Your mother dying."

"Thanks, but I'm not. She and my father gambled away the family fortune and when they were down to the last dime she got drunk and crashed the car. My father was soused on the seat beside her. They'd been to the track, wouldn't you know. Varina knew my mother, who was a classy bitch while she lasted. An aristocrat down at heel. I never wanted to be anything like her. And I'm not."

Fifty-Three

WE WALKED through the marble lobby of Pearl's building to the elevator, the clang of Susan's jewelry echoing through the polished hall. As we entered the apartment a maid took the Persian lamb stole, giving it a look of decided distaste.

"Pearl! Hey, Pearl!" Susan shouted, standing on tiptoes and waving madly at Pearl, who stood at the far end of the vestibule greeting her guests. There were hundreds of people at the party, and it was difficult making our way through the crowd to Pearl. She was talking with the mayor of New York. Next to her was Hayton, and on her right was David Spane. The Ambassador and Varina were a few feet from Hayton. Twenty press photographers were shooting pictures, crushed in an excited, clamoring group in front of the Ransomes and Spane. "Look this way, Mayor! Smile a little, Mr. Spane! Pearl, shake hands again! Don't look at the camera!"

I was surprised that the press was there, as you normally wouldn't expect to find them at a private party. I figured Spane wanted the publicity to promote the movie. As we moved through the crowd, I looked more closely at Hayton and Varina, and saw their obvious discomfort. The Ambassador, however, was greatly enjoying the press attention. He was grinning for the cameras like a man running for office.

Finally we reached Pearl, and Susan and I embraced her. I was introduced to David Spane, who already knew Susan. He was tall and broad-shouldered. Dressed in black tie, with his blond hair and his dimples and teeth so perfect you half-expected to see "Steinway" printed on his upper lip, he exuded both power and sexuality. His appeal to Pearl was clear.

"When are you coming back to the Coast?" he asked Susan. "You never should have left."

"My brain was turning to rice pudding," she replied. "And my acting career was nonexistent."

"You Easterners," Spane said. "You New Yorkers, you never give the Coast a chance. It's a great intellectual center. You should've taken extension courses at USC. Or better yet, gone to the Center in Santa Barbara, where Robert Hutchins is. There's a mind for you!" He shook his head, marveling at the brain power in Santa Barbara, an upper-middle-class enclave up the Coast from Los Angeles. That's where my mother lived with her car dealer, so I had some sense of its intellectual stature. It was on a par with Burbank.

"I was bored," Susan complained. "Everybody eats birdseed out there."

David Spane laughed. "Did you hear that, Pearl? She said everyone in California eats birdseed!"

We moved away.

"What a fool he is," I said to Susan.

"I know. And everybody in the movie industry buys that crap that he's a heavy intellectual. Who the hell cares? He's the best goddamn lay in town. He shoots right away, as soon as he's hard."

"That's a good lay?"

"Yeah. Because after he comes he stays hard, and he can go all night long. Now, that's a good lay."

"So that's his trick. Hayton said Spane had a trick to keeping it up."

"He did, did he? Well, Hayton ought to learn it himself. Hayton couldn't get it up in a wet dream. He never could with me."

"Did you date him very much?"

"Me? A couple times. It was my brother he was close to. That's how I met Hayton, through Rick, who'd met him at some party at Warhol's Factory. And after Rick dropped dead, Hayton hung around with me for a while. He likes to watch, and I like to be watched. I like it best when a couple guys do it to me, and I don't mind an audience. So it worked. I felt sorry for him. He was very broken up about Rick, but he couldn't talk to anyone about it. He wants everybody to think he's this great stud, this lady's man. He's not that way, not really. It was Rick he loved."

"Your brother was Hayton's lover?" I asked. It seemed extraordinary to me that I'd never seen an aspect to him as central as that, although I had known him most of my life. I made no moral judgment on it. It merely served to increase his vulnerability in my eyes, and to soften and sadden the vision I had of him. There can be nothing sadder than to be possessed of a love you cannot acknowledge.

"Hell, no. Just close friends. Rick was like his little brother. I never knew anybody as lonely as Hayton. He's empty inside and desperate for affection . . . I know. That's what Pearl gives him.

He's like a child with her. She makes him feel that he's not alone anymore. That's what he had with Rick. He liked to take care of him and give him things. I thought it was dear. And then Pearl blew into town. When she came to the agency we met and hit it off. She shared my apartment for a couple months, she and that boy-friend of hers, the Dixie cracker?"

"Piers?"

"That's the one. Nice kid. But God, is he mixed up. He's too pretty to trust. She was mad about him, and I think it was sick."

"In what way?"

"I mean, he could get her to do anything. She loved him too much. I think Hayton had eyes for Piers, too. Piers was a lot like Rick."

"You're getting carried away. He hates Piers."

"But why, huh?" she asked. "Did you ever think about why he hates Piers so damn much? Piers never did a damn thing to him."

"He hates him because of Pearl. Because he's jealous."

"He *likes* being jealous. He gets pleasure out of being hurt."

"Maybe."

"Listen, it's so obvious," she continued. "Pearl had to choose between the Southern stunner, who didn't have a penny, and Hay-ton's money. And she went fast for the bread. And so would I if I had the chance. She's already rich, and she's getting famous on top of it. God, look around you! Look who's here tonight. The mayor, senators, half the celebs and money in New York. Look at this goddamn apartment. I'm still living in a hole downtown, and you think she didn't choose right?"

"I didn't say that." I felt defensive, and I couldn't account for it. I resisted believing that Pearl was as cynical and calculating as Susan thought. I was a romantic and preferred to believe that it was affection not money that cut the mustard. Greeting-card convictions.

After we got a drink at one of the four bars, I took Susan on a tour of the apartment. She was impressed, to put it mildly, most of all by Pearl's bedroom, which was larger than Susan's entire apartment.

It was done in pearl-white with rose accents, and very feminine in the gentlest sense. Her bed was canopied. There was a white marble fireplace, and the walls surrounding it were mirrored. In a near corner was a large round table covered with a rose-colored throw, with two sitting chairs on either side. On the table were silver and gold and malachite boxes, and photographs of Hayton and the family, and of friends, in exquisite frames. On her bedside table, by the white telephone, was the malachite box I had given her. And near it was the malachite picture frame she had purchased just days before at La Vieille Russie. I lifted the frame and touched the diamonds and seed pearls forming the oval at its center. She was right. It was worth the money. In the frame, under glass, was a photograph of two young children, around four years of age. Both were dressed in identical sailor suits. They stared at the camera stoically, their pale, wide eyes as joyless as lost children. The photograph was yellowed with age, and it was cut from a strip of dime-store photos, the kind you have taken for a quarter in a Photomat booth at Woolworth's.

I put down the Fabergé frame and picked up the malachite pillbox I had given Pearl as a wedding present. Inside was a tiny heart-shaped locket, like a baby would wear, made of silver. It was the size of a thumbnail. There was no chain, just a length of pink ribbon soiled with age. I had seen the locket before, but where? Then I remembered. At the airport in New York, when I first knew her and drove her and Piers to the plane for their flight to New Orleans, she was wearing it then.

I opened it. The lining was vermilion. Engraved on its lid was "MATT 13:46."

We left the bedroom. In the living room we discovered Sir Cecil Chard. "Lucky girl! Lucky girl!" Cecil kept repeating to anyone who inquired about Pearl. He felt himself responsible for her success, and in many ways he was. "She's going to be a dazzling movie star, my dear. I'd invest my own money in that bloody picture, but Hayton's the only outside investor that chap Spane will permit. Hayton's underwriting a goodly part of the film."

At midnight a small band arrived, and dance music was played in the vestibule. The lights were lowered, and Hayton and Pearl and the senior Ransomes took the first dance. It was all very formal and impressive, and dated.

I danced several times with Susan Vanderlip, only because she was my date. She was a terrible dancer. She sweated fiercely and didn't appear to notice. The sides of her cocktail dress were stained dark from her armpits nearly to her waist. She danced on, laughing, shouting asides to the other dancers, her jewelry jangling away.

I finally dumped her on Prince Rupert von Tallenberg, who was too stoned to care.

Around one-thirty the orchestra played a flourish, and Ambassador Ransome strode slowly to the center of the dance floor. Hayton and Pearl and Varina stood beside him.

"My dear friends, it isn't my house but I would be pleased if we could all raise our glasses in a toast to my dear son, Hayton, and his lovely wife, and to many years of happiness in their new home . . ."

"Hear, hear!" The guests applauded.

"And . . . and," he said, raising his hand to quiet the group, "I soon hope there's a Ransome baby to live with them here. You know, I help Hayton and Pearl as much as I can, but a baby is one thing I can't help them with."

And we laughed.

The music started again, and I went up to Pearl and asked her to dance.

"Not tonight, Beau."

"Ah, you're tired." I smiled. She looked so lovely and serene.

"Yes, and I think . . . for my husband's sake."

"Oh?" I was embarrassed and hurt. I shouldn't have been.

"Why give the gossips a tale?" She smiled.

"You're probably right." I didn't believe it for a minute. What was the harm in a dance? "Let me see you tomorrow, away from the gossips."

"I leave for L.A. tomorrow."

"Why so early?"

"Why not? The sooner I get there, the sooner I'll be back. I think the movie's a mistake. I don't want to be a public person. I'm tired of trouble. I don't want any more. Hayton's right. The family has to come first."

"I wish you had never married him," I said, suddenly bitter, feeling cut off from her life.

She shrugged. "But I did. What you can't change, you accept."

I kissed her goodbye, and I smelled sandalwood again. I was overwhelmed by memory. I could not and cannot even now forget the night I first touched Pearl's body in the heat above the traffic of that slum.

"You should say goodbye to my husband. He's your host."

"Yes, of course."

"And . . ." She began and then hesitated.

"Yes, baby?"

"I don't think we should see each other much anymore, not like we have been. I love you. But I have to think of the family now."

Hayton, Ambassador Ransome, and Binky Rockefeller were in the library, sitting near the fireplace in leather chairs. It was a comfortable room, paneled in fruitwood and filled with art and books, many from the library at Timberton. I paused at the threshold and looked at them, two young heirs and an elder, vastly rich, thoroughly comfortable with wealth and station and the prerequisites of their class, sitting before a blazing fire in a coldly air conditioned room, on a warm September night, talking about the politics of South America, where both dynasties, these economic royalists, had vast holdings. And for the first time in many years I was angered by their wealth, embittered by their smug security, by their having a free jump ahead in any race, the timekeeper and the referee always in their pay. Old resentments rooted in my childhood, in a noose my father fashioned, in the fact that Orin Ransome tried to save my father's neck but not enough to imperil his own. How could one compete when the scales were so weighted in their favor. "I have to think of the family now," she told me as she pushed me aside.

How incomplete I felt, how inadequate, between two worlds, part of neither but belonging nowhere else. I think it had paralyzed my will all my life. I think it was why I didn't fight to marry Pearl. I'd conceded the game before the first round was called. There would always be someone better than me, and richer, so what was the point of the try?

That wasn't true, but it was a convenient excuse not to admit any vulnerability into one's life. If one refuses to feel, one cannot be hurt. If a question is never asked, rejection in reply is never invited.

It went back so far, to the banalities of childhood. In the jealousies of children, and in their petty cruelties. In the life of a father who was a traitor—or so I was allowed to suspect and live as if it were true. In a mother who really didn't want me growing up in her house after my old man hanged himself, not that I blame her now; she had her reasons. In growing up an unofficial ward in a household of great power and wealth, and yet not belonging there with any rights beyond their sufferance. Being a Yankee until the suicide, and then finding myself the token charity of one of the Deep South's illustrious names. I didn't know who the hell I was. And how, I ask you, can you fight for anything if you don't know what's rightfully yours?

Looking at Hayton seated there with his father and Rockefeller, I hated him. Not only for mucking up his life, for his wasteful refusal to put to proper use all he had, but I hated him because he was monied and because he was a Ransome and because he had married Pearl and because, I thought, whatever he does, short of killing himself, however much he fucks up, there will be legions in his pay to set it right.

"Oh, Mikey, there you are," the Ambassador said as I crossed the room. "Forgive me for not seeking you out tonight. The press of the crowd, son. What a fine party, eh? I felt I was a youngster dancing the light fantastic!"

"It was a smashing party."

"That's my Pearl," he declared, grinning. "Knows how to do it right. Just goes to show—it's a natural thing, this matter of style and doing things right. Pearl didn't have our benefits, Mikey, but still in all, she fits right in. She's one of us. What say?"

"She is by now," I replied too gloomily.

"Father," Hayton said, standing. "I think Michael's got to get home."

"Quite right, too. Sorry, son. I can't seem to shut my mouth tonight. I feel too damn good."

I shook the Ambassador's hand, nodded at Rockefeller, and walked out.

"Let me walk you to the door," said Hayton, catching up.

"I can find my own way. Don't bother," I said.

"I have something to say, old f-friend."

We walked through the apartment together, his arm around my shoulders, a gesture very unlike him. Hayton was not a casually tactile person. But he seemed particularly convivial tonight, probably because the party was a great success, and also because, for once, he wasn't stinking drunk. I was pleased by his sobriety.

"Thanks awfully for the wine glasses you sent. My wife loved them."

"I'm happy she liked them."

"Pearl's off to California tomorrow to do the bloody picture. I don't think she'll be doing another. It's not appropriate, really. M-Mother's right about that. A touch vulgar, don't you think?"

"No, I don't agree with you."

He stared at me, narrowing his eyes, his expression intense like his father's.

"Well, that's none of your concern, is it?"

"What are you getting at, Hayton?"

He put his hand on my arm and pulled me aside. "We don't want you around for a while. We think you're an unhealthy influence on Pearl."

"What? Who the fuck is 'we'?"

He was angry, and I could tell he was fighting to keep his rage under control.

"Let me be p-p-plain, Michael."

"Please."

"If you ever swim naked with my wife again . . ."

"Hey, hold on a minute. That was perfectly innocent. *You're* the one talking about people fucking her, not me!" Now I was angry.

He took a deep breath. He gripped his hands together. "That's my prerogative, and it's just talk, not to be repeated. It's booze talk."

"And we were drunk when we went swimming, goddamn it! Why don't you fuck off, Hayton, and cut the shit."

I turned to leave.

He slammed his hand on my shoulder and pulled me around, his face white with rage.

"You get the fuck out of our lives! If you so much as touch her again, I don't care how fucking innocent it is, I'll blow your fucking brains out. *Comprende?*"

Fifty-Four

"CHEER UP, ducky!" Susan Vanderlip shouted as she came into Rupert von Tallenberg's immense living room waving a plastic bag of cocaine and a small silver spoon in her right hand. "This is just what you boys need to fuck right. Some snow!"

She was naked, and she had thick thighs and a flabby stomach, and large breasts that sagged. In fact, we were all naked. I was slumped on a sofa, and Tallenberg sat in a chair opposite under a Renoir. His eyes were closed and he was slowly masturbating.

"Don't spill it, bitch," he said, not opening his eyes. "Susan, she always spills the dope. You pay a thousand dollars, and she drops five hundred on the carpets."

"Do you want me to help you?" she inquired, leaning over me, her breasts swaying sloppily, her hand shoving the silver spoon toward my nose.

"I don't want any. I'll stick to the booze. Hell, I'm drunk."

"Boo . . . Ouch! Careful!" She giggled and slapped at Tallenberg, who had come up behind her and was trying to enter her from the rear. "Wait," she commanded. "Put some snow on it." She turned to me as she bent over. "It kills the pain. A little coke on the back road kills the pain."

I nodded.

She got down on her knees with her large bottom in the air, and he applied more cocaine, then he spit on his hand and wiped it on his penis and started to have at her.

She groaned, and then her mouth was on me. "Lay back," she mumbled. "I want to try to take it all in."

I lay back and closed my eyes, and I thought of Pearl, that it was Pearl, not Susan, and that we had never met Hayton. That we had met years before, and there was never any Piers, and my father had not been what he was, nor my mother, and I had never married and had a daughter who died or a son who didn't but in a way might as well have. Just Pearl and me someplace where people are happy.

"Do you think people are happy ever after?" I asked.

"Uh . . . no," Tallenberg grunted. "Only when they are fucking, yes? Only then."

"You're probably right," I said. "What you can't change, you accept."

Susan took her mouth off me and looked up, her hair in a mess, strands of it caught in the perspiration on her face.

"Give me some help, man. I can't do it alone."

Part V

The Way Out

Fifty-Five

I N AUGUST 1974, two years after Pearl's housewarming party in New York, I was having lunch at the Ritz Hotel in London. It had become a popular place for show-business types to eat. On any given afternoon you were likely to find, seated at the row of tables along the windows, movie stars, agents, producers, directors and the like. I was lunching with Lord Harry Ruthstein, a life peer, chairman of the major film-producing organization in Britain. He was in his seventies, and he was fat and good-natured. He was known as a generous man to his friends, and a brilliant, if somewhat too sharp, producer to his competitors. He had begun his career in Europe as a manager of circuses and specialty acts and, during the war, after he settled in England, he worked as a promoter of British music-hall shows. He was a bit of a P. T. Barnum in that he believed you could sell the public anything if it was packaged and promoted right. In recent years Lord Ruthstein had worked to rebuild the British movie industry, which had practically ceased to exist.

I was lunching with him because he had bought one of my scripts, a rewrite of the play I never finished. It was a story about a Jewish family in Austria just before the war, and about a love affair between one of the daughters of that family and an American journalist stationed in Vienna to report on the fall of that country to the Nazis. Lord Ruthstein had a special interest in the project because he himself was an Austrian Jew who had fled to London before the war. His sister, who'd refused to leave, was murdered at Treblinka in 1944.

I had done the last rewrite on the script, the blue pages, and we had reached the point where it was possible to discuss casting. The director had been chosen long ago.

"You don't work enough," Ruthstein said, puffing on his cigar which was Cuban and very long, "You young men who have it too good, work you don't appreciate. Sixteen, eighteen hours a day I work. People ask me, 'Harry, how come you are seventy-six and you're not in some National Health home for the old and decrepit?' Because all my life I work."

Good for you, I thought. "I work when I feel I have something to say. And when I don't, I don't," I explained.

"On this script you worked hard, and I'm proud of you. Now, this woman, the young Jew, she's very important in the picture. She *is* the picture, no? She must be sensitive but not weak, and above all she must be beautiful so we weep, but not one of the actresses you see in the films and the telly all the time. But someone special, someone with mystery. Some actress whose appearance in a movie is an event in itself, sort of news, or where we can make it *seem* like news!"

Ruthstein's face was flushed with high blood pressure, and spittle seeped from the sides of his large mouth down to his chin.

"Whom do you have in mind—Greta Garbo?" I was being facetious. I didn't trust producers. In fact, I didn't trust anybody connected with the production end of the movie racket.

Ruthstein laughed and wiped his chin with the back of his hand.

He gripped his wine glass in his hand like someone grabbing a beer stein, the whole paw tightly clutching it. He drank generously from it and banged the glass down on the tabletop in a gesture reminiscent of a laborer.

"For Garbo I'd kill! No, Mr. Hot Shot Writer, for us we must have Pearl Ransome." He nodded sagely. "That would be perfect . . . box office, my friend, promotable."

I must have looked astonished, because he raised his eyebrows. "Pearl Ransome?"

"You don't think so?" He hated reservation. He was after enthusiasm and submission. Life was too short to argue.

"She hasn't made a movie in two years," I said lamely. "And she only made one movie in her life, that thing with David Spane . . ."

"*The Shoot-Out*. I know."

"Yes, and after that she said—and it was in all the papers—that she'd never make another film."

"But *what* a movie it was! Her first, and it grossed seven times its cost. That's bankable, my friend, no? And it made her a star. But a different kind. Mystic she still has. Class like Audrey Hepburn or Grace Kelly. You read about her in the gossip sheets all the time . . ."

"No you don't. Not much, anyway. I don't think she'd agree to do it. But, then, I really wouldn't know."

"The publicity we could make. And David Spane, he would do it too. *If* she was in it. He hasn't done so hot since that last picture with her. His last movie, that thing with music, that bombed bad, my friend. Now, listen to me," Ruthstein leaned his elbows on the table, his belly bulging against its edge. "You, you are a friend of hers, maybe for you she'll do it."

"I haven't seen her in a year, Harry. I know little more than you do. She lives quietly and very privately in Paris with her husband."

"This I know," he said, sitting back, his cigar shoved to the side of his mouth, his chin glistening.

"They have a baby son. That's why she never made another film. Because of the child."

"So how old?"

"Philip? About a year."

"So we get a nanny. Listen, you go to Paris and you talk. You see what she'll take. Everybody's got their price. She's too good a property not to work. And the public loves her. *I* love her, and the lady I never even met."

"Harry, did you think of Pearl all by yourself?" I was suspicious of Ruthstein. He always knew far more than he let on.

"I let you in on a secret. Sir Cecil Chard—the great photographer who shoots the pictures of the royal family . . . ?"

"Yes?"

"Sir Cecil sees her in Paris a few weeks back. We're both in the same fancy club, and we get to talking in the bar. Maybe Sir Cecil does the designs for our picture, no? He said that Pearl Ransome is very unhappy and seems despondent. Now, that I don't like. Too beautiful to be sad, yes? We help her, you and me. She needs work. That's why you should go to Paris, my friend. Wine and dine her, buy her things. Treat her like a princess. Save your receipts, though."

"Harry, I'm sorry if she's unhappy. But you're not going to impress her with lunch at Maxim's."

"Dinner then. I don't care. Spend what you must. But get her for the picture."

It wasn't sinking in. "She doesn't *need* money. You can't buy her."

"You think I don't know?" He threw his hands up in disgust. "Like a Rockefeller, she is, a Grosvenor. A princess, an American princess. That's why the people want her back in the movies. Grace Kelly, you think she needs money? She lives in a real palace, but for the right *part,* ah, there's a chance. I almost got her to play the Virgin Mary in a television picture about Fatima—you know, the place in Portugal where the three kids saw the ghost? Almost," he smiled. "What great actress needs money? Who cares about money? *Work* they need. *Applause* they need. See what you can do."

Fifty-Six

I HAD SEEN Pearl twice since her houswarming party two years ago. The first time was immediately after the film opened. It was two weeks before Easter, and I had been in Palm Beach visiting friends. I had gone to the airport to catch the flight back to New York, and when I arrived at the terminal there was a limousine parked in front of the Eastern Airlines entrance. As I walked by, I glanced in and saw Pearl in the back seat.

I knocked on the window. She was startled at first. And then she recognized me and rolled down the window, smiling.

"What on earth are you doing here?" I asked, delighted at seeing her.

"I'm picking up a friend. What are *you* doing here, Beau?"

"I'm catching a plane back to New York. I've got to run to the gate in a minute. Where are you staying?"

She hesitated. She was wearing a tennis dress and bubble sunglasses, and her hair was brushed back and held in place with a ribbon. "Where am I staying?" She really didn't want to tell me. "At the Breakers. But I'm registered under a false name. The movie so exhausted me I wanted to get away by myself. Just three days. Keep it secret. The press is hounding me like crazy."

I understood. There had been a great deal of conjecture in the media about her having an affair with David Spane. But then, that was a standard item. Whoever Spane's costar was, the press assumed a torrid love affair.

"I always keep your secrets, baby." I smiled. "Do me a favor?"

"What, Beau?"

"Take off your sunglasses, and let me see your eyes."

She removed them and fluttered her eyelashes. "They haven't changed color."

"I know, Pearl. I just wanted to check to make sure. I haven't seen your pretty face since your movie premiered."

"My God, were you there? I didn't know."

"No, I wasn't there. I saw it on television."

She laughed. "I should have done the same thing. Wasn't that a mob scene? I thought the crowd was going to tear David and me to pieces. Real hysteria. It scared the daylights out of me. I never want to go through that again."

The movie premiered in Los Angeles, at Grauman's Chinese Theatre on Hollywood Boulevard. It drew the reigning stars of the movie colony, and thousands of excited fans. Fistfights broke out as people fought for places along the street.

I threw Pearl a kiss. "Got to run or I'll miss my flight."

"Oh, Beau?"

"Yes?"

"I'm truly sorry about the party and what Hayton said to you. I heard all about it. He was under a lot of stress . . ."

"It's okay. I had it coming, baby. Kisses."

I hurried through the airport. When I reached the gate I was told my flight would be delayed for twenty minutes. I decided to go back and see if Pearl's limousine was still there.

As I quickly walked from the departure gate to the main terminal, at the far end of the building I saw Piers walking toward the main doors. I waved, but he didn't see me. He was dressed in white slacks and a blue summer blazer with an open shirt. He was deeply tanned, his hair sun-bleached. And he was heavier than I recalled. I watched him leave the terminal, enter Pearl's car, and be driven away.

I didn't see Pearl again for nearly a year. After her film was released, she moved back to Paris, where Hayton had a job as an investment banker. I received an announcement that they were the proud parents of a baby boy, christened Philip Orin Ransome. I cabled congratulations, and sent the baby a set of antique toy soldiers he might play with when he was older. I had loved toy soldiers when I was a child. A month later I received a short and polite note of thanks from Pearl. Her handwriting seemed unfamiliar, and I suspected the note had been written by a secretary.

I heard little about Hayton and Pearl—very occasionally something in the social columns, or Sabina would pass along a bit of news. Nor did I see much of Orin and Varina. The Ambassador's health was fast failing. He had suffered a small stroke that slurred his speech and made writing difficult for him, and they now spent most of their time at Timberton. They had closed their apartment in the Riverhouse and the estate in East Hampton. When they did travel, it was in the winter to Palm Springs.

In 1973, in the summer of that year, Maurice was murdered in his apartment on East 78th Street. It was a nasty business all around. The elevator man discovered Maurice's naked body hogtied and lying on the floor beside his bed. His throat had been cut from ear to ear. He had been dead for twelve hours.

His slaying received heavy newspaper coverage of the most sensationally lurid kind. The papers wrote that the crime was sexually motivated, a sadistic, even racist, act. Since nothing was taken from his apartment, the police ruled out robbery. The only damage, except to Maurice, was to the framed photographs of celebrities on his white baby grand piano. They had been smashed and hurled about the room.

The police also discovered a large collection of homosexual pornography. Among the pictures were some of Maurice himself posed in various sado-masochistic positions; in a few he was even bound in the manner in which he was later found murdered.

Among the pictures were Polaroid snapshots, apparently taken by Maurice, of hundreds of anonymous hustlers in his apartment. Many of the photos were released to the press, and a sampling of them was run in the New York *Post*, carefully edited, to be sure. The only person pictured the police could positively identify was Paco Moralez, who of course was also dead. The cops wanted the public to come forward and help identify the others.

Among the anonymous was a photograph of Piers, stripped from the waist up. He glared unsmilingly at the camera, which had been held by Maurice years before. I stared at his picture in the news-paper. There was something in his eyes that reminded me of Pearl, something of her features I had never noticed before in his face. And there was something sinister there, too, a hatred of Maurice, of what he was subjecting Piers to.

Three weeks after Maurice was killed, a seventeen-year-old drifter from West Virginia was arrested.

I attended the memorial service, which was held a month after his death, partly because I thought Pearl might fly in from Paris for it. I was right. There were many celebrities present, but of them all Pearl caused the greatest excitement among the photographers crowded outside Saint James Church on Madison Avenue.

After the service, I spoke briefly with her. She seemed moved by the memorial, and horrified by the bestial manner of his death.

"Beau, he was so gentle," Pearl said.

"It's tragic how he went."

"Yes. And the way the press played it up, the vulgarity. I gave off reading the papers. You couldn't escape the scandal, not even in Europe. Even the *Herald-Trib* in Paris was obscene. But what can you do? That's how the press is. Did you see the bouquet Piers sent? We both owed Maurice a lot."

I assumed she hadn't seen the New York *Post* and Piers's picture. She never mentioned it at any rate, and it was just as well if she didn't.

I asked if she could stay in New York and have dinner with me.

"I'd love to, but I'm being driven right back to Kennedy. There's a plane waiting to take me to Timberton. Orin's not well, and I want to see him."

"Are you returning to New York later?"

She touched my cheek, a gesture so typical of her and so gentle. "No, honey. I'm flying from Dallas directly to Paris. I have a little boy, you know. He needs me."

"How's he doing?"

"Perfectly fine. He's the sweetest little baby in the world."

"And Hayton?"

"Fine. He's at the bank a lot. So I'm alone a good deal. *C'est la vie.* But little Philip is such a comfort. Oh, you'd love him. He's so dear and so pretty. He keeps me alive. I'll send you some pictures." But she never did.

Fifty-Seven

I T WAS the hottest day I could ever remember in Paris.

I was staying at the Hotel Crillon, courtesy of Lord Ruthstein, in a suite that overlooked the Place de la Concorde.

The Crillon was my favorite hotel in Paris. It had once been a princely palace, and its elegance and security on the unobstructed plaza was why the Nazis made it their headquarters during the Occupation.

The American embassy was across the street, and after the Liberation my father often worked there as De Gaulle established the Fourth Republic. He told me stories about drinking at the bar of the Crillon, which remains to this day a favorite watering hole for American diplomats and journalists. Whenever I was in Paris I liked to have cocktails there. It was a good place to meet Americans, and I far preferred them to the French.

Both my sitting room and my bedroom had glass doors leading to a small balcony, where you could take the air. Because of the exceptional heat on this visit to see Pearl the balcony was useless. Even so I stood at dusk outside and watched the traffic circle the fountains and the Luxor obelisk, heading toward the Rue Royale and the Madeleine or the Champs Elysées.

I was trying to catch sight of Hayton's red Buick convertible. I think it was the only Buick in all of France, certainly the only red one. Hayton had come across it in Belgium, of all places, and paid ten times what it would have cost him in the States. But he loved tooling around Paris in the thing. Hayton, like Southerners generally when they are in foreign places, tended to exaggerate his American attitudes and tastes. I found myself doing it too.

It wasn't far from where I stood, across the square by the gates of the Tuileries, that the Revolution beheaded Marie Antoinette and about 2,600 other royals and aristocrats. And directly across the Place de la Concorde, on the Left Bank of the Seine, I could see the stone façade of the Palais Bourbon burning yellow-orange in the setting sun.

I never saw the red Buick. Pearl came by taxi instead.

When she entered my suite she was on edge, but she soon relaxed. I think she was relieved to see that the bedroom was separate. Pearl had aged more than her years, but it only increased her beauty. She was thin, and dressed in a silk summer dress and soft leather pumps. She wore a Cartier slave bracelet on her right wrist, her wedding and engagement rings, and a small pearl and sapphire brooch, designed in the form of a rosebud.

"Where's Hayton?" I asked, after I made us drinks at the bar in the sitting room. It was one of those mechanical bars that you find in American motels. They were new to France and considered chic. I put in a few twenty-franc pieces and out came a little bottle of liquor, like you get on an airplane. Still, I had to call room service for ice before Pearl arrived. I also ordered caviar and champagne, having forgotten that she never did acquire a taste for it.

"Hayton has to work late, or whatever, so we're to meet him in an hour at the Café de la Paix. I hope he's sober," she said with curious calm.

"Is he having trouble with the bottle again?"

"You'll see him tonight. It's hard for me to know, since I'm usually home in bed most nights long before he gets in, if he gets in at all."

"Mixed blessing, that." I smiled. "Sit down beside me, Pearl."

She came over and sat on the sofa. She seemed preoccupied, her speech a tired monotone, as if she were making a great effort to be pleasant and congenial, and she couldn't quite pull it off.

"And you? What brings you to Paris?" She sipped her drink, and stared blankly out the glass doors.

"I'm here to see you, baby. Why else would anyone come to Paris in August?"

"I don't know why *we're* still here. No, I know why. But all of Paris is empty in August. All my friends, such as they are, are in the country or abroad. And here Hayton and I sit like tourists. You could've chosen a better time to come, although I'm happy you're here. Have you seen much of the city?"

"I just arrived this morning from London."

"There's a splendid show of Rouault at the Orangerie. Hayton said you fancied Rouault?"

"I do. But I didn't come to go museum-hopping. I came to see you." I took her hand. It was cold.

"The Comédie-Française, then." She withdrew her hand. "It's diverting, I suppose."

"Pearl . . ."

"I love to walk around Paris. Every weekend I take Philip in his carriage to the Luxembourg gardens, along the Seine where the band plays under the trees? Nearby, on Saint Michel, there's an old organ grinder . . . I spend my days walking, or going to movies on the Champs Elysées with the tourists. I love the commercials best of all. Y'all know the ads that start about twenty minutes before the feature goes on? I always arrive early so I don't miss them. The heat has been something awful this summer, like New Orleans, but the theatres are cool. I usually try to keep Philip indoors as much as possible. He gets the most terrible heat rashes. I want to take him back to the States, and raise him as a proper American, but . . ." She shrugged.

"Why won't Hayton go back? You seem so miserable here."

"Ask him. Do. Ask him tonight. I'd be interested in what he tells you."

"Then why don't *you* leave?"

"Ask him that too," she replied. "Do you have a cigarette? I'm dying for a real American smoke. They sell Kents and Marlboros here, but they're fakes like so much in France."

I gave her one. "Keep the pack."

"We have an English nanny for Philip. He's learning to talk. He speaks baby talk in either French or with a British accent. It's very odd to have a child who says 'Mama, I want a sweet' with a foreign accent. It makes him seem so powerfully much older, not a baby at all." She laughed. "This is a pretty room," she remarked, looking about.

"It is, isn't it?" I decided to take the plunge about her making another movie. "You know, Pearl, I've been thinking—"

"Darling," she interrupted me and touched my thigh, and then she put her hands to her face and wearily rubbed her eyes with her fingers. "I'm so glad you came to see me. It was so generous and unexpected. I've been a very bad friend to you."

"Nonsense." I took her hand and kissed it. "You've been the best of friends."

"No, that isn't true. But *you've* been. It's been very difficult for me. You know that Hayton and I were separated for a time?"

"No, I didn't."

"Varina didn't tell you?"

"Varina and I don't speak much about you. I don't know why."

She nodded. "We separated a month after Philip was born. Hayton didn't want the child at first. It was Orin, God bless his heart, who forced the issue. I think he wanted an heir more than Hayton."

"And?"

"Hayton was going to file for divorce and disown the child. My baby. I was terrified. I flew with the baby to Timberton and told Orin. I was frightened for Philip's future. Orin ordered Hayton home, and there was a terrible row. I know how Hayton felt. But I had to protect my son, I had to. Orin told Hayton if he went through with a divorce he'd cut him off without a cent. It was as harsh as that. I don't know what will happen if Orin dies . . ."

"Varina will be there."

"You think so?" She looked at me, and I could tell she didn't agree.

"Yes, I do. I've known her a long, long time. She's fair-minded."

"She sides with Hayton. Varina wanted us to divorce."

"My God!"

"Exactly. I couldn't believe it either."

"But why, in God's name? It sounds so unlike her."

"Can't you guess why?" she said.

"No. It doesn't make any damn sense. Varina was pushing for your marriage. She wanted a grandchild as much as Orin or more so."

Pearl finished her drink. She put down her glass and lay back against the sofa. She closed her eyes. "Varina," she said in a quiet voice, "Varina doesn't believe Hayton is Philip's father. She thinks someone else is."

"Ridiculous."

She said nothing for a few minutes. And then she sat up and opened her eyes. She smiled sadly, and tapped my nose with her finger. "She's right. Hayton isn't the father. Can you make me another drink?"

I went to the bar, surprised by what she'd revealed, and put in several franc pieces and waited for the bottle of vodka to come banging out. "Does Varina know that for certain?"

"What does it matter?" she asked tiredly.

"Here's your drink. It matters the world to your son."

"No, she isn't sure." She sipped her drink. "And now that Philip's a little older and beautiful and sharp as a tack, oh, so precocious, and now that he's legally a Ransome, I might add, Varina acts like she never had a doubt in her head. I've agreed to let Philip spend two months a year at Timberton with them, without me, only the nanny and Orin and Varina. For two months she plays mother with my son, and she's happy as a lark."

"Why aren't you with him those two months?" I asked, going back to the bar to make myself another drink, a double.

"Because Varina resents my presence. I think she's jealous of me, as far as Philip's concerned. After Orin had his stroke she transferred so much love to Philip. I really believe, Beau, that if she could she'd take my child away from me. And Hayton couldn't care less if Philip was with us or with Varina. She calls from the

States at five o'clock every afternoon to check on Philip and God help me if I'm not there to take the call! It's crazy, isn't it? What a web they've spun around me. I'm trapped, and there's no way out. No way out."

Pearl started to cry. I put down my drink. "Don't, baby." I took her in my arms and kissed her forehead.

"Don't, please." She pushed me away and went into the bathroom.

She returned a few minutes later, composed and smiling.

As we left the hotel and hurriedly hailed a taxi, we saw four tourists gathered on the sidewalk. They looked German to me, and three of them had large cameras dangling around their necks. They were snapping pictures of the *place* and the hotel.

"Lady, lady!" one called out, smiling, and started shooting her picture as we entered the taxi.

"Goddamn press. I hate them! Oh, how I hate them!" she angrily declared, holding her arm in front of her face. "One crummy movie, and they won't let a body be."

"But they were tourists, Germans probably. It wasn't the press."

"No?"

"No, dearest."

"Still, it frightens me." She put on her sunglasses. "You never know what the press will discover. That's why I wanted to back out of David Spane's movie. I only went to the damn premiere because I was contracted to, but I refused to do any publicity tour. I didn't give a single interview. Not one, and still they wrote as if I had. I'm afraid of them."

Fifty-Eight

WE HAD dinner at the Café de la Paix. Hayton was tipsy when he arrived and immediately ordered bottles of champagne and vodka at the table. We had a round, and then ordered dinner. Hayton was very loud with the waiter, refusing to speak French, and it was a battle between him and Pearl to make our orders understood.

When the waiter left, Hayton said, "The sonofabitch speaks English. Most of the frogs speak English, they just won't do it. The bastards."

"I suspect you're right," I agreed.

"Damn right."

Pearl, attempting to keep the conversation civil, asked me about what was on Broadway, and we discussed current plays and films. I spoke of the London theatre, and suggested, "You should come over to London for a few days, the two of you. It would do you some good."

"Oh let's, darling!" Pearl said to Hayton.

He wasn't listening. "Do what?"

"Go visit Beau in London and take in some plays. It'd be real fun. It's too hot in Paris."

"I like Paris. What the fuck's wrong with Paris? All you do is complain. What a drag you've become," he said.

"Do you remember on our honeymoon, Hayton, how happy we were? Oh, how I'd love to go to Venice again and see it one more time. We had planned to go, after the movie was finished, but then I got pregnant with Philip and we didn't go . . ."

"Your fault. You fucked that up, no pun intended."

"Do you remember the view from the terrace of our hotel? It was on the water, Beau, and we'd sit there at sundown and watch the water turn to gold, the whole city turn golden and shimmering like what heaven must be like. Hayton, you were so sweet then. I loved you so much—"

"You never loved me, sweetums. You never loved anybody but yourself."

"Can't we forget the bad times, darling? Can't we forgive the mistakes? Think of the beautiful moments, the beach in Australia where we met that funny lady, the painter, who said we had the purest souls because our eyes . . . our eyes . . ." She stopped talking. There was no memory that he cared to recall, no evocation in what they shared. It was obvious, embarrassingly so, that he wasn't listening to her anymore.

In fact, he was studying a fat, old man who occupied a corner table. A young Arab youth had joined him, and the old man had risen unsteadily to his feet, and touched the boy's neck with his hands, heavy with rings, and kissed his cheeks in the French way, murmuring too loudly in his Breton accent, "André, *mon trésor! Mon petit chou!*"

He was no more than sixteen years old. He had an exquisitely delicate face, huge dark eyes, wary and quick. A sensuous mouth that seemed, like his eyes, too knowing for his years. His laughter was high-pitched and light, laced with disdain. Its rhythm fluid and easy. It made one think of water.

"Who's that you're staring at?" Pearl asked.

"That old man and boy."

"Oh, the grandfather? That must be his grandchild. Isn't that sweet," she remarked. "French families are very close. I wish I'd known my grandparents. Still, in France they feed the babies wine, you know, which I don't think's at all healthy. I'd never let Philip drink wine, not while he's young."

"Do you know what the old man is whispering to the boy?" Hayton asked, smiling wickedly. "He's saying, '*Guerre aux cons, paix aux trous-de-cul*—'War to cunts, peace to the assholes'."

"Hayton, *please!*" Pearl admonished. "That's so offensive."

"But it's true," he went on. "Do you know who that old man is? That fat, ugly gnarled old roué?"

"I haven't a clue."

"He was Marcel Proust's lover, and at one time he was supposedly the prettiest boy in France."

"Look at him now," I said.

Hayton laughed, delighted with the spectacle and, I'm sure, pleased by Pearl's evident embarrassment. "Pathetic old bastard. I've seen him here many times before."

"I've never seen him," she countered.

"My dearest," he replied with sarcastic sweetness, "I'm rarely here *with you*, faithful wife. The old man always dines here in the company of a boy, usually that one, André. He's the best looking of the lot. All his boys are Arabs. You know, when Proust died he left the old man a fancy male whorehouse on Saint Denis. It's still going strong. When he was a boy he was a whore in that brothel and Proust used to buy his ass. And now, the kid he's with, he's a hooker, too. As are all the other boys he drags in here."

"And I thought it was such a nice restaurant," Pearl said morosely.

"Do you know what I often do at night, little wife?"

"I don't want to know. Your food's getting cold."

He laughed. "My own wife doesn't want to know! Do you believe that, Mikey? I don't bother coming in most nights, and I certainly don't bother to fuck *her*, and she doesn't want to know who I ball. Or why."

"I know why," she said, looking down at her plate. The fork in her hand trembled.

"I suppose you do."

"Why is it that the only time we talk," she said, slamming down the fork, "the only time you say things like this, is when we're not only in public, but with *friends* in public? No wonder we're never invited anywhere in Paris anymore. Everybody's bored silly with your drunk act and your self-pity and your bad manners. Do you think Beau wants to hear all your drunken crap?"

"Drunken? Crap?" He laughed. "Oh, how high and mighty our Mrs. Ransome has become!"

"Cool it. Let's all cool it." I was very uncomfortable, and I resented being used as the occasion for their mutual abuse. I didn't know how to shut him up without risking a scene.

He ignored me. "Little mother, when you're asleep, don't you wonder where hubby is tonight? Where he goes until the wee hours? I'll tell you. I take my beautiful Buick convertible, which I frankly love more than you, and I drive along the Champs Elysées or into the Bois de Boulogne, where I cruise the parkways under the trees until one of the prostitutes catches my fancy. I take them to a cheap hotel. They're only really comfortable in cheap hotels, like me . . ."

"I'm not listening," she announced, closing her eyes tightly, holding her hands against her ears.

". . . and I pretend I don't know French. I play the American hick, the redneck cracker. I always leave a thousand francs in plain and larcenous view. And guess what? Invariably the francs are taken because invariably I turn my back. And sometimes . . ." He gave off, unable to go on. He dropped his head into his hands, suddenly exhausted of bile. And sometimes, he was about to say?

Hayton looked at Pearl. He reached across the table and pulled her hands from her ears.

"I'm sorry," he said.

"I didn't hear a word."

As we followed Pearl out of the restaurant, Hayton paused at the door and glanced at the old man's table.

The boy turned and stared at Hayton and, while Hayton watched, he lifted his finger to his mouth and pressed it to his lips in a kiss.

Fifty-Nine

AFTER DINNER we drove in the Buick to the Left Bank, stopping at Le Flore on Saint Germain-des-Près for a nightcap. Pearl complained of being dizzy with the heat.

The café was crowded on the sidewalk, tourists filling the seats around small tables under the awnings, watching other tourists promenade along the avenue. But inside the place was relatively empty.

"Have you met the baby?" Hayton asked after ordering drinks.

"Not yet, but I'm anxious to."

"I bet you are," he said.

"What do you mean by that?" Surely he didn't think I was the father.

"Honey, *please*," Pearl begged, "Let's not start in on Philip tonight."

"Why not? What's so special about Philip, or any kid? Frankly, I don't really like kids very much. They're messy, and they're loud."

"But I think that's dear," she heatedly countered. "That's the way babies are supposed to be. And Philip, wait until you see him, Beau—"

"Tell me who you think he looks like when you do," Hayton snidely remarked.

"He's the prettiest child in the world, and so smart. Only a year and a half old, and he can talk and crawl, and he has such *curiosity*. I swear I can't keep up with him."

"I have the strangest dreams about Philip," Hayton interjected. "He's so mysterious to me, like something from another world."

"All children are mysterious in their way, that's their charm. Their mystery and their helplessness," I said. "They know things we've forgotten we ever knew."

"I dream of his mouth open and wet as a knife wound . . ."

"That's obscene!" Pearl exclaimed. "It's my *son* you're talking about."

Hayton laughed. "My son. My son. How my wife has played that tired card. You know, don't you, that she's got me over a barrel with my old man, who stubbornly refuses to die? Through Philip. It wouldn't surprise me if Daddums left every dime to the little bastard. Excuse me, dear wife, but that's what he is. Even Mother has been taken in. Gramama Ransome. You know something? Varina has not dyed her hair since the little brat was born. She's white as the driven snow now, and she wears it on top of her head like a spinster schoolteacher. She's playing Grandmother to the hilt. You want to know the truth? They're both gaga senile and ought to be packed away in a rest home somewhere . . . Oh, shit. I don't think that at all."

"Let's leave, honey. You've had enough to drink."

"Yeah," he agreed.

I called for the check.

"Do you ever read Rimbaud?" he asked me.

"I did in school. Not since, I'm afraid."

"Rimbaud?" Pearl brightened. "He was a favorite of . . ." She was about to say Piers, but caught herself in time. She glanced anxiously at me. "A favorite of Maurice's, before he, before he was killed."

"He probably had it coming," Hayton said. Then he laughed. "It wouldn't surprise me if old Piers cut his throat—"

"Stop it! Stop it! I can't take it!"

"What the hell's gotten into you tonight?" I asked him, "You're being cynical and boring. You know Piers had nothing to do with it. They arrested somebody else, some drifter . . ."

"Did you see his picture in the New York papers, Pearl? I meant to show it to you. Seems Maurice took porno shots of Piers jacking off. Nice focus, good composition. They were in all the newspapers, along with shots of a couple of hundred other boys selling their butts to Maurice—"

She slapped his face, and he grabbed her wrist as she did, and squeezed it hard. I pulled them apart. She started to cry.

"I'm going . . . to the ladies," she whimpered, as she hurried from the table.

I stood to follow.

"Leave her be. Stay the hell out of it. You always got to butt in, don't you? So self-righteous, so fucking understanding, so square and liberal and goody-goody. God, I've always hated your sanctimonious bullshit—"

"Thanks for the news. But don't hurt her again. Not while I'm around," I warned him. I was livid, and he was a mess.

"Sorry." He hit my arm playfully with his fist. "I apologize to God and man and General Motors. I mean it. I'm sorry."

"Forget it. It's the liquor."

"Wish it were, old man. *'N'eus-je pas une fois une jeunesse aimable, héroïque, fabuleuse, à écrire sure des feuilles d'or, trop de chance. Par quel crime, par quelle erreur, ai-je mérité ma faiblesse actuelle . . .'* " Hayton threw his arms wide, enjoying the performance. " *'Moi,'* dear friend, *'je ne puis pas plus m'expliquer . . . Je ne sais plus parler!'* "

"Rimbaud?"

"Right you are, old buddy. What the hell happened to me that I'm so much less than I was. Screw it. I haven't the slightest idea."

I paid the check. I leaned over the small marble table and gripped his arm. I sensed what he was going through. It was more than simply a marriage that was falling to pieces. It was his life itself, buffeted and broken by his own self-hatred. He seemed to me like someone who wanted to make everyone who loved him despise him as he despised himself, even as he longed to draw close. His violence had turned inward, his rage targeted against himself.

"You wait for Pearl," he said, stumbling to his feet. "I've got to get some air."

Sixty

WE WENT up Saint Germain toward the car. It was parked near the old church. We said nothing as we walked, all of us a bit embarrassed by the scene in the café. I held Pearl's hand, and Hayton walked behind us, sheepishly staring down at the pavement. He'll be all right in the morning, I thought, but he's got to get off the bottle.

On the way we stopped to watch a group of acrobats performing in a courtyard. A small crowd had gathered around the troupe, laughing and applauding their antics. There were five acrobats, two terrier dogs dressed in pink tutus, and a monkey in white tie and tails with a top hat in his hand.

We smiled as the monkey waddled about the edge of the crowd holding out its top hat for money, bowing like a Persian in thanks for the coins contributed. A woman tossed in what looked like a five-franc piece. The monkey retrieved it from its hat with its small hand, sniffed it, bit it, and then angrily threw it at the woman. The crowd laughed. And in the laughter I heard the high boyish sound we had heard several hours before at the Café de la Paix.

On the other side of the court, among the spectators, was the Arab boy called André. He stood in front beside Proust's old lover. I glanced at Hayton, and he was staring in fascination at the boy, like a mongoose eying a snake. The boy stared back knowingly, beneath his look something coiled, menacing, alert. The look was too direct, and so provocative and insolent. The boy looked away.

"Honey," Pearl complained, "the humidity is killing. Let's go."

Hayton either didn't hear her or he chose to ignore her. The youth intrigued him.

She followed his eyes and finally saw what had caught his interest. "Oh, there's that old man from the restaurant. He's probably here to pick the tourists' pockets. They're very skillful at that, especially the Algerians. You have to watch your pocketbook all the time."

"It *is* hot," I said, feeling the sweat roll down my back. "Let's find the car, Hayton." I wanted to get back to my air-conditioned room.

"In a second. I want to see them finish the trick." He pointed to the acrobats forming a human pyramid on the sidewalk.

"They aren't even professional. I'm heated to die! If they were any good, honey, they'd be in a real circus and not out here in the blazing heat performing for nothing!"

But we stayed and watched until the pyramid toppled and the crowd applauded and we threw coins toward the performers.

We walked to the car and Pearl and I got in. Then Hayton went around to the driver's side and, rather than open the door, he jumped over it into the convertible's seat. As he turned the ignition,

I looked down the street to see the Arab boy standing a few yards away. His arms folded on his chest, his legs spread apart, an expression of arrogance in his stance. He had followed us, and I didn't like it.

Sixty-One

WE DROVE to their house on Rue Bixio, past the Invalides with its floodlit dome. Pearl asked me to come inside and see the baby.

"Go on," Hayton said. "I'll wait for you here and give you a lift back to the hotel."

"Come on up, too."

"I've seen the kid. I'd rather take the air. I'm a little queasy."

When we entered the house, Pearl said, "We have to be quiet now. I don't want to wake the nanny."

We walked through the hall to the stairs to the upper floors. "Watch your step. It can be mighty slippery."

There was no carpet on the steps.

"Have you ever fallen?" I asked.

"On the steps? Oh, no. But Hayton has. A lot. This house is a hazard for drunkards."

A light was burning in the nursery. "He's afraid of the dark," she said, "just like his father."

Philip lay on his back in the crib, his small hands curled into little fists and held back against his chest like someone doing chin-ups on a bar. He was a beautiful child, with masses of light-brown hair and rosy cheeks. The room smelled of baby things and powder and infancy, all of which brought to mind my own children.

"Such sweetness," I whispered.

"Not when you try to wash his hair," she whispered, "then he's a regular little hellion."

I reached down and touched his cheeks and gently ran my finger over his soft hair. He gurgled in response, and in his sleep tried to clutch my finger when I touched his cheek again.

"Come," she said.

We went to her bedroom. She turned on the lights and went directly to a bookcase by her bed from which she pulled a scrapbook of baby pictures.

"Sit on the bed and look. They were taken a few weeks back."

I turned the pages and she explained that this was Philip in the Luxembourg gardens; and here he was with his new push-pull toy; in the bathtub playing with his rubber ducks; dressed in a new baby outfit, with a ribbon in his hair, when he entertained four other local babies at a Sunday brunch. And so on. She described each scene lovingly, with that maternal pride that is nurtured by adversity, and strengthened as the center of one's life is reduced to the child itself. She was so completely a mother with such love for this baby that I could conceive of no other possible love that would ever again equal what she felt now.

When we came to the end of the book, she asked excitedly, "Can I show you more? I have so many scrapbooks of Philip."

We heard a car horn blare.

"I'd better leave. No point in getting Hayton riled."

"I'm afraid of him," she suddenly confessed, grabbing my hand. "I can't help it. He hates me so much sometimes, and he hates the baby. I'm scared."

"You shouldn't be. He's more of a danger to himself than to anyone else."

"You don't know him like I do. Sooner or later, one of us will kill the other."

"Don't be silly, baby. He's unhappy. It'll pass." I stood up. I glanced at the small bureau by her bed. Next to a porcelain lamp was the Fabergé frame she had bought in New York. Beside it was another frame, of gold. I picked them both up. In the first was a picture of Philip. In the second, the old picture of the two children dressed in sailor suits taken in a Photomat booth somewhere long ago. I looked at one and then the other. I was struck by the similarity between the little boy in the sailor suit and Philip. The resemblance was extraordinary.

"Oh, look, baby," I said, holding the frames up for Pearl to see, "Who's the child in the sailor suit, the little boy on the left?"

"There?" she asked, pointing. "Why, that's Piers, when he was about four years old. It was taken in Atlanta at a dime store."

"But he looks just like Philip . . ." I said, and then froze.

We faced each other, and in my look she saw that I knew . . . Piers was Philip's father.

Sixty-Two

WANT a drink?" Hayton asked, pulling a large flask out of the glove compartment of his car.

"What is it?"

"Vodka."

I took a swig and handed it back to him.

"Let's go back to the Flore and see who's there."

"Why don't you take me to the hotel and then go home to bed?"

"Because, old buddy, I don't want to. Anyway, I get scared at night when I'm alone. I detest being alone."

"But you're with Pearl."

"I know. But I still feel alone. I didn't, not for a long time. I felt complete with her. But after the baby miscarried . . . I couldn't get it up anymore, not with her. And that sort of takes the kick out of a marriage. What the hell."

We drove back to Saint Germain and parked the car a block from the café.

"Let's walk," he said, taking the flask with him.

"Is that going to be enough for you?" I sarcastically asked. It held at least a fifth.

He laughed, not catching the sarcasm. "You must have known an awful lot of alcoholics in your time. Don't worry, I always keep a case in the car trunk. You never know."

We walked down the avenue, and then turned to follow the Seine toward the Palais Bourbon.

"Why don't you ever get drunk?" he asked, slurring his words.

"Why don't you ever stutter in Paris?" I replied. I had noticed that all evening.

"I don't know. Maybe because I'm away from the Ransome family. America. I'm more myself here, which is why Pearl wants to get away. She's seen the real me at last and hell is she appalled. But answer the question. Why don't you get drunk?"

"But I do. I can drink one martini after another and not show it until the lights go out. People think I'm sober when I'm dead drunk. But you can tell, the non sequiturs, the bits of verbal disconnection. All those slight jolts that show my mind has shifted gears. Oh, and my palms get red. And when I've had too much I crash."

We sat on a bench beside the Seine and watched the water, traced by white lights from the lamps along the promenade, and red and yellow lamps glowing on the barges moored at the base of the embankment. Hayton wanted to sing Southern songs, so we did. "Crying Time" and "Born to Lose," and "Your Cheating Heart." And we finished the flask.

We started back toward Le Flore.

"When Father dies I'm going to divorce Pearl. But I can't until then."

"Does she know that?"

"I haven't told her, but I think she probably does. Does it surprise you?"

"Not really. She told me tonight that sooner or later one of you will kill the other. Do you think she's right?"

"I don't know. Maybe. But I hope it's me who dies. I'd like to die, but I can't get up the courage to do it myself. You know how it is. Anyway, I'll divorce her as soon as Daddums kicks the bucket. And then you can marry her, Michael." He laughed. "I know you're in love with her. I used to be, too. I'm not anymore. But you've been in love with her for years. I knew it the night you brought her to my house, the night I first saw her. You loved her then. Come on, 'fess up."

"Yeah, I love her. What of it?"

"Nothing. You know, I was an ass to hate you so much. What I said at that damn housewarming dinner. I didn't mean a word of it. I thought I had to say it. But I didn't care anymore. That's when I knew I didn't love her anymore, when I saw you naked together in East Hampton by the pool. I felt no jealousy, and that's a good thing to feel, and when I didn't feel it I knew I had died inside. When Father goes I'm going to take what's coming to me and split. I'm not worth shit, and I know it. My being a banker's a bad joke."

"Don't be too hard on yourself," I said. And then I asked him, "Are you gay? It doesn't matter to me if you are." I don't know why I asked. I shouldn't have. Maybe it was the booze asking.

"No, I don't think so. I loved Susan Vanderlip's brother, Ricky."

"She told me."

"Yeah. I assume the bitch's told everyone in New York. And you want to know why I stutter when I'm in the States! Susan was the friend who sent me the picture of Piers in the New York papers after Maurice was murdered. A troublemaker, that's all she is. She never wanted me to marry Pearl. She was probably right, but for the wrong reasons . . . But to answer your question, I've only been to bed with a boy once."

"You know what Voltaire said, 'Once, a philosopher. Twice, a pervert.' "

Hayton laughed, and put his arm on my shoulder. "You know who the boy was?"

"No," I replied. But I thought, probably Piers.

"It was André. The Arab kid we saw tonight."

"The boy with the old man?"

"That's the one. I'd seen him around. He hangs out at Le Flore.

I picked him up. I was drunk, but that wasn't why. I wanted him. Sheer, unmitigated lust. I took him over to the Ile Saint Louis. I rented a room at this dump hotel there . . ."

"What did you feel like, I mean, having picked him up?" I couldn't understand it. There was no point to it. And yet I knew it obsessed many people.

"What did I feel?" He laughed. "It was like seeing a train coming you'd waited all night for. A small satisfaction, I guess, like the resumption of a journey. There wasn't much to it. He just lay quietly on the bed, staring at the ceiling. There was a crucifix on the wall. Near it was a wine bottle holding paper roses. His mouth smelled of Pernod. Do you know where that line comes from— 'Pernod green as the distance, warm as the vagrant heart'?"

"No."

"Well, neither do I. But that's what I thought of. That, and how I didn't deserve to live, and didn't know how to die."

"That's booze talk."

"You're probably right." He laughed again. "I'm a lousy drunk. Listen, you want to know something? I won't ever go to bed with a boy again."

"What difference does it make?"

"It doesn't suit me, that's all. I like women better. Whores. I feel in control then. I've never been impotent with a whore."

"I know what you mean," I said. "Neither have I."

Sixty-Three

I LEFT Paris for London the next day, and that afternoon had a meeting with Lord Ruthstein. I gave him the bad news. Pearl was not going to make another picture.

"We'll give her some time to think it over. The rich Americans, they get bored easy, if they have brains. Money isn't enough for them. Soon she'll want to act again. That's the way it is. In two months or so, we'll approach her again, no?"

I stayed on in London, planning to spend the summer there. I called Pearl and invited her and Hayton to England for a week. I suggested that we drive to the lake country and perhaps take a cottage for a few days. She was delighted by the idea and said she'd try to convince Hayton.

"If he doesn't want to join us, why don't you and Philip come alone? We'd probably have more fun in the end."

"I just might do that," she said.

We never did see the lake country together because on August 3, 1974, Orin Ransome died in his sleep at Timberton of a massive stroke.

Sixty-Four

THE FUNERAL for Ambassador Ransome was private. The public memorial would come a month later, a state service at the National Cathedral in Washington attended by the President. Averell Harriman would deliver the eulogy, an irony that wouldn't have been lost on Orin Ransome.

The funeral was held on August 5 in the east drawing room of the main house at Timberton. I flew in from London for it, and Hayton, Pearl, and Philip came from Paris.

The Ambassador's flag-draped casket, made of bronze, rested on a bier by the open French doors. There were ten funeral bouquets arranged around the casket, one of them sent by Richard Nixon. Outside on the veranda were nearly a hundred more.

The service was brief. The only people present were the family; Charles Eddings, the Ransome's lawyer and investment manager;

the household servants; and myself. The service was conducted by a Baptist minister from the village, who read Scripture. The twenty-third Psalm. And this: " 'Though I speak with the tongues of men and of angels, and have not love, I am become as sounding brass, or a tinkling cymbal . . .' "

Then it was Hayton's turn to read. He stood and took the preacher's place in front of the casket, and started to read the collect for the dead.

"O Merciful God, the Father of our Lord Jesus Christ, who is the resurrection and the life . . ." he read, but when he came to the line "Come, ye blessed children of my Father . . ." he could not go on. He lowered his head silently, his shoulders shook and tears rolled down his cheeks. After a moment, I went up to him and put my arm around his shoulders. "It's all right," I whispered. "I'll finish."

I took the prayer book from his hand.

"Go sit down, Hayton."

He looked at me, his face full of misery, "I loved him. I loved my father."

"I know."

He went back to his seat, and I completed reading the collect. ". . . Receive the kingdom prepared for you from the beginning of the world . . ."

As often happens at funerals, one person's crying sets the others off, much like children in a nursery. When one starts to bawl, they all do.

Hayton's quiet sobs were contagious, first among the servants. Aunt Kattie started weeping, and then the others took it up, and it spread to the front of the room, where the baby started to cry, and then Pearl did too. Only Varina sat dry-eyed. She had shed her tears days before in private.

"Let me hold the baby," she said to Pearl, taking Philip from her and rocking him on her lap until his crying stopped. When Pearl reached to take him back, Varina said no.

We all stood and said the Lord's Prayer. And it was over.

The casket was wheeled out of the room on an aluminum carriage. There were no pallbearers. At the veranda steps the under-taker and his assistants loaded it onto an old wagon. Jeremiah, who was driving, snapped the reins and yelled, "Giddyup, Bessie!" to the mule.

We all followed behind the wagon as it slowly made its way down the road to the burial plot in the fields. As we walked, Jere-miah began singing "Hold My Hand, Precious Lord." It was the Ambassador's favorite hymn. We all joined in.

Orin Ransome was laid to his rest in a grave next to his mother's near a very old cottonwood tree.

The preacher read First Corinthians 15: 51 through 57. Behold I show you a mystery; We shall not all sleep, but we shall be changed, in a moment, in the twinkling of an eye, at the last trum-pet . . . And so on. Then came the dust to dust, and the benediction for the dead.

The undertaker folded the American flag that had covered the casket and carried it to Varina.

"Hayton, you take it," she said, not wanting to give up Philip, who was enfolded in her grasp. She was dressed entirely in black, her hair as white as Hayton had described it, and gathered in a bun. She wore no make-up, and she looked old but strong and willful. She held her body straight, her head back, and she radi-ated pride and endurance and command, much as her late husband had.

We turned away from the grave and walked back to the house. When we reached the top of the hill, I gazed behind to see the gravediggers lowering the bronze box into the red earth. And I was overcome by a feeling of emptiness and a curious forboding, as if in some way Orin Ransome had held all our lives together, had been their center and focus, and now that the discipline of his presence had passed, things would spin out of control. I felt the loss of him, not only to his family and to me, but to the nation and the world, to history itself, which he had influenced so strongly and at times bent to his will. He was among the last of that generation of aristo-crats who shaped and directed public life and events for half a century—the Roosevelts, Churchill and Eden, Acheson, Harriman,

De Gaulle, and the others. That class, and its power, was fast fading from the West's public life. And in a way we were the worse for it, because the values they embraced and defended, however hypocritically, their patrician liberalism, had seen us as a people through hard times and kept us more or less intact. And what would follow them? Nixon. Agnew. Ford. Harold Wilson. And all the other small, mean and petty men of limited vision who tried to play it safe.

Sixty-Five

THE NEXT DAY, before I left Timberton for New York, Varina asked me to come into the library. Charles Eddings was there, sitting behind the Ambassador's immense desk, the top of it piled with manila folders and accounting books and stacks of computer print-outs. The financial summing-up had begun.

"Do you wish to tell him, or shall I?" Eddings asked Varina.

"You do it. I can't keep the facts straight anymore."

"Sit down, please," he said to me. He didn't smile. I had seen Charles Eddings many times, and I had never seen him crack a smile. I think he felt it was unlawyerly to show good humor. He was a short man, with white hair, who dressed in dark, pin-striped suits and always wore a Kings College, Oxford, rep tie, although he had gone to school at the City College of New York and changed his name from Weinstein when he began to practice law. He was in charge of Room 206, the headquarters for the Ransome family's holdings at 425 Park Avenue. It was from this office that investment decisions were made, philanthropic gifts bestowed, foundations and trust funds managed, taxes audited and paid, personal family accounts balanced, and wills enforced. It was a quiet, discreet, formidably sober operation, as befitted a fortune in the hundreds of millions.

"Ambassador Ransome, as you know, looked upon you as a son . . ."

"I appreciate that," I said. "He was like a father to me."

"Yes, well, he was always proud of your ability to make your own way, financially that is, in a difficult world. But he wanted to protect you from any possible financial reverses that might occur in these unsettled times. Do you know the property in East Hampton, Long Island?"

"The estate?"

"Yes. It consists of two hundred acres of the finest real estate in the Hamptons, or on the East Coast for that matter. The family purchased the property last year for three million dollars, which was a very reasonable price, given market conditions now. The land and its development rights are worth many times that. The estate is legally held through a company called Eastlands, which is incorporated in the Cayman Islands for tax purposes. The Ambassador has instructed me to give you twenty-five percent of the shares in that company. His son Hayton and Mrs. Ransome own the remaining seventy-five percent. At any time, you may sell your shares to the Ransomes at fair market price. But I advise you against that. The property, in this inflationary economy, can only increase considerably in value as the years pass."

"My God," I said, genuinely surprised. I had expected nothing. "So Hayton and Pearl and I are in business together," and I smiled, amused by the idea.

"Not *Pearl*," Varina snapped. "Pearl hasn't a thing to do with it. Hayton and *I* are the other co-owners."

"But what about Pearl?"

"I don't think that's any of your business," she said.

"Mrs. Ransome is the financial responsibility of her husband," said Eddings, "she wasn't named, as such, in the Ambassador's will."

"And Philip?" I asked Varina.

"Philip has a trust of thirty million—"

"Thirty-one million," Eddings corrected her.

"Whatever. And until the child is twenty-one, Hayton is the executor of the trust, if you have to know. I'm rather surprised that you would think Orin would forget his only grandchild. As you see, he didn't."

Sixty-Six

I RETURNED to New York, only to be surprised three days later when Pearl called me from East Hampton and asked me to come out to the country.

"But what are you doing there?"

"I felt in the way at Timberton. All day it was business conferences and talk about foundations and bequests. I wasn't a part of it. Hayton finally suggested I come here and get out of his hair."

"Is Philip with you?"

"Varina wanted him to stay with her for a little while. She's terribly attached to the baby. He helps take her mind off Orin's death."

"So you're alone."

"No, Piers is here. He arrived this morning."

"Good God! Does Hayton know?"

"Of course not. Can you come out tomorrow?"

"Not tomorrow. But I'll drive out on Friday afternoon."

Which I did, driving a rented Ford the three hours to the estate. It was a sunny, warm, and altogether delightful day. I looked forward to swimming and tennis and, most of all, to being with Pearl.

I drove up the long gravel driveway through the acres of estate land planted with potato and barley and fields of flowering grass.

It was about four o'clock, and the sun was still hot. There was a pleasant wind off the ocean smelling of salt and seaweed, and as I passed the last clump of trees and approached the great, weather-beaten clapboard mansion, faded gray over three centuries, I had the happy sensation of coming home. I now owned a part of this place, twenty-five percent, and what a grand feeling it was. In my heart I blessed the Ambassador.

I drove through the second set of gates and along the fence separating the household section of the estate from the working farm. I parked the car in the large gravel area in front of the former stables, now a garage, and carried my luggage across the lawn toward the house. When I came to the swimming pool, Piers saw me from the water and yelled hello. He swam over to the side.

He reached up and I shook his hand.

"Well, I'll be damned!" He wiped his hair off his forehead. "Aren't you a sight for sore eyes? You ain't changed a damn bit since I saw you last, years back when I took sick. It must be all that Bible reading and clean living." He laughed, throwing back his head. "You still got Sunday School looks, I declare," he drawled.

He was naked, except for the Imperial Russian emeralds around his neck that Varina had given to Pearl at her wedding.

I ignored the Sunday School looks remark, although it surprised me, since it seemed to indicate that Piers thought of me as a goody-goody, or perhaps a liberal patsy. I wasn't sure.

"Do you normally swim wearing jewels?" I asked, baffled by the sight.

He pulled himself out of the water. He grinned. He was the type of person who knew to the most precise degree the strength of his physical charm, and it was considerable. "Man, when I saw those rocks of Pearl's, I couldn't rightly believe my eyes. They must be worth a hundred thousand or more."

"A lot more."

"So I thought, what the hell, I'd see what it felt like to wear that much money around my neck. Well, not surprisingly, it feels damn good."

"Where's Pearl?"

"She went shopping for supper."

"Do you know what bedroom I'm to use?"

"Yeah, I sure do. The blue bedroom in the east wing. Hurry and change. You can still get some sun."

"I'll be back in a second."

"Oh, wait, watch this!"

Piers ran to the far end of the pool, and climbed onto the diving board. He stood there a moment, the emeralds glittering brightly in the sun.

He was well built. He had narrow hips and thin legs. It was remarkable how much he had changed since I had seen him sick and yellow with hepatitis almost seven years ago. His face was still exceptionally handsome, but it had lost its boyish softness. His eyes? Green and large as the emeralds around his neck.

"You watching?" he yelled. "Now, watch close." He walked to the end of the board, where he jumped up and down several times showing off. It was rather comic, the emeralds and his genitals bouncing together in time with his jumps. Suddenly he lifted into the air and turned over, twisting beautifully in the air twice before his body slipped into the water with barely a splash. He surfaced and I applauded, impressed.

After unpacking my luggage and changing into trunks, I went to the pool and swam ten laps. Then I lay on a chaise in the sun next to Piers. We were both drinking kir, which he said he had never heard of before. He thought it tasted like soda pop.

"I've never been in a house as big as this mother. You know, it's still hard for me to believe Pearl's this rich. I tell you the truth. We were so poor once we'd go to the back of cafés and beg for scraps. That was when we were on the road, trying to find a place for us where we could live a half-decent life. We stuck together then, through the worst shit they threw our way, and it ain't going to be any different now. We're like one person that got cut in half, and it's only when we're together that we feel complete. But, God, I hate this sneaking around. When we were in Palm Beach, we had to register under a fake name so the goddamn Ransomes wouldn't trace us—"

"Or the press."

"Well, that too. But it was a happy time. Man alive, we lived like we were the two richest damn people on God's earth. It wasn't the money exactly. It was being there and remembering the times we had nothing, and knowing we could pick up the hotel telephone and order any damn thing we wanted and it would come to us. We felt safe then. And we've felt safe so seldom in our lives. Only pity is she's married to that bastard."

"He isn't so bad. Not really. He drinks too much, and . . ."

"And he beats her up, did you know that? That's why she lost the baby. He threw her down a flight of stairs over there in Paris. It about broke my heart. I wanted to kill the sonofabitch then."

I had long suspected that was how the child was lost. Hayton had confirmed it in his way, but how did Piers know unless Pearl had told him?

"You know," I said, "people when they're married sometimes do terrible things to each other that they don't mean and cannot help. And unless you're there, unless you know her heart and his—"

"I don't give a shit one way or another about his heart and his problems and his drinking. But I do care that he treats her right. And that she's happy. That's all that matters to me, that she's happy. But the day she isn't, when she knows the game's up or wants a way out, I'll be there. Listen, I'm nothing and I know it. I've got no education. The only thing I've got that was ever good in my life is Pearl. Just her. And I'd do anything she wanted, and she'd do the same for me. And I know she wants me to stay out of it and keep my nose clean. And I will. Until she asks me to move in."

"What do you mean, move in?"

"Well," he smiled, "when you love somebody and you're a man, and you find out they're hurting bad, you move in on the case. You cut down the bastards causing them pain. I done it before, and I can do it again."

I was alarmed by what he said, or rather by the manner in which he said it. I had known many young men of the South, men without much education, with few if any options, streetwise, alert to the main chance, in and out of trouble, who strutted with a self-conscious, self-enforced pride through life, and they inevitably hit all the trip-wires, the ground under them forever blowing up in their faces just as they were about to make the killing that would set them up for life. Piers, I thought, was like all those others. And like them he justified what he did by an oddly antiquated blend of personal and public values that no longer fit the situation. Good values are like a map for living without too much bad faith or avoidable regret or intentional cruelty; how to survive intact as men with at least a little self-respect remaining at the end. With Piers, his map did not apply to the terrain. Long-standing loyalty or love was the one virtue that justified any crime. You look out for your own. And that, in the case of Piers and Pearl, said it all.

"You ever kill a man?" he asked.

"No."

"I have." He paused, and glanced over at me as if anticipating censure or shock. I didn't blink. "I didn't want to," he continued. "Sometimes you got to do things that ain't right, but you want to do them. So you do. But killing I never wanted to do. I've known me some fellas who got a thrill from it. I knew two crackers in Mobile who got their kicks out of running down drunks at night with their car. They'd see them staggering across a street and they'd gun the pedal and knock the poor wino to kingdom come. I'd never do something like that. But when Pearl was about fifteen in that Baptist home and that bastard was doing real sick things to her, I had to get her out, and to do it I had to kill the sonofabitch, and it was right to do. Between Pearl and somebody else, there's never a choice. Not for me. No choice."

A car drove into the driveway. "Piers!" Pearl called. "Come help me with the groceries."

We ran to the car. It was a Jensen, a new one. I gave Pearl a kiss, and we started to unload the groceries.

"You bought out the store."

"Well, there was absolutely nothing in the house when we got here, so each time I go shopping I try to buy more to fill up the larder. This ought to hold us through the weekend."

"Or the month."

"Honey," she said to him, "why on earth don't you wear some shorts? Lord knows who might see you running around bare naked."

"But it feels good," he said, with a touch of petulance.

"And you're still wearing that silly necklace. You're going to break it if you're not careful. That one's the real thing and if you break it or lose it there isn't enough money to replace it. It's a museum piece, honey, it's priceless."

"I won't hurt it none," he said, lifting two bags of groceries.

We walked toward the house. "We'll eat early, about eight," she explained. "And I want us all to get dressed up real fancy. Wear your best clothes. We're going to have caviar, and then the thickest steaks. And brandy and coffee. I have so come to love fine brandy . . . You know, it's really nice not having any servants around to be fussing at you night and day. I do believe this is the first time since I married that I'm living like a normal soul doing for myself. And I like it."

That night we gathered in the living room at six for cocktails. I opened the Russian caviar, which Piers tried and hated. He said it tasted uncooked.

Pearl was still upstairs dressing but Piers and I, as per request, were dressed to the nines. I wore a blue summer blazer and white slacks. Piers was dressed all in white with an open blue silk shirt, an outfit she had bought him the day before in Southhampton.

While we waited for Pearl I made cocktails, and Piers said, looking about the enormous room with its elegant décor, "I ain't done so bad myself, to tell the truth. I mightn't own a mansion but I got me my own boat." He spoke defensively, as if telling me that he belonged as much to the world of wealth, in his way, as did Pearl. "It's laid up for repairs though. As soon as Pearl lends me the bread to fix it, I'll hit the Gulf again. Do I love that salt water! Yes, sir. I was born to be a sailor. I think I always did know it deep down inside. I must have been born part fish. You know, I put on a good ol' boy act from time to time, it's good to let folks think you're dumber than you are because it makes them put down their guard.

They get clumsy that way, and they think you're too dumb to notice what they're about. Like I knew about Hayton the minute I met him. I knew Pearl could get him. He was a fish jumping to bite. There's nothing inside him that a man ought to be."

That was the second time today he had criticized Hayton, and done it gratuitously.

"Pearl must have seen something in him, she married him, after all."

He laughed. "Hell, yes. She saw what I saw. Money. And she married the sonofabitch, and I thought she should. But, goddamn it, it sure did hurt like fire. For a couple years I was shooting smack. I kept trying to break it, but I couldn't. I get off it a few days, or off the booze, and then I start thinking of that bastard fucking her, and I'd rile up and spin out . . . I guess that's why I hate the bastard. He made me feel so bad; and because he never invited me in, not to the wedding, not even for a drink. And Pearl and I, when we see each other, got to sneak off somewhere and hide away like criminals. It ain't fair."

"Well, you're here now in his house."

"Yeah. But he don't know it. And as soon as I get some bread from Pearl I'm heading south."

"How much do you need?"

"For the boat? Not much. Fifteen grand maybe. Another five to pay the fines. A little more than twenty should do it fine."

"Twenty thousand. That's a lot of money."

"Not for her. She's given me a hell of a lot more than that."

"But that wasn't her money. That was her father-in-law's, Orin Ransome. She got the money from him."

"But he's dead now. So it's hers to give."

"Don't you know," I asked, astonished, "that she doesn't *have* any money of her own?"

"She what?" he exclaimed. "You putting me on?"

"The only money she has is what she gets from Hayton, and whatever she has left from the movie. But I think that's about gone."

"Gone? Hell, she married into one of the goddamn richest families there is. Look around this place! You telling me the old man didn't leave her anything in his will?" Piers was both disbelieving and angry. He gulped down his drink and slammed the glass down on a table. He scratched his head, and then began to pace. He was very agitated and more than a little confused. Pearl must have led him to believe that she, personally, had a small fortune.

"Orin Ransome," I explained, "left his grandson Philip a trust fund, and the rest of his estate went largely to Hayton, his widow Varina, and assorted charities. Pearl didn't get a dime." I wasn't about to mention my bequest, since I didn't relish the idea of Piers hitting me for money.

"You mean she ain't going to come into money until Hayton dies?"

"I suspect not . . ."

"Shee-*it!*"

"Or she divorces him, of course. Then she might get a good deal of alimony. It depends . . ."

"Darlings," Pearl said, coming into the living room. She looked radiant. She wore a silk caftan of blues and turquoise, and sandals embroidered with crystal beads and seed pearls; and the emerald necklace with matching emerald earrings. I thought, seeing the jewels, and her carriage, the elegance with which she moved, and the beauty of her face and body, that if history had ever once truly imitated art, then at some time during a summer long ago a young grand duchess of equal beauty and poise must have appeared on the shores of the Crimea in these gems.

As soon as she appeared, Piers's mood calmed and he brightened. How could he believe, how could anyone think it possible, for someone like Pearl not to be able to give him whatever he wanted. The setting and the costumes and the jewels belied the truth.

We went out to the patio. It was dusk. The pool was lighted, and beyond the dunes the ocean lay pinkish-blue in the dying light, the first evening stars just appearing in the sky. I looked at Pearl and Piers, tanned and healthy and elegantly dressed, seeming so young and favored by nature, like the pets of God, and I remembered W. Somerset Maugham's remark that it is better to be born lucky than to be born rich. At that moment, it occurred to me that if they were endowed with anything that set them apart to their advantage, it was the luck of physical beauty and charm and the capacity to seize an opportunity when it was there. They looked born to this place.

Most people who are rich, certainly those in the Pack, look as if they shouldn't be. Physically they don't look the type. And there's something vulgar and grotesque in that incongruity. We resent it. Perhaps that's why the Kennedys so captured our imagination. They *looked* princely. They were handsome and suave and superbly educated and passionate and blessed with an elegance of wit. And rich. They seemed royal. And for Americans they were what they seemed.

With Pearl there in that shimmering caftan, crowned with a fortune in jewels, Piers beside her with a beauty equal to her own . . . they looked born to it, as if they had lived a life of pampered leisure on estates where the extravagance of their beauty matched the excesses of the Ransome wealth.

The magazines once hailed Pearl and Hayton as the Beautiful Couple, among other press-agented salutes. It never fit Hayton. But tonight, that veneer of handsomeness and ease in each other's company and, yes, love, they were indelibly present before me. Two human beings perfectly complementary . . . *they* were the Beautiful Couple, the Golden Pair. And I envied them.

After dinner we played poker in the library, and we drank as we played. They were both expert players, Piers in particular, and I didn't win one hand out of ten.

"You're too damn good for me," I complained, after losing six in a row. "Where'd you learn to play so well?"

"Me?" Piers asked. "Why, I picked it up in New Orleans. I'd run away, I guess I was about thirteen or thereabouts. And I got a job working as a gardener's assistant. He took care of the grounds of four of the mansions down there, and we'd play poker when we finished work. He had a room over a bar on Bourbon and I slept on a cot there. His name was Danny. He was also the one who got me interested in poetry. There were a lot of poets in the French Quarter and they hung out at cafés and drank at the Absinthe House, and Danny was one of them. He kept saying one day he'd be famous and not have to do other folk's gardens, but he'd have his own. He's still there, mowing rich people's lawns and spraying their roses and reading his verse to tourists in Jackson Square. But he played a good hand. The only one I ever knew who played better straight poker was Paco—"

"You mean the fellow who got killed?"

"He had it coming!" Piers declared heatedly, as if I had suggested otherwise. "He pushed drugs, and he cheated. He cut the smack with too much quinine. He used to deal to Maurice, too. Coke that Maurice sold to his customers at the club."

"Was Maurice involved in Paco's killing?" I had never known. And I had always avoided finding out, I think because I suspected that Piers was intimate in both their deaths. And because of my love for Pearl, I did not want to learn that I was right.

"Hell, no. It was a couple of spades from Jersey. They came to the project, that's after I got sick, and when I opened the door there they were. They wanted Paco. I told them he was up on the roof. How was I to know they'd off him? About thirty minutes later there was all this yelling and hollering, like to raise the dead. And Bonita came screaming to my door saying they done in Paco and it was all my goddamn fault. Man, she was some crazy bitch to think that."

"Your deal," Pearl said. "And let's change the subject."

I shuffled the deck. Piers broke it, and I dealt five-card stud.

"Damn. Honey, you know the time?"

"It's a little before ten."

"I have to call Mississippi and check on Philip. I promised Varina I'd call before this."

Pearl left the room, and we stopped the game, leaving the three hands face down on the card table.

"I'm going to get myself another drink," he said. "You want anything?"

"A glass of white wine would be nice."

Piers went to the bar. I stood up and stretched. I felt tired but good, and I looked forward to a fast sleep in the ocean air. It was a treat being out of the city and at the shore.

I noticed a small leather volume of Yeats's poetry lying on one of the sofas, and picked it up. On the first page was pasted a name plate: EX LIBRA PIERS GOODPASTURE. Below his name was a drawing of two hands cupped together, their thumbs linked. The hands held two roses entwined. It was delicately if somewhat amateurishly drawn, but it displayed a fine eye for exact detail, a sweetness of motif and a lovely balance in composition.

"You like it, huh?" Piers asked, handing me my drink.

"It's very pretty, really."

He smiled with pride. "I did it myself. I drew that picture and designed the whole damn thing, and then I had it printed up. Got that pasted in all my books so they don't get stole. Those are Victoria roses. They're my favorites. They grow good where there's a lot of humidity, like in the delta."

How complicated he was. Roses and a love of poetry and an intensity of loyalty and passion for Pearl; simplicity of taste and manner and a sense of humility coupled with a knowledge of his own strengths and his courage to violence . . . and all of it shadowed by a history of hustling and reform schools and petty arrests and the murder of a Baptist elder to protect his Pearl. And he was freer than I, despite it all, not only by the quite remarkable openness of his acts and his intentions and the weakness of his moral limits, but in his freedom of any trace of remorse. I think Piers had known sorrow and pain and jealousy and rage, but remorse, moral regret— that whipping boy of the liberal middle class—was unknown to him, and with it the vulnerability to guilt. And if you cannot feel guilt, I thought, then any act is possible.

"Your name, Goodpasture, is that English?"

He laughed. "Hell if I know. It was the name of the only foster parents I had that I liked. So I took it. And when I ran into Danny— remember the gardener?"

"Yes."

"Well, for a time I thought I'd be a gardener and a poet too, and Piers Goodpasture seemed like a damn good name for a poet. You know where Pearl got her name?"

"No, I never thought to ask." I kept forgetting that Pearl was an orphan.

"From Oxford, Mississippi. She was in an orphanage there, and she took the town's name. That's where William Faulkner drank himself to death, don't you know?"

I glanced at the nameplate again. "What's it mean, the hands holding the roses?"

"What's it *mean*?" he asked, as if the question had never occurred to him.

"Why hands holding roses?"

"Well, let me see. One of the hands is mine, the other's Pearl. And one of the roses is me, and the other's Pearl. So it's our hands clasped together holding us as roses. And the thumbs are linked together, see, because I was once told that it was in your thumbs where stubbornness was. And there ain't two more stubborn people than Pearl and me. And that's the truth."

Pearl came back into the library.

"Let's finish the game," Piers said, moving toward the card table.

"We can't," she said. She looked very upset. "Hayton's on his way here. Any minute now. Piers, darling, you're going to have to leave."

"I ain't afraid of him. Fuck that."

"How do you know?" I asked her.

"I called Timberton. Varina said he'd flown to New York to see some lawyers this morning. And then I called the apartment in the city and cook told me he had left by limousine for East Hampton about seven o'clock. That means he'll be here any minute."

"Shit." Piers was having none of it. "So what if he comes here? What's he going to do, stamp his feet and cry? I'm tired of having to sneak around and hide like—"

"Honey, go up and pack. I can't face a scene. Darling, please!"

"Where the hell am I to go? I'm supposed to sleep in the fields like a tramp?"

"Stay at a motel. Take the car. There's a nice motel in Bridge-hampton. Oh, you can't miss it. It's called the Blue Angler, and it's right on Highway 27. Please, dearest. I'll call you there as soon as I can. Everything will work out, you'll see."

He stared angrily at her as he slowly drank his bourbon. And then he shrugged, "What the hell. I'll leave, but I tell you, sweet stuff, I am getting mighty sick and tired of always having to run and hide every time that goddamn pussy of a husband comes around. I ain't going to live that lie much longer, and you better believe it. It's time you cleared the decks, sweets, it's time you trimmed the tree." He said it coldly and slowly, and there was a threat in it that was unmistakable.

He took his time packing his clothes, but twenty minutes later he borrowed my rented Ford, since it was clear that Hayton would notice the missing Jensen, and headed off to the motel.

But Pearl couldn't relax. She drank a glass of brandy and paced the floor, smoking cigarettes as she did.

"I shouldn't have made him go."

"You had no choice."

"No, he's right. What's there to hide anymore? My whole life has become a farce, Beau. It's like a bad French bedroom comedy."

"Hayton would blow his top, and you know it. Or worse."

"Why did I ever marry him? I should have seen it coming to this. Dear Lord, please don't let him arrive drunk! I can't face his anger anymore, his rages. I think he's lost his mind. I'll leave this house. I swear, I'll leave him if . . ."

We heard his limousine drive up the gravel road to the house. The car door slammed, and the car backed away.

"He's sending the car away," Pearl said ominously.

"Pearl!" he shouted as he entered the house.

"We're in here."

"Who's we?" he asked as he walked into the library. "Oh, M-Mikey, what a nice surprise. Hello, Pearl. How's tricks?"

Hayton was drunk. Pearl looked at me and rolled her eyes. "I was just about to go to bed," she said, putting down her drink. "Nice of you to call and say you were coming."

"I thought you enjoyed surprises. Stay up another minute because I've got something to t-tell you, dearest. And get me a drink while you're at it."

"You know where the bar is."

"Oh, chip chip. Listen to her. You can't even make your goddamn husband a goddamn d-drink anymore? I hate to bring up bad memories, but when I first saw your ass, precious heart, you couldn't afford a Dr P-Pepper, to say nothing of the hundred-dollar brandy you so like to sip. Get me a vodka, bitch."

"Hayton, is it necessary to be so offensive?"

"It doesn't matter," Pearl said, leaving the room to make his drink.

"Every time I see you you're stinking drunk."

"Why thank you," he bowed to me. "I still have a lot farther to go tonight before I'm done. And what a treat to have you here, Michael, the professional f-family friend. The wifey's bosom buddy. Everyone's goddamn confidant. Don't you ever get tired of always being someone's houseguest and mooch? You should incorporate yourself as a charity, then Father could have written off the land he gave you. You're such a kiss-ass, little Mr. In-The-Way."

"Here's your drink. I'm going to bed."

Hayton swirled around. "Not quite yet, you're not." He took his drink. "Sit down, Pearl. I've got news hot off the wire."

"What news?" she sat at the card table.

"Playing cards?" he asked.

"Just some poker."

"Yes? Who was the third hand?"

We all looked at the table, the three hands of five-card stud lying where we had left them.

"Helen Mellon was by to play," Pearl lied. "She left a few minutes before you arrived."

"That's a rather c-clumsy falsehood. Bridge is her game, darling, surely you remember that. Poker is far too vulgar a game for Helen."

"What do you have to tell me? Let's get it over with, I'm tired."

"Don't you want to know how your precious son is? Or your mother-in-law?"

Pearl sighed. "How are they?"

"In the pink. But you . . . My dear, I have made a decision I should have made a long time ago . . ."

I looked at Pearl and saw her stiffen with dread. We all knew what was coming, but Hayton alone was enjoying the game. He delighted now in toying with her, keeping her off balance, punishing her.

"I saw some of the family's attorneys in New York today. I'm filing for divorce on Monday morning, bright and early. It's bye-bye time, beloved. It's the last stop on the line."

"You can't do that!" she shouted, standing. "What about the baby!"

"Not only am I divorcing *you*, I am naming Piers Goodpasture and David Spane and every other tatty lover of yours as correspondent in the action. And I am going to see you leave my life without a dime to your name."

Pearl glanced at me. She was terrified. She shook her fist at him. "You can't name Piers. I won't let you!"

"You don't have a choice in the matter. I want it *all* to come out."

"Hayton," I interjected, "this is madness. What's the point? If you want a divorce, fine. But give her a decent settlement, and don't drag in anyone else. Think of the family's name, and think of your son."

"Ah, another country heard from, the family lap dog . . ."

"Think about Philip, your son," I repeated, beaten. And suddenly I thought, He's right. The family lap dog. That's about the size of it. Maybe that is all I was to Orin Ransome, an amusement and an investment against bad faith.

"*My* son!" He laughed.

"You're not going to have Philip, I won't allow it."

"Poor Ginger Snaps, wrong again. Varina wants Philip. And what Mother wants, she gets. I don't think a judge is likely to grant an unfit mother custody of what is legally my son, although in fact—"

"You won't get away with it! I'll fight you every inch of the way."

At that Hayton laughed very hard and very, very long, in a kind of hysterical outburst.

"He's mad as a hatter," Pearl said in disgust. "I told you he was crazy. He's sick."

"Sick? You little fool. It's you who are sick. You and that goddamn Piers. I've got enough on the two of you . . . You think I
don't know the truth of it? You think I'm that *blind*? Sick? That's
a twist." He put down his drink. "Where are the car keys?"

"They're in the car. Why do you want them?"

"I'm going out for some fresh air and a few drinks with barflies
who are far better company than you, my dear. Sick, huh?" And
he laughed again. He went up to her and put his arms on her
shoulders, and I thought he was going to kiss her and say he was
sorry as he had always said in the past, that it was the booze talking, that he meant not a word of it. But instead he simply unclasped
the emerald necklace and stuffed it into his pocket.

"You won't be needing it anymore."

"He's gone mad," she said after he left the house. "Do you think
he'll really do it?"

"You want an honest answer? Yes, I think he's unhappy enough
and sufficiently out of control to do it. And I think there's not much
you can do about it."

"I can't give up Piers," she said, more to herself than to me. "I
can't do that. I've been down and out before, I can survive it again."
She cocked her head, and smiled sweetly. "Beau, you win some.
You lose some. Now I have to go call Piers. He'll know what to do."

She went upstairs to her bedroom to call the motel. I had
another drink, and turned on the stereo. About an hour later, when
Pearl hadn't returned, I went upstairs and down the long hall to her
bedroom. She had fallen asleep on her bed.

"Pearl?" I whispered.

"Oh, Beau. Just let me rest a bit."

"Okay, darling. I'll see you in the morning."

Sixty-Seven

AROUND eleven-thirty that night I heard a car drive slowly up the road. I looked out the window but I couldn't recognize it. It was too dark outside. Whoever was driving parked the car on the other side of one of the cottages. I assumed it was the caretaker, who I knew lived somewhere on the grounds.

I read in bed for another hour or so, and then I turned out the light. As I drifted off to sleep I thought back on the day, on Hayton's crazy plans, his self-destructiveness. He was trying to drive her into a corner, to humiliate and demean her, but to what profit? A scandal that would bring him down with it. How could any man hate himself so deeply that he would publicly seek to have his wife's infidelities, and his own tacit approval of them, exposed in a court of law? It made no sense. I remembered arguments with my wife at the end of our marriage. They were as wounding and as irrational, but all the terrible things we said we would do to each other, in our hurt, in the end we never did. In the light of day it was always different. So it would be with Hayton and Pearl. I would talk to him, I decided, and get him to see reason.

I woke when I heard the Jensen crash into the fence outside the house. I heard Hayton swear loudly. There were several thumps, like he was kicking the car in anger. I turned on the light and looked at the clock. It was 5:12 A.M. I turned the light out, but I was fully awake now. I prayed he would quietly make his way upstairs to bed and that would be it.

He stumbled on the stairs. "Goddamn it," he said, and stumbled again.

I was in the east wing of the house. His bedroom, which was where Pearl slept, was in the west wing. The room adjoining it, that Piers had used, was empty.

It was about four minutes later that I heard the first pistol shot. It was followed for several seconds by the most complete silence I have ever known in my life. And then I heard Hayton cry out "No, not yet!" and three more shots rang out in rapid fire.

I heard a heavy weight hit the floor.

I bolted up in bed and ran to the door. As I opened it and stepped into the dark hall, I heard someone running toward the stairs.

"Who's there?" I called out.

I saw Piers run down the stairs and out of the house into the night.

And then Pearl screamed. For the shortest time I hesitated, thinking, I'm naked, I should go back to my bedroom and put on a bathrobe. It was irrational, but that is what went through my mind.

I ran down the hall to her room. The light was on inside. It shone through the open door and fell in a yellow rectangle on the hall floor. Pearl stood outside her room, her hands cupped over her mouth, her body rocking back and forth as she moaned and stared down at Hayton's body. He lay on his stomach in the doorway of his bedroom. His left arm was bent back and twisted in a grotesque way. He's broken his arm, I thought.

I went up to her and pulled her to me.

"Come away. Come to my room. Don't look at him."

"No, no," she said, and lurched away from me. She went into his bedroom, carefully stepping over her husband's body like someone hopping over a rain puddle to avoid wetting new shoes. It was all unreal. I stood where I was watching her.

"Where is it! Where is it!" She was searching the room for something. She reached down and picked up a .38 revolver with both hands. She stared at the gun, oddly, as if she didn't quite know what it was. Then she pointed it at the body.

"Don't!" I yelled. "You can hurt yourself."

"Is he dead? Is he really dead?"

I knelt down by Hayton's body and turned him over. I knew immediately. He had been shot through the chest twice. The last bullet hit him below the left eye. There was blood everywhere.

"He's dead, baby." I stood up. I stared down at him, unable to accept what my eyes were seeing. "Poor man. Poor, damned, unhappy man . . ."

"I killed him. I killed Hayton. I shot my husband . . ." She said it mechanically, like a child learning lines by rote, "I thought he was a burglar. It was dark. And I shot him."

I didn't believe her. I was convinced it was Piers who had fired the gun. "It was Piers, baby. And you know it."

It was as if I had slapped her face. She threw back her head, and then she shook it as if trying to clear her thoughts. She stared at me, fiercely, and in a voice that was both commmanding and pleading, she declared, "*I killed my husband!* You must believe me! I thought he was a burglar. If you ever loved me, you must believe me now."

"I believe you," I said softly. Because I loved her.

She suddenly threw the gun aside. Her hands flew to her hair. She pulled at it, throwing her head from side to side as she wailed, "No, no, no! My sweet darling! My dearest!" And she fell on his body and for a moment sprawled there in sudden grief. Then she sat up and struggled with the corpse, finally succeeding in lifting his upper body onto her lap, her arms embracing him awkwardly as she caressed his hair, sobbing, "It'll be all right, my baby. Pearl will make it all right, you'll see. Mama loves you, baby . . ."

I was overwhelmed by the horror, and the inordinant sorrow and a weakness at once overpowering and relieving. I sank to my knees and felt I was about to pass out. I sat on the floor at Hayton's feet, unable to move, trying very hard to breathe, trying not to vomit as everything inside me was in indignant rebellion against what had happened. I was immobile. I hadn't the strength to speak. If I close my eyes tight, I thought, when I open them it won't have happened.

I closed my eyes.

"My dearest, my dearest, my little baby . . ." Rocking him. Out of the cradle endlessly rocking. I looked at her, and then turned my eyes away and I saw, glittering near Hayton's shoe, the emerald necklace fallen from his pocket.

Sixty-Eight

Don't call the police," is what Charles Eddings instructed me when I reached him around 6 A.M. at Timberton. "I'll tell his mother when she wakes. Someone will call you from my office in New York. Stay off the phone until he calls, and then do exactly what he tells you."

"I will."

"You're sure it was accidental?"

"Yes. She had taken a sleeping pill. They'd had an argument earlier last night. Hayton was drunk and burst into her room about an hour ago, and she fired thinking it was a burglar. There've been a lot of house break-ins out here lately."

That was her story. She would stick to it until the end, never wavering. And so would I.

Ten minutes later, someone from Room 206 called and instructed me not to touch anything in the house. In a few minutes a private ambulance would arrive from Southhampton to take Pearl to Doctors Hospital in New York, where she would be secluded from the press and the police. I could feel the power of the Ransome name, the legal machinery at the command of its wealth, mobilizing to protect the few Ransomes who remained alive. An old woman and a child. And Pearl.

The Ransome lawyers would handle the police, but they wouldn't be called until Pearl was in the ambulance and safely on her way to Manhattan. I was to say nothing more to the police than what I had told Eddings. Not one word.

She was still wearing the caftan she had fallen asleep in the night before, and the emerald earrings. When the ambulance arrived she refused to be sedated. It didn't seem necessary in any event. She was staggering drunk from the brandy and the horror.

Within minutes of the police being called and informed of the accident, and told that Mrs. Ransome was on her way to Doctors Hospital in New York, within minutes the press was alerted and photographers and television crews started gathering outside the hospital entrance on Gracie Square. Late that morning they would film Pearl, supported by two nurses, stumbling her way up the hospital steps still in her bloodied dress.

Sixty-Nine

IN JUNE 1980, six years after the killing of Hayton Ransome, my son graduated from White Plains High School. My ex-wife had, although belatedly, told the boy who his real father was. And Alexander, that was his name, insisted that I be invited to his graduation. I was more than delighted to attend.

It was held in the gymnasium of the high school. Because of traffic, I was late in finding the place, and the program was well under way when I took a seat in the back. I listened to the student choir sing a selection of songs from *Camelot*, which I thought an appropriate choice. The musical had reopened on Broadway that year, starring Richard Burton, who had, twenty years before, played the original King Arthur in the first production. And it was associated in the public mind with the Kennedy family, whose remaining brother, Senator Edward Kennedy, was battling President Carter for the Democratic nomination. In many ways a cycle, not only in my life but in the history of the nation, had been completed and renewed in the years since Alexander had been born. There was a certain irony in it all. I had worked for John F. Kennedy, and I had worked for his brother Robert. And now, twenty years later,

I found myself working as a volunteer fund-raiser for the surviving brother. And among the people also raising money, and a lot of it, was Varina Ransome from her home in Switzerland, where she lived with her grandson Philip, who attended school there.

I first saw my son Alexander when he received his diploma. I had no idea what my son looked like until then, having seen him but once, and that briefly when he was a little boy on the downtown IRT subway. The assistant school principal announced: "Alexander Michael Goldstein," and I stared intently as a tall well-built young man climbed to the stage. He had, I thought, a face much like my own, the same light-brown hair, a small nose and large ears, and blue eyes. When he was handed his scroll by the principal, he let out an Indian whoop of joy and waved the diploma in the air. And I felt like crying.

At the end of the ceremony all the seniors hurled their mortarboard caps into the air and made a great, jubilant shout. I stood on my chair in the back of the gym and saw my former wife and her husband, Professor Goldstein, and Alexander's younger brother, all run to embrace him. Watching them, I knew it was wrong to have come. I was a ghost from the past, and I had no part in my son's life, I had earned no right to it. So I left without greeting him.

Fortunately, Alexander called me the next day and angrily told me that he was disappointed that I hadn't made the effort to be at his graduation.

"But I was. I sat in back. I didn't want to intrude."

"Intrude. Jeez. How could you intrude, Dad?"

Dad, he called me, and in so doing made me happier than I thought it was possible ever to be again.

The following night I took him to dinner in Manhattan. He drove down from White Plains in a MG Triumph his stepfather had bought him for graduation.

He picked me up at my apartment and drove very fast through Central Park to the East Side. We had dinner at Jim McMullen's restaurant, a pleasant place done in mock *Belle Époch* décor and always filled with flowers. We ate in the garden room under the glass ceiling and the hanging plants.

Conversation was difficult at first. Not for him. He chatted away excitedly about his plans for the future (he was off to Stanford in the fall), about the kind of political career he wanted to pursue. And the more he talked, the prouder I was of him. Not because he was handsome and on his way to a fine school and had definite and, I considered, very mature perceptions of himself and the future he wanted. But because his values were so damn good. Immodestly, I must say I felt that they were good because they were so similar to my own, that by now old-fashioned and somewhat tarnished liberalism, that respect for basic Western values, for fair play, for giving everyone a fair shake. His grandfather would have been proud of him, too.

Alexander was tremendously impressed by Senator Kennedy. When I told him I had known both John and Robert, he nearly fell off his chair.

"You did? I'll be damned. My father worked for Jack and Bobby Kennedy? Wow!"

I spoke about the two slain brothers, and gradually conversation became easier for me. I had feared rejection. I felt, or so I told myself, dated and out of touch and unneeded. And suddenly through my son, I knew I had connected with life again—something I had, like a monk, withdrawn increasingly away from in the years after Hayton's death and Pearl's journey out.

After dinner he asked to see where I lived. We drove back to the West Side, roaring through the park again in his sports car. I gave him a fatherly admonishment about speed limits and moderation behind the wheel, and he laughed and stepped on the gas.

Upstairs in my apartment he asked me if I had any marijuana. I said a little, and he rolled us some joints.

"They never let me do this at home. Mom thinks grass leads automatically to heroin addiction and a junkie's death."

"That sounds like your mother. She was always one to cry alarm when there was no threat. She likes drama."

"She sure does. Can I bring my girlfriend here? I really want you to meet her."

"Any time. I thought you might like to come to London with me this summer. And, if you like, we could go on to France and Italy? What do you say?"

"Dad, why don't you stick around New York this summer? I've got a part-time job in a law office downtown. I've got to earn money for school in the fall. But if you stuck around, on weekends . . ."

"Say"—I remembered East Hampton—"you know, I own part interest in a place in the Hamptons. I haven't been there in years. I have use of a cottage on the beach. Why don't we go there some weekend soon, and you bring your girlfriend?"

"That's really cool. I didn't know you'd be such an easy guy."

"No? What'd you think I'd be?"

"A drip."

We both laughed. I made us drinks. We sat out on my terrace, and he talked about his girlfriend, Linda Summers, and her beauty and the rest of it that men who are in love praise in those they love. And I thought of Pearl, and my mind drifted captive to her memory, and I found it difficult to talk, remembering being with her on this terrace and so much more.

"What is it?" He looked closely at me. "You feeling okay?"

"I'm fine. I was remembering a woman I once loved. You know, son"—how good it felt to say that word, son—"sometimes you can never stop loving someone, despite everything that happens. You think it will hurt less as the years go by. That love will fade with time like clothes too long in the sun. That you won't feel the remorse and the pain of what you loved and came to lose. It isn't like that. It gets worse with the years."

"Tell me about her."

I smiled at him as he sat forward in his chair, his elbows on his knees, a look of intense curiosity on his face. He'll make a great politician, I thought. He has the knack of it and the charm.

"I haven't had such a good audience, son, since I don't know when. Well, here goes . . ." And I told him all there was to know of Pearl and Piers, and the love between them and me, and the end to which it led each of us in our own way. And when I came to the killing of Hayton, he suddenly exclaimed, "Bingo! I remember that. It was on television and in the newspapers for weeks. I was about thirteen then. God, she was a beauty. Did she really kill him accidentally?"

"That's what the coroner ruled. Only he was wrong. Piers killed Hayton. My guess is that he hid in Hayton's bedroom waiting for him to come home while Pearl stayed in the other room. Maybe he didn't plan to kill him, maybe he only wanted to talk him out of the divorce. But he had a hair-trigger temper, Piers, and he had killed before . . . So when Hayton came home drunk, he went to his room expecting Pearl to be there, and discovered instead Piers with a gun pointed at him. And a few seconds later he was dead."

"What did the cops do?"

"Pearl's fingerprints were on the gun. She picked it up after Hayton was shot. And I lied at the inquest and testified that we were the only people in the house. I loved her. I had to protect her and to save what she loved, and that was Piers. I can't get over her even now. You know, the other day I got on an elevator in the RCA building. The car was empty but it smelled of sandalwood. Some-one who had just left it was wearing that fragrance, and I almost broke down. I had to leave the elevator at the next floor. The memory was too great."

"But the *truth* is worth something?"

"Truth? If I had told the truth it would have destroyed her and Piers and Philip. That's too many lives to ruin. Hayton was dead. He wanted to die, he said as much many times. And as for truth? Pearl used to say the truth won't buy you a corn roll."

"But the truth is Piers killed someone and you covered it up."

I lit a cigarette. How could I make him understand? "Alexander, it wasn't the truth about the murder that I had to suppress, it was another truth even more lethal. If Piers had been arrested for mur-der it would have invariably led to something else much worse . . ."

"Which was?"

"That Piers was Pearl's twin brother."

He fell back in his chair.

"Before she left New York she told me. Pearl loved him. They were obsessed with each other. She loved him, not only because he

was her twin but because of all they had suffered as children together, and what he had risked and gone through for her. For most
of her life Piers was all she had she could count on, and she
couldn't break away from him. And in a way she tried, at first with
me, and later with Hayton, but she couldn't do it. Perhaps if I had
been a different kind of man, or Hayton a better and stronger one,
perhaps then. I don't know. Why people love each other and cling
together even as that love brings them down, why they become
snared in a trap of mutual affection and need, I don't know that
either . . . Anyway, Hayton left her nothing in his will, and so she
was dependent on Varina, the mother of the man she had confessed
to accidentally killing. Varina kept her in seclusion for a year, because of the press and the scandal, first at Doctors Hospital and
then at Timberton. When they returned to New York, the two of
them ate lunch in public every week so that the Pack, their social
friends, would know that Varina did not consider her daughter-
in-law a murderess."

"Did you ever see Pearl again?" he asked, sympathy in his voice.

"Once. Just once more, shortly before she left New York for
good. She and Piers ended up living in a small hotel in San Miguel
de Allende in Mexico, and they died there in a fire. They're gone,
and what does it matter now? They paid for what they were, for
the love there, they paid too goddamn much. She's gone, and yet
sometimes I think I see her on a crowded street or in a taxi speed-
ing by. Or I go to a party, someplace she might have been, and I
half expect, even now I hope, to feel her come from behind and
whisper to me 'Beau.' "

I stood up. "The dead never let go, son, And there's no one to
tell them how."

Alexander stood. "You want another drink?" He took my glass.
"I'll get it for you."

"Please. Oh, but first I want to give you something. It's a little
pillbox of gold and malachite that was made for the Romanovs.
Your girlfriend might fancy it. I know Pearl did."

DOTSON RADER, former contributing editor to *Esquire* and *Evergreen Review,* is a frequent contributor to the *New York Times, Partisan Review, Rolling Stone, Harper's Bazaar,* and other major periodicals here and abroad. He is the author of five widely praised books: *I Ain't Marchin' Anymore!* and *Blood Dues,* nonfiction accounts of life on the American Left. His fiction includes *Government Inspected Meat & Other Fun Summer Things, The Dream's on Me,* and *Miracle.*

Dotson Rader is consultant to the National Committee for the Literary Arts at Lincoln Center. He is single and lives in New York.